Death in Paraíso

Jack Polo

Black Rose Writing | Texas

ISBN: 978-1-68433-336-3
PUBLISHED BY BLACK ROSE WRITING
www.blackrosewriting.com

Printed in the United States of America
Suggested Retail Price (SRP) $19.95

Death in Paraíso is printed in Palatino Linotype

Dedicated to Leslie/Stripey Geraci,

who was far braver than any character in any book.

And more beautiful, too.

"Everybody's got a secret ... something they just can't face.

They carry it with them every step that they take.

-Darkness On The Edge of Town

Bruce Springsteen

Death in Paraíso

1

Abbey McDougal's beautiful green eyes were staring at me and Jamal.

Staring...but not seeing.

Not seeing anything except the black hole of eternity.

She was a crumpled island in a sea of crimson, her blood having spread wide and deep into the expensive Persian Isfahan silk carpet of the enormous bedroom suite she shared with her husband, Stephen.

Detective First-Grade Mike Gillette of the Paraíso del Mar police force looked at Jamal. "And you know nothing about this?" Mike asked.

"No," Jamal said, still looking at this once stunning woman who had been—and there was no other word for it—*slaughtered*.

"Then you mind telling me what your Derek Rose boxers are doing over there?" Mike said.

I looked at the cream-colored boxers at the bottom of the entangled silk sheets of the McDougal's custom-made circular bed. Then I looked at Jamal.

Jamal was a suspect?

"But those *are* yours?" Mike said. "The ones with the embroidered JW?"

"They're mine, but I didn't kill her."

"No, but you *were* fucking her."

Jamal stood up...

... and up, a black monolith rising.

Jamal is 6'4", weighs 230 and has about 5% body fat.

"Let's go, Matt," he said.

"Hey," Mike barked at us. "We're not done here!"

"Yeah, we are," I said. "Until we get a lawyer."

I followed Jamal through the double-sized front door, its Brazilian wood panels shiny with wax. As we crossed the enormous emerald-green lawn, six burly cops glared at us even after we'd ducked under the black-and-yellow crime scene tape.

Like *we* were the bad guys.

"There goes fifteen-million-dollars," Jamal snarled and kicked the real estate sign so it sailed over one of the cop cars, clanged loudly on the street, cartwheeled several times like a steel gymnast, and came to rest faceup so you could read the name of the company: Singer & Wade Real Estate.

That's us.

Matt Singer, Jamal Wade.

And that's our listing, the $15 million McDougal mansion. Total luxe. With a view that goes not just to the shining blue Pacific but to forever.

A mansion that's now a crime scene.

"We going to need our other licenses?" I asked Jamal.

"Never know."

Our other license is our *real* job, our DNA: Singer & Wade, Private Investigation.

"When were you going to tell me?" I asked.

"I's wuz biding mah time, Mastah."

"Uncle Remus? Now?"

Jamal graduated from Emory with honors. He speaks four languages, but he does this cornpone accent when he wants to defuse a situation. He was about to give me grief, but then he shook his head, his dreads swaying slightly and said, "This is trouble, Matt. Big trouble. And not just because of seventeen-ten."

Seventeen-ten or to be precise, § 1710.2, is the California real estate law that requires the seller and the listing agent to disclose that someone has recently died on the property within the last few years.

"The property being a crime scene is the last thing we've got to worry about," I said.

"And how do you figure that?" asked Jamal.

"Once things quiet down, and that will be just a few days on the media spin cycle, the sheer notoriety of it—"*Wow, this is where she was murdered!*"— will send traffic through the roof with all the lookie-loos, curiosity-seekers, and the plain weird types. And after that, the real buyer will appear."

"And the real seller hasn't disappeared."

He had a point. If Jamal was a suspect or even only a person of interest, Stephen McDougal had every right to go ballistic. And while I knew Jamal was innocent, Stephen would not like the notoriety. He was a tough cookie—even without all his millions.

Stephen and Abigail McDougal were one of the most photographed couples in town. Whether it was the opening of the new wing of the city library, to which they'd contributed a hundred grand, or dining out at the very latest restaurant, there wasn't a photo op they'd miss.

Money and the things it buys can be the most opaque screen or a panoramic window into your life. So when the first tremor hit, that something was wrong in their seven-bedroom mansion in the richest section of town, it was like an 8.9 on the Richter scale—disaster, the sky is falling. Then when Stephen moved into the Marriot Hotel and Abbey went to dinner with a different beefcake young stud every night, the proverbial had hit the fan.

Stephen had called me about listing the house. We met with him and Abbey, and their attorneys, Jerk One and Jerk Two, and after a long session, signed them up. That was two weeks ago. During that time, Abbey seemed as if she was on a mission to prove she was still hot by screwing, supposedly, a different guy in each of their seven bedrooms. And on the granite counter in the kitchen. And according to a peeking neighbor, on the diving board by the infinity swimming pool.

There's a song by rap artist, Ludacris, that crudely talks about women being so hot for him that their panties are soaked-- that *...they so wet, they be leakin'.*

And while it might be a fantasy for Luda, for Wade, it's reality.

Jamal's size attracts a certain type of female, but its his looks that pull women to him like some romantic magnet. Women of every color love his ebony skin and his face with its sleek cheekbones, and the tribal scars he got as a teenager when he and his sister Andriel went back to Africa to trace their ancestral roots. So it shouldn't have been a surprise that Abbey found him attractive. But it was a surprise that he'd succumbed.

Beautiful as Abbey was, sex with her was wrong on so many levels.

"You want to confess now?" I said. "Clear things up before it gets nasty. You know the old saying, '*The first one to report has the advantage. After that, everyone else is on the defense.*'"

He opened the door to his tuxedo-black BMW 750iL and looked at me over the roof. "Get in." He stared past me at the cops who were still giving us attitude. "This is between you and me."

I buckled up and waited.

"You remember last week when Avery Tillman was supposed to bring his client over?" Jamal asked.

"Yeah, and he didn't show."

"Right. But I was there, while you were out doing something."

"This was *my* fault?"

"No, I'm just sayin'."

"Well, say it."

"Abbey says, 'Let's have some wine while we're waiting.' So we do, and we're chatting and having a nice time. Then one glass leads to two and Avery's not returning my calls or text messages, so I tell Abbey, 'Sorry, it's a no-show.'" He pushed the starter button, and the powerful engine roared to life. "And then she showed me everything."

"Damnit, Jamal, you do realize how this looks?"

"I'm not proud of it. But Abbey was a nice person. Behind all the glitz and money, a *good* person. The divorce and Stephen had really hurt her."

"Be sure and tell that to Gillette and Ben Black. No doubt they'll be very sympathetic to you."

"You don't seriously think I did it, do you?"

I looked at him. Jamal's been my partner for over a decade, my friend for almost a decade before that. I was almost offended at the question. But I realized he was in a bad place. And not just because of the possible loss of the sale and the commission. Or the negative publicity Singer & Wade Real Estate would get from this. He was hurting because I think he cared for Abbey.

"I can't believe you asked me that. But I understand. This is FUBAR to the tenth level."

Which made me realize that Singer & Wade Private Investigation had just acquired its biggest and most important client ever—*us*.

3

"How we going to handle this?" Jamal asked.

"First we call Duncan."

"You really think we're going to need him?"

Duncan Fitzgerald is easily the smartest attorney we've ever met. I'm sure he's lost a case, but not in the fourteen years we've worked with him.

"These things can get funny in a hurry. Having Duncan in the on-deck circle is just being ready for whatever they throw at us."

"You going to be able to concentrate on this?" he said.

"What're you talking about?"

"You know, as you get older, harder to stay focused."

"I'm still not following."

"Proves my point. You've got a birthday coming up, remember? You're metamorphosing into a *Mattasaurus*? A really old beast. Estimated to be about forty-three years old."

"Forty-two, asshole. And you know it."

Heh-heh.

That, for Wade, was a big laugh.

We drove down the block and then Jamal turned for the ocean.

"It was a mistake, Matt. No ifs, ands, or butts. I called her the next day," he said.

"And?"

"And I apologized. And she was insulted."

"Insulted? You didn't ...?"

Suddenly it seemed vulgar to be talking about a dead woman's sexual history.

"Insulted that I thought she didn't know what we were doing." He looked at me again and shook his head. "This gonna be gale-force shit-storm."

"Yeah. From Chief Black for sure. He'll send goddamn Ken Purdy around. Tempt us…no, tempt me. "

"True dat. Last time the Chief called you into his office? Didn't turn out so good as I remember."

It didn't turn out so good for anybody.

And even though it was so long ago, when I was still a Paraíso cop, none of us would ever forget it.

Ben had brought me in to tell me he was recommending me for a promotion. And I told him I was quitting.

It hit him like a right hook.

Although *that* hit him later too—the right hook.

I didn't give him too many reasons, and after a few minutes he said, "You sure I can't talk you out of it?"

"No, sir."

"What if I put you with Remington?" he said.

"He's a lieutenant. He doesn't have a partner."

"This would be a new, special assignment. Glenn's taken on a lot more responsibility. He could use an aide. You."

I stood up. "No, thank you."

"You fucker, you tell me no?"

He grabbed me by the throat with both hands.

I just reacted.

I drove both my fists up through his arms and smashed outward.

That broke his grip, and when he drew back to clobber me, I hit first.

My right fist crashed into his face and sent his ass back over his desk, and he took his carafe of hot coffee with him, so he was a soggy mess. Technically, I was still on the force since they hadn't signed me out, so when he busted me back down to patrolman, it was after I was gone and already studying for my real estate license. So it was a posthumous demotion.

But that was later.

First, they threw my ass in a cell. Ken Purdy, the Chief's version of Luca Brasi, roughed me up pretty bad. The second time he came to do it, I evened up the score. My dad posted bail and the Chief, I think because he didn't want all the internal shit to get outside the department, didn't take it to trial. It never even made the local papers.

My life was shit for a year or so. Got parking and moving violation tickets up the ying-yang. But then Wade and I got the inside scoop on one of the nicest homes in town, connected our client with the seller, which meant we got both sides of the deal, and in closing the deal we met the seller's attorney Duncan Fitzgerald. A few months later, I was able to pull a rabbit out of a hat for Duncan to buy a movie producer's house behind the gates in Holmby Hills at what the producer called "monkey points" money.

A few weeks later Duncan called and said, "Your tickets are dismissed. And there should be no more contrived problems with Chief Black and the Paraíso del Mar Police Department. Any real ones, of course, moving forward, would be your own doing."

I found out through one of the cops who would still talk to me, off the record of course, that Duncan threatened harassment, coercion, and fifteen other issues. He also asked some pointed questions about the Chief's lifestyle that made Big Ben apoplectic.

One night somebody shot out both front windows of my little bungalow. They aimed high, just at the top panes, so I'm sure it was *quid pro quo.*

Time heals all wounds, they say.

I did what I thought was the right thing at the time.

The police take care of their own. Just like every family.

And I wasn't a member anymore.

I miss being a policeman. But not if it means being a cop under Ben Black.

"So what'd you think?" Wade said, bringing me back to the present.

"I don't know," I said.

Stephen McDougal could cancel the listing and also file ethical charges with the California Real Estate Commission. And while in time we'd be exonerated, there would always be that shadow of doubt about us: Could we be trusted? Were we rogues who made their own rules?

Once people found out, we would be pariahs.

Then I thought about that—*once people found out.*

"Anyone else know about it?" I said.

Jamal caught it immediately. Just another reason he's my partner.

"No one. And I'm not volunteering to talk to Gillette or Ellie or anybody."

"And Abbey wouldn't have said something to her friends?"

"No, she understood the game. Abbey was counting on a huge settlement from the divorce from the prenup."

"Sounds like Stephen."

"No, it was Abbey who insisted on it."

"Abbey?"

"Yeah, it was *her* money. You look up 'trust fund baby'? It'll have her picture beside it. Huge family wealth, all in Manhattan."

Wade turned onto Laurel Street. He pointed out the window.

Two cop cars were parked at angles in front of another house for sale.

"Looks like property values are causing a crime wave."

4

"Thirty years here and I've never seen anything like it," Bruce Lewis said. "That's how long I been building houses here, thirty years. And I've dug up a lot of shit getting ready to pour the foundations. But never a set of bones."

Bruce had built some of the biggest, most expensive homes in town. His reputation was money, in that he cost a lot and did a helluva job. He started to say something else but saw a cement truck grinding up the street and hurried off to turn it away.

"Guess he won't be needing that today," Wade said.

I saw the assistant city coroner, Hal Bartkowski, in his white lab coat directing a couple of city workers struggling to push a gurney with a body bag on it through the dirt and rubble of the construction site. After a couple of feet, they just picked it up and lumbered with it toward the van.

"At least they put Hal on it," I said.

Official medical work for Paraíso del Mar was handled by two men: Head Medical Examiner Gerry Kelly, and his assistant Hal Bartkowski. Gerry was a toady of Ben's while Hal was aces. Gerry played a lot of golf, hit all the bars on the days he wasn't on the links and was drunk by two o'clock.; so Hal did all the work.

"This has got to be the first real forensic autopsy work in Hal's career," I said.

"Bad luck," Wade said to Bruce when he returned.

"Not really," Bruce said and smiled. He lowered his voice and headed toward us, "The city will do my job for me. They'll dig all over.

We'll have to fix things, smooth out the soil, but they'll have done all the heavy work."

"You'll lose time," I said.

"That's okay, I'm behind on a Strand house. Big project, right next door to the Mayor's."

"Oh, right," I said. "I know that. It's huge."

"Yeah. And Mayor Lockhart's always on my ass about regulations, making sure we don't violate the rich folk's peace by starting early or working past five. And yet, he's always bitching about how long it's taking. So I'll just put this crew on that job. Make His Honor happy."

The coroner's van pulled away.

"Long way from the cemetery," Wade said,"those bones."

"So?"

"You don't think that's unusual?"

"We could use some excitement. Nothing much ever really happens around here. Or if it does, everybody treats it like being caught in a riptide—just go with the flow and pretty soon it'll have run its course, and you can get back to solid ground. And watching your property's value go up."

"The key is how long they've been there. The house that was on the lot was about thirty, forty years old."

"Yeah, but I bet the bones been there over a hundred years."

"Why?"

"The Spaniards were in California a long time before the *gringos*. And the Native Americans long before either of them. Those bones are probably some sailor who died of scurvy or a pioneer who lived long enough to see the Pacific Ocean, or maybe a *Gabrieleños* who just passed on."

"*Gabrieleños*? Now you just showin' off."

"I had *Mestizos* ready, just in case you weren't impressed by the breadth of my cultural knowledge."

"Maybe you should tell that to Mayor Lockhart. He'd like that spin. Add more history to the town. Help property values go up even higher."

"Hey, Hal," I called out and waved to catch his eye.

Hal's vision is probably 40/220. He's close to being legally blind and wears fifties-style thick black frame glasses, probably to hold the lenses which look about as thick as the bottom of a shot glass.

Hal and I had spoken a few times about surfing. Hal wanted to ride the waves in the worst way. And, unfortunately, that's how he rode them—in the worst way. He took more headers off his board, got churned up more times than anyone I ever knew. It seemed like he always had a raw patch on his forehead or some part of his body, or a sore shoulder from being pile-driven into the sand. But he kept trying.

For a while, I had given him lessons, and it had helped some, but I think the longest ride I saw him make was a tiny baby wave and then just as it petered out, the board and Hal shot straight up, and he bombed into the water on his back.

Maybe that's why he has trouble surfing. He can't see without his glasses and his equilibrium's off.

"Matt and Jamal?" he said. "You guys heard about this already?"

"Bad news travels fast." I didn't want to tell him we were just driving by and happened to see the cop cars.

"So what's the story on the bones?" Wade said. Hal stepped around to move past us, but I blocked his path and frowned at him. "Hal…?"

Hal looked around as if Gerry Kelly was watching him. "C'mon, Matt, I'm just the bottom Indian on the totem pole."

"Matt thinks the bones were from Native Americans or *Gabrieleños* from the eighteen hundreds," Wade said. "I'm thinking not so far back in time."

"Wade's right," Hal said. "Judging from the length of the femur, the overall mass of the bones, this guy benefited from a healthier diet and was larger than individuals from the nineteenth century. Most Native Americans weren't very big. Plus, it looks like some kind of silver bracelet that certainly wasn't made back then, is still attached to the left ulna."

"You said, guy, so it's a man?" I said.

"Hip structure told me that right away."

"If it's within the last half-century, then this was a homicide that was covered up, so to speak."

"I've gotta get going," Hal said. He checked around again, then lowered his voice as he said, "That poor bastard's skull was *caved in!*" He took a couple of steps past me and looked back. "But you never heard that from me."

5

"You think we're going to hear from Stephen McDougal?" Wade said.

We had gone back to my office. My office, because while Wade and I are partners, we each need our own space. And also because he doesn't have an office. Unless you count a bedroom with a desk and computer setup.

"No way to tell. He's got to be devastated by this."

"Going through a divorce has to be bad enough – all that money you're kissing goodbye, other men kissing, and screwing, your soon-to-be-ex-wife. Then she's murdered! Then you've got Chief Black grilling you. "

I dialed my cell.

"Who you calling?"

"Jennie, down at the station."

"Ah, the old heartthrob."

I rolled my eyes in response.

"Jennie *loves* you, Matt. Why you think she helped you out all those times?"

Her cell went to voice mail, and I left a message asking her to call me back. "It was only that once," I said. "And I think it was more because she hates Purdy so much."

"Everybody hates Purdy."

Purdy's reputation for brute force is well known throughout the department, as well as in town. He's been called on the carpet by several citizens and their attorneys, which meant Ben had to read him the riot act and on two occasions demote him. That's why, after more than twenty years with the department, he's still just a corporal.

"And not just because of his face," I said.

"Ouch," Wade said.

"You're right, that was a cheap shot."

"But true."

You would feel sorry for Purdy's looks if he wasn't such a dick. He must have had the worst case of teenage acne in medical history. His face, as another cop put it, was that Purdy's face caught fire and somebody tried to put it out with a fork.

And then there's his nose. That *I* get credit for.

Back when the Chief and I had our little waltz in his office, they'd handcuffed me and threw my ass in a cell. Then Purdy came back about two in the morning. He was drunk, but he didn't need booze to crank up his cruelty.

"Assaulting a police officer," Purdy said. "You don't know how much trouble you're in."

I didn't say anything and rolled over to face the wall, my back to Purdy.

"Hey, asshole!" he yelled. "I'm talking to you."

I didn't say anything again.

Purdy grabbed my shoulder and spun me off the bunk. I hit that damn concrete hard. Mostly because I was surprised he'd touched me, but also because the handcuffs didn't allow me to break my fall.

I maneuvered my body around, started to push up, and had my feet kicked out from under me, accompanied by Purdy's nasty, evil laugh. "You want to try hitting me, Singer? Huh? C'mon, I'll even give you first shot."

"I just want to get to bed." I eased up, watching him.

Good thing. Because he aimed one of his size-thirteen boots at my head that I just barely avoided, rolling away fast.

I scooted my hands under me and made it to my feet.

"Oh, good," he said. "Now you and me are going to do a little waltz."

"Look, I don't want any trouble," I said. I backed away and glanced over in the other cell. "*Hey!*" I yelled at the top of my voice, "*Alan! Wake up.*"

Alan Saunders was in the next cell, lying on his back with his hand over his eyes.

"*Alan!*" I yelled again. I think Alan moved, but couldn't tell because Purdy was coming at me, his fists balled.

"Pussy. He ain't gonna help you."

Purdy launched a huge roundhouse that I ducked…most of.

It hit me on the crown of my head and staggered me back.

Shit. I was going to take some serious damage.

Purdy moved in, winding up again. Obviously, he'd forgotten or never learned any of the police tactics for offense or defense. He was wide open.

I took a half-step to my right, his eyes—and attention—went with me, and dropping my hip, somehow remembering the movement perfectly from all those hours of instruction, I shot my leg out, snapped at the moment of impact, and drove my foot into his left knee. It was probably the best karate kick of my life—power, speed, impact. If it had been a field goal attempt, it would have been good for seventy yards.

Purdy howled, lurched down on that side, exposing his big ugly face. I stepped into my next move and head-butted him right in his nose. His blood and snot geysered over the concrete as he collapsed.

I moved back into a defensive stance, my hands useless because of the cuffs, and waited for the son of a bitch to get up.

But he didn't. He started gagging and gasping. And I knew he was choking on his own blood and body fluids. He croaked out some garbled sounds that could have been a call for help; no way to know. His eyes bulged as he grabbed his throat. He was running out of oxygen fast.

I went to him, managed to get my hands on his enormous bulk, and rolled him over on his side, so the blood from his nose went on the floor and not into his lungs. It wasn't easy, working behind my back, but I got his mouth open and stuck my finger in and felt something sticky and wet. I scooped out a thick blood clot and flicked it to the floor. Probably saved the whale's life.

I wasn't aware of Alan shouting for help, but the cell door flew open and Annie Meyer burst in with two cops, weapons drawn, behind her.

"Get back, you bastard!" Officer Jon Daniels shouted. "Get back!"

"Shut up, Daniels!" Annie snapped.

Annie is the only female on the force. She does all the menial duties: mans the front desk, puts drunks and other people who've committed misdemeanors into the holding cells, dispatches patrol cars, and all of the other little jobs that none of the macho cops think they need to do.

Annie does them all without complaining. Mostly because she's far too smart for any of the men who think they can order her around.

"Purdy," the other cop shouted, "you okay?" About as dumb a question as I've ever heard, but Tim O'Halleran, was a rookie.

Purdy's eyes rolled back, and he hacked up a huge glob of snot and goo and then blacked out.

"Tim, call the ambulance, now," Annie said. "He need CPR?" she asked me.

"Don't move him," I said and pointed at Daniels. "Make sure his blood clears his body."

Daniels looked at me, then at Annie.

"Do it, for Chrissakes," Annie said.

"Loosen his collar," I said.

He did, and Tim came back into the cell. "The ambulance is on its way."

"Good," Annie said. But there was a flatness to her voice that was the opposite of her speech as if she secretly hoped the wagon had a flat tire. "Shit," she said, "I didn't know it was Purdy that needed the wagon."

"What the hell happened here?" Daniels said.

"He fell down."

We all looked over at the other cell. Alan Saunders was standing at the bars, probably holding onto them to stay upright.

"What do you mean he fell down?" Jon asked.

"This mutha came in to uh...his cell, yelling and screaming. Asshole woke me up." Alan fought down a gag reflex and continued, "I seen him come in, and start yelling at...uh..."

"Matt," I volunteered.

"Right, Matt. Yeah. He yells at Matt and goes for him, and I don't know, maybe he was drunk; in fact, I'm pretty sure he was drunk. I mean, I know a thing or two about being drunk..."

"Get on with it," Jon said.

Alan nodded, warming up to his audience. "So he comes in, swaying, so I knew he was drunk. And all of a sudden he does a face-plant right into the concrete floor. Splat. Blood all over." Alan looked at me, and a small smile bowed his lips. "And Matt there saved that lardass's life. He was chokin' and gaggin' and Matt got up and rolled him over and stopped him from choking on his own blood and puke"

Tim and Jon didn't know what to say or who to believe.

Annie looked at me and nodded in recognition, then smiled.

"That the way it happened?" Jon asked me.

"Fuckin' A, it did!" Alan yelled. "You fuckin' sayin' I'm a liar? Just 'cause I drink doesn't mean I can't see and can't tell the truth."

And that's the way it went down.

There wasn't even a hearing.

Purdy didn't want to admit to Big Ben or anybody else on the force that he'd screwed up again and was too embarrassed to acknowledge that he'd been so easily overcome.

But a week or so later after Duncan had gotten all of the charges dropped, I was coming out of Ralph's supermarket, and Purdy limped up. His knee was really screwe up and he needed a cane to walk. Once the swelling was down, he was scheduled for major surgery.

"You chicken shit," he said, his words adenoidal and garbled since he had gauze up his nostrils and several white ribbons of tape across his nose. His eyes were puffy and shadowed by deep purple-and-yellow bruises.

I guess my head's harder than I thought.

"You pulled that dirty fighting shit," he said. "You didn't fight fair."

"I don't know what you're talking about," I said.

"The hell you don't."

"No, Purdy, what I meant was I don't know what *you're* talking about when you say a fair fight. There's no such thing as a fair fight. There's no *dirty* fighting. There's no *clean* fighting. There's *only* fighting. And you either win, or you lose."

I looked into his bloodshot eyes. "How do you think you did?"

Our little war had just begun back then. And it's never stopped.

I looked at Wade. "I'm going downstairs to get some coffee. You want anything?" I said.

"Just a mini-me."

"What?"

"A tall black."

Heh-heh.

"That was terrible," I said over my shoulder. "Absolutely terrible."

My cell rang: Annie.

6

"She definitely likes you," Wade said. He took a sip of his coffee and smacked his lips.

"She'd have told anyone who called," I said and shifted into third gear and steered into the diamond lane on the 405, going north.

"Bull. She'd have said she would pass that request on to the appropriate staff member and have them get back to you."

"So she gave me some insider's stuff."

"How many people in town know Stephen McDougal, who called it in, has been down at the station since nine-thirty?"

"Not very many."

"And that he said he didn't need his attorney. Because he didn't do it."

"Because he was at the Marriott all night."

"A guy can slip out the door; hotel isn't going to know," Wade said.

"They checked with the staff. All the Marriott room doors have electronic keys. The door closed at 9:26 last night, didn't open again until 8:31 this morning when he left the hotel. During that time, he called room service once for extra towels, and at 7:20 this morning he ordered the most expensive breakfast special they had, including a fifty percent tip. He checked out via the hotel's internal computer system."

"Annie tells you all that, and you still think she ain't hot for you? Hell, if it wouldn't look unseemly, she'd have given you the file."

"Unseemly?"

"I'z a college graduate."

"Internet universities don't count."

"Dat mean I has to gives back my deeploma, suh?"

"You eat grits or something with all this Southern-fried, cornpone talk?" Wade shrugged for his answer. "Besides, if you're going to pimp the cops with the black thing, shouldn't you be doing Swahili or something?"

"I could, but then I would be reinforcing the cultural repression that truly was part of my ancestry."

"Not the ancestry lecture, please."

Wade ignored me and in his James Earl Jones imitation said, "The hometown of my people…"

"Karona," I said, to cut him off, "was the stronghold of a famous Arab slaver name Mlozi. So his followers and your natural ancestors, in some cases, blended. And not just in the languages."

"Okay," Wade said, "that gets you a day pass. Mlozi, no shit, you remembered."

I put the Snake into fourth. We passed a lot of cars on our right.

"You know I'm right about her," said Wade. "When you work it out, wake me." He shifted to get as comfortable as he could. A Shelby Snake is tight, and when you're as big as Wade, there isn't much room for anything.

"Asshole."

"I heard that. I ain't asleep yet."

"Possum-playing asshole."

"White honky retard."

Some fool cut across the double yellow lines into the diamond lane. It wasn't bad enough he'd pulled a dangerous stunt and broken the law, he was riding alone. Rather than slow down, I just blipped the gas, cut into the right lane, now as guilty as he was, and flipped him the finger as we went by. I doubt he even saw it.

"So why we goin' to see Duncan?"

"Because right after I hung up with Annie, he called."

"And when Duncan calls, you go. Because fo' shore, da mountain ain't coming to you, Mohamed."

"Where do you get this shit?" I asked.

"Internet University. And yes, this will be on the midterm."

I took the off-ramp for Santa Monica Boulevard and got into the far right lane so I could make the turn for Century City. We were fifteen cars back from the corner.

"Lots of people in a hurry going nowhere," I said.

The left lane seemed to be going a little quicker. I looked over.

"You thinking of jumping and then cutting back at the corner?" Wade asked.

"Not worth it. Besides, I hate gutter snipers."

The light turned green, and everybody moved up. In my side mirror, I saw a red Porsche Carrera 4S accelerate and the driver check over his right shoulder. I nudged the gas and hit the brakes a nanosecond after—just enough to close off any opening Mister Porsche might be planning on violating. He leaned on his horn and flipped me the finger. I didn't take my eyes off the car ahead and gave him a thumbs-up without looking over. Then the car behind him honked. Because Porsche-Man had stopped in the left lane. He flipped that guy off too and then floored it…only to slam on his brakes when the light had turned red, and the traffic stopped.

"Asshole must be one of the accessories that comes with the car," Wade said.

Several other cars followed the Porsche, and we moved up too but were still behind him. Then a blue VW, blinkers on, came alongside. I looked at the driver who was looking at me for help—a very pretty coed. At least she looked young enough to be a coed. Probably in pre-med at UCLA. I nodded yes and waved her into the lane. Her smile alone was worth it. She gave me a big, happy wave of thanks.

"You're obviously a chauvinist," Wade said.

"Only if the chauvinism includes a pretty face. Like that UCLA coed."

"And you know she's a coed how?"

"Superior intellect," I said.

She turned right onto Santa Monica Boulevard.

"And that you saw her UCLA parking sticker in the window," Wade said.

"You saw that too."

We had pulled even with Mister Porsche who was obviously talking on his blue tooth because he was waving his hands and looked like he was yelling. Probably telling his girlfriend or wife about the assholes in "some fuckin' Ford" that had cut him off.

He looked over, and his window came down. I slid mine down too.

"What the hell was that all about?" he yelled.

"Beauty and the beast," I said.

He glared at me, checked the left lane, and shot out into it. He squealed his tires as he cut us off before we could make the turn, and he roared up the street.

"Hostile," said Wade.

All of a sudden we heard the *whoop-whoop* of a police siren and a motorcycle cop maneuvered his Harley in between the other lane and ours. I eased the Snake over to the right, and he cranked the gas and his siren as he took off after the Porsche.

"I didn't see him back there," I said.

"Neither did Mister I'm-about-to-be-out-three-four-hundred-dollars-for-a-ticket," said Wade.

It took us about five minutes to go the two blocks until we were by the Porsche driver, who was out in the street, waving his hands, while the cop kept writing the ticket. I tooted my horn two short little hits as we passed him.

"Justice is served," I said. "A little lagniappe of life."

"How long you been waiting to drop that word into a sentence?"

"Just a couple of days. Why? Internet University's curriculum doesn't include English?"

"It does. Just not the English spoken by weird white folks."

I took the ticket from the machine, drove down the ramp, pulled into a parking spot, and cut the engine. Wade opened his door and levered out. He looked over and leaned his elbows on the car's roof.

"What?"

"This whole thing with McDougal. It seemed hinky to me from the jump."

"A little, maybe. But how could we say no to listing a house like that?"

"No such thing as easy money. You told me that. Only you said it, how?"

"I gotta hear a lecture? With my own words?"

"Humble pie always good to serve."

"No free rides in life. Somebody wants to give you something no strings attached? You just haven't looked close enough for the strings."

"So now we see just how tangled the strings are with McDougal."

I punched the button for the twenty-first floor. Duncan had the penthouse suite, but his rent was literally bargain basement. Years ago Duncan had saved the owner of the building some highly embarrassing legal issues. "Priceless, actually," is how Duncan had estimated the value of his work.

The elevator doors opened. There were only two offices on this entire floor: Duncan's and some oil sheik who visited once or twice a year when he would fly in with a planeload of beautiful women and hit every hot nightspot in Los Angeles.

7

"Well, hello, gorgeous," Wade said, but only so I could hear it.

A stunning redhead smiled at us as we walked up to the desk. Every time I came to see Duncan, there was a new receptionist, each one as beautiful as the next. And while I only see him three or four times a year, it's always a surprise to see the new face. And body.

"Good morning, I'm Tamika, "she said, standing up and making good on the body part. Sexist or not, *pneumatic* was the apt word to describe Tamika. She was wearing a tailored navy skirt that stopped just short of risqué, but certainly in the neighborhood of tempting. "You must be Mister Singer." She held out her hand, and we shook. Nice, warm, dry grip. "And you," she said, pausing to take in his total effect and rewarding Jamal with a wonderful smile, "must be Wade."

"The one and only."

"I'll let Mister Fitzgerald know you're here." Tamika turned and walked back toward Duncan's office. A cop told me a funny story once of a guy he and his partner were grilling because they thought he was a voyeur. The cop asked the guy, "What's the first thing you notice on a woman?" And the guy answered, "Depends whether she's coming or going." Tamikawas definitely the definition of that in both directions.

Wade gave me an in-your-face smirk and said, "You must be Wade."

Heh-heh.

"Well," I said, "at least she called me *mister*."

"Like I said, old."

The door opened, and Tamika crooked her "come-hither" finger, and of course, we obeyed. What man wouldn't? She held the door open for us, and we walked into Duncan's hangar of an office. I wasn't sure, but I think Tamika's hand brushed Wade's arm as he passed before she closed the door behind us.

Duncan was dressed in a pink striped shirt with white collar and cuffs. His rose silk tie probably cost more than our day rate. He stood up from behind the 747 of his desk, his charcoal slacks unwrinkled even though I'm sure this was the first time all day he'd gotten up from his leather chair.

"Ah, the Beach Boys," Duncan said.

"Duncan," said Wade and shook hands.

"Matthew," Duncan said, examining my face. "You're looking troubled these days."

"Yeah," said Wade, "he be troubled can he afford your bill."

"Spoken just like a Comparative Lit graduate from Emory."

"You're never going to let me live that down, are you?" Wade said.

"If Professor Hankins wasn't a friend of mine and didn't still occasionally ask if I had any news on the book you had started in his class, I wouldn't." Duncan went back behind his desk. "Imagine my chagrin when I have to tell him that, alas, you are still in the company of…" He looked at me and shrugged to complete his answer.

"Alas?" I said.

"And also lack of day," Duncan said.

"Thank you, George Gershwin," I said.

"Really?" said Duncan. "You know *But Not For Me?* That's before your time. In fact, it's before *my* time."

"That's why they call them classics."

Duncan looked at me. "That's your father's influence."

I grinned for my answer.

"And how is he?"

"Perfect, according to him."

"Also according to his young blonde girlfriend," Wade added.

"Okay," Duncan said. He pulled a thick manila file folder from a drawer but didn't open it. "One Stephen Jonathan McDougal. You can read all the background information on him later. It's all in here." Duncan tapped the file with the manicured nail of his middle finger. "And exactly how did you come to work for him?"

Uh-oh, I thought. "Well," I said, "he called about two weeks ago and wanted to know how fast we could sell his home. And for how much."

"And what did you tell him?"

"Fourteen, nine, and probably less than thirty days."

"So he accepted that?"

"He tried to negotiate us down from our usual percentage, but I held firm."

Duncan appraised me for a moment. "That seems appropriate for him."

"That he tried to get us down?"

"Yes. A rather flamboyant persona, this Mister McDougal." Duncan opened the file, ran his pointer finger down the various colored tabs, stopped at a yellow one, and opened that section. He turned the file around so Wade and I could see. "Likes the ladies and the high lifestyle. Emphasis on high."

The photos showed McDougal at various parties, sporting events, restaurants, each time with a different beautiful woman. The women looked slightly trashy, definitely enhanced, and at least a decade or younger than McDougal.

As I flipped through the papers, Duncan kept talking.

"Seems to have a serious cocaine addiction. Gone through several detox programs. The fact that I said several shows you the seriousness of it."

"Or that he didn't really want to quit," said Wade. "Which is a serious problem."

"When were these photos taken?" I asked. "I'm not a big fashionista, but some of these women's clothes and hairstyles…they don't look like the latest and greatest."

"Perceptive," said Duncan. "They're all from about six, seven years ago."

I turned a page. And stopped. "This is…Abbey."

"More points," Duncan said. "Yes, who was on her way to be the third former Mrs. McDougal."

"Third?"

"Yes. His first wife, Martha, stayed with him about two years and then split for some peace and love commune someplace up in Montana. Divorce was *nolo contendre*, and they went their separate ways." Duncan took back the file folder, flipped to the last section, a black tab. "But here's where it gets interesting." He turned the folder around and pointed to a photo of a beautiful brunette. "He and number two, Jennifer, were going through a very nasty divorce. She had moved back to New York and was living with her younger sister and her family on Fifth Avenue." Duncan stopped and looked at us. "And on the morning of September 11, 2001, Jennifer was on her way to make arrangements for a friend's birthday party at Windows of the World restaurant."

Wade and I looked at each other and considered what Duncan had just said.

"Shit," was the extent of my brilliant analysis.

"Her sister had a Fifth Avenue apartment? Jennifer came from money, right?"

"Jennifer's maiden name was Titlebaum," Duncan said. "Her grandfather helped broker the original deal for the Empire State Building. He would have eaten a dilettante like Trump for breakfast."

Duncan shook his head, almost as if he was bewildered. And perhaps he was, because he said, "How that buffoon got to the White House is beyond comprehension."

Duncan very rarely showed his true feelings, but I knew he had a special category for bombast.

"So, back to Mister McDougal. Unlike the traditional blue-collar-white-collar back to blue-collar cycle, none of the next generations squandered the money. Jennifer's father doubled the family fortunes, her older brother tripled it."

"So, in a macabre way, McDougal hit the lottery."

"That would be the natural assumption. But her brother's financial acumen was, and remains, cutting edge. Of course, he also hired some very savvy attorneys."

"You one of them?" Wade said.

"I am not of counsel to the family, although I do qualify for the savvy ranking." Duncan smiled at us, giving some back. "Nonetheless, Jennifer's share of the inheritance was protected by a boatload of covenants, clauses, and restrictions. McDougal only got five thousand dollars from her estate."

"Five thousand? Jesus, that's not even chump change for him. So where did he get all his money? His house is in the most expensive part of Paraíso del Mar."

Duncan took the folder back, flipped to the red-tabbed portion, glanced through the notes for a moment, and then looked at us. "Jennifer had life insurance policies worth ten million dollars. The..."

Duncan paused, searching for the correct word, "...the tragic events of 9/11 come under an accidental death clause, so..."

"So the policy tripled," Wade said.

"Exactly. There were two extenuating circumstances. The first, that her body or remains were never found."

Wade and I looked at Duncan. My hands went out in a "What?" gesture.

"In fact, there was never any proof that she made it anywhere near the Towers."

"So she didn't take a cab, or the insurance company would have found that out by now. And nothing on Uber or Lyft? And the family didn't have a limo driver?"

"Nothing. Naturally, the insurance company argued that since the McDougals were going through a divorce, pernicious as it may seem, perhaps she used the events to disappear and collect illicitly."

"That doesn't make sense," I said. "She wouldn't collect, he would."

"Well, money is money," Wade said. "And insurance companies like to hold onto it."

"Yes," Duncan said. "But McDougal had some viper for a flack and the first few stories painted such a negative picture of the insurance company taking advantage of a 9/11 family member that their public relations department recommended that they abandon that tactic. I would have advised against it. They could have held out and settled for ten cents on the dollar."

"They never found anything connected to her?" I said.

"Her name isn't part of the memorial wall."

"Sounds like bullshit," I said.

"I concur," Duncan said.

"What was the second problem?" I asked.

"The insurance company tried to continue the divorce tactic, but..."

"But," I interrupted, "they were stuck because the divorce wasn't final."

Duncan looked at me, and then cleared his throat, a mild reprimand. "Your stalwart client claimed that they were going to reconcile and brought all of his cell phone records as proof. Her sister said they talked so much because Jennifer would discover more shit that he'd pulled and call and scream at him. Of course, that's all hearsay and inadmissible."

"So what did they settle for?" Wade asked.

"The insurance companies caved in. He got thirteen point seven." Duncan closed the folder. "That's why I don't do family law. Such a cesspool."

"Getting harder to see him as the killer," said Wade. "He got that kind of settlement, the prenup didn't mean squat. He didn't need the money."

"Yes," Duncan said. "But here's the great part about this guy. He and his attorneys went out to celebrate, and Stephen hoists a glass to the late Osama Bin Laden."

"What?" I said.

"No fucking way," said Wade.

"Absolutely," said Duncan. "He tells them: 'It sounds pretty offensive, I know, and I'm truly sorry for those that lost their lives, but truth be known, the man made me a multimillionaire.'"

"Jesus!" Wade said. "I don't want this listing."

"Don't be foolish," said Duncan. "The money isn't tainted, just the client."

8

"Why did Duncan run the numbers on McDougal?" Wade said.

"Don't know. Unless he's got a mole in the police department and he or she told him what had happened to Abbey."

"Let's dump this, Matt. I know it's a lot of money, but for Stephen to say that..."

I punched the elevator button, and it lit up. A businessman came up and punched the button again, several times.

"Definite A-type personality," Wade said, loud enough for the suit to hear. "Once the light is on, the system's in motion. Doesn't matter how many times you hit that button, it isn't coming any faster."

The suit snapped his head around ready to deliver some pithy remark I'm sure, and then saw Wade, and that Wade was definitely in a pissed-off mood. The suit turned back and kept his focus on the buttons.

Wade's got a direct connection to 9/11. He didn't lose any family members or friends, but his youngest sister, Andriel, who'd just finished her residency at Johns Hopkins, joined the Army on September 12, 2001. Her first tour was as a MEDEVAC doctor, saving lives, usually under heavy enemy fire, and getting our men and women to the nearest U.S. forward operating base for Provincial Reconstruction Team Kunduz in north-central Afghanistan. She's now Major Wade, but still in-country. And there isn't a day that goes by that Wade doesn't worry about her. So when an asshole like McDougal toasts the monster that was Bin Laden, it stirs emotions in Wade best left untouched.

We didn't say a word going up in the elevator; neither did the suit. And when we got off on the fifth floor, I'm sure he let out a deep sigh of relief.

"You know anyone who doesn't hit the button several times when the elevator's slow?" I said.

"Me."

"I meant normal people."

I hit the button to close the doors, but a man's hand broke the beam and the doors shunted back. And who walks in? Mister Porsche. Jesus, talk about a bad news day. He looked at us, and it was obvious he knew who we were. He wisely decided to keep quiet.

For about ten seconds.

"You drive a Ford?" he asked me.

"Why do you ask?"

"Yeah, it was you. Goddamnit, you fucking cost me three hundred and seventy-five dollars," he snarled. "I don't appreciate it."

"You forgetting traffic school," Wade said. "That'll' be another hundred or so."

He whirled around and was talking before he really saw Wade, so his sentence started out strong, "Goddamn it, you...think...this..." Then he looked at Wade, and the rest of the sentence just ran out of steam, "...you...you think this is funny?"

"Actually, yeah," said Wade. "It's a real gut-buster."

"That's not cool," Porsche-Man said. "And I was late for my appointment."

"Sounds like you need to leave a little earlier or get a faster car."

"What?" He didn't know what the hell to say to that. "Really? Really? You think you could beat a Carrera?"

"I don't think that. I *know* it."

"I'm not just talking a street drag. I mean real driving, curves, and turns."

"Absolutely. Want to race for pink slips?"

"I wouldn't do it," said Wade.

Porsche-Man wasn't sure how to proceed. Considering I hadn't backed down from his challenge and had upped the ante, he was at a loss for words. The elevator stopped, two businessmen got on, and suddenly Porsche-Man stepped off into the corridor.

"Hey," I called and held the door from closing. "Some people call it a Ford. I call it a Porsche-eater." I stepped back, and the doors closed before he could figure out a snide reply. The two businessmen couldn't figure out what the hell was happening, so just stared at the elevator numbers.

My cell phone rang. I checked the ID: Duncan.

"In the past four months, your client," Duncan said, without a hello, "has spent over sixty thousand dollars. Not significant enough to dent that thirteen-seven, but it does draw attention."

"His coke habit?"

"His nose would blow out before he even dented the interest that kind of money throws off."

"He go to Vegas much?"

I could hear clicking on the keyboard. "No," Duncan said. "Airline tickets to…Cabo…Rio… and last December, to Interlaken, stayed two weeks at the Victoria Jungfrau Grand Hotel."

"Sounds expensive."

"Five stars. Reasonable skiing, but better known for their hospitality."

"The Swiss?"

"Efficient, if not necessarily warm. You want warmth, go to Italy."

"Duncan, I'm just curious, why did you run the background check on Stephen?"

But there were only the two electronic bleeps of a broken connection.

"Good-bye to you too, Duncan," I said, not wanting Wade to know. Fat chance.

"Just hung up on you, didn't he?"

9

Surfers were hanging ten, jammed together on the blue-green moving landscape of the Pacific as I drove home along the coast, their black wetsuits punctuation marks on the wild colors of their boards.

A long time ago I was one of them, riding the nose of my '67 Greg Noll Duke Kahanamoku stick, hoping some beach bunny surfer girl embodied in a Beach Boys song was watching.

Wade looked out at the water. "Had a philosophy professor at Emory," he said, "when he was trying to get us to understand the scope of the universe…"

"Don't you mean a science professor?"

"There are more things, Horatio Singer than are dreamt of in your philosophy. Besides, this is my story."

"Where wilt thou lead me? Speak."

Wade looked at me, surprised I think.

"You aren't the only one who read Shakespeare. Dude."

"Okay, so this professor said to get an idea of the size of the universe, imagine a golf ball in the middle of the Pacific Ocean." He waited a moment. "I mean, look out here, just this small little bay and one little golf ball. Then imagine the Pacific."

"Titleist or Nike?"

Wade backhanded my shoulder. And damn, it hurt. But being a macho man, I covered my pain.

"Asshole," he said. "Educating the heathens be hard work."

"So what's your point?"

"Just that it doesn't take much to see that the problems of three little people don't amount to a hill of beans in this crazy world. Someday you'll understand that. Schweetheart."

"Philosophy, Shakespeare, and now Bogart. What's with you?"

"I'm trying to figure out what the hell happened. McDougal, dickhead that he is, not only has an alibi, I just don't see him being able to do that kind of violence and remain so cool about it."

"Unless we're losing it."

"I ain't losing it. You, on the other hand, do have that damn berfday comin' up."

We passed the two road signs that identify Paraíso del Mar. The first is the official city limits sign: white letters on a green background, it's pock-marked by all of the chips in the paint from where teenagers shot at it with BB guns, or sometimes a .22. The other sign is simple black script lettering on a white background: *Paradise By The Sea.*

And this *is* paradise. For the most part.

Like every other Southern California beach town, we have McMansions stuffed on tiny oceanfront lots. And you can't look north without seeing the jumbo jets taking off in the distance from LAX. But it's easy to imagine, especially if you're sitting on one of Paraíso del Mar's higher bluffs, a tri-masted Spanish galleon gliding into our little bay a couple hundred years ago and the sailors and the *conquistadores* on board thinking they'd reached the Promised Land. The pristine white sand beaches are long and deep. The water, in spite of all the pollution we humans dump into it, still clean and pure. Even now on the rare times, I go out and boogie board, I can look down and see the ocean's sandy bottom through the waves.

Ever since Big Ben Black became police Chief, crime in our sleepy little beach town has been pretty much small potatoes: petty theft, some drunks getting too loud or crashing into one another with their cars, the occasional domestic disturbance, and the odd B&E. The Chief is a law unto himself. Has been for over two decades. Abbey McDougal's murder had hit Paraíso del Mar like a tidal wave.

The Chief didn't like it.

Neither did the one man who's richer and even more powerful than him: Mayor Reed Lockhart. The Mayor isn't just the Chief's boss, he's also his best friend of over forty years. Nothing happens here without their say-so; or more importantly, say *no*. Reed Lockhart is up for his seventh consecutive term. It's a wonder they even print another name on the ballot.

Reed has power.

And he has money.

And he wields them in an inexorable combination.

Need a city building code exemption so you can go up *just an extra foot or so* to get that perfect unobstructed view of the water? Talk to Reed.

Wouldn't it be nice if those multimillion dollar homes a block from the Strand didn't have all those goddamn telephone poles interrupting the view? Talk to Reed. He'll get a bond issue put on a referendum to pay to put everything underground. So what if the only residents that receive the benefit are those that live just along the Strand? This is our town. One benefits, we all benefit.

Bullshit.

But through all those elections, no one's been able to stop him.

Mostly because no one's been able to figure him out or is smart enough to plan ahead and see his moves coming.

When he's not swaying voters to his side or strong-arming the city council members with his slicked-back charm, Reed controls the biggest real estate company in town, RL Real Estate. Reed doesn't own *all* of the town, just the most expensive parts.

Singer & Wade is small potatoes compared to him. And about to get smaller.

"I think you're right. We dump McDougal."

"You sure?"

"Screw it. It's only money."

"A lot of money."

"Feels like blood money now."

I turned up the side street to Wade's house. He has a little two-bedroom bungalow, built in the thirties, that's been significantly remodeled, but not so it shows. New copper plumbing, total new electric, double-paned windows, all of it. But as the Mayor likes to say when he's into his real estate agent mode and pitching a house for sale, "the owner kept the 'bones' of the house and its original charm." However, if you were a "buyer with vision," he'd tell you the highest and best use of the land would be to raze the cracker box and put up a two-story mansion.

I pulled up in front, and Wade got out and leaned back to me, "Seven okay?"

"As long as that's the time and not the number of drinks you're having."

"Absolute–lee," Wade said and strolled for his front door.

10

Wade was already at the bar when I walked into Kincaid's. Next to him was my father. What the hell? Something was up, or somebody was in serious trouble. I hoped it wasn't me. Or my father.

I was ten feet away, and like a radar scope tracking incoming, my dad's silver-white head turned and locked onto me. "Ah, Signore Singer," he said and got off his stool and gave me a big goombah hug.

Our original family name is Signorelli, but around the time my dad was nine years old, his mother, Flavia, decided the reason she couldn't get the jobs she wanted was that people discriminated against Italians. Singer, in her mind, seemed fairly close to Signorelli and when she and her little boy moved from Brooklyn to the San Fernando Valley, where I think she expected to see cowboy stars Gene Autry and Roy Rogers riding Champion and Trigger among the orange groves, they got off the Santa Fe El Capitan as Flower and Mario Singer.

The newly minted Singers came west because of the newly minted three grand that Flower got from a National Service Life Insurance (NSLI) policy that Giovanni, my paternal grandfather, had taken out before he shipped out. Giovanni had gone down in a B-17 bomber over Berlin in September '44.

Based in Foggia, Italy, the 5th Bombardment Wing of the Fifteenth Air Force would take their Flying Fortresses in tauntingly low over the Alps and bomb the shit out of German industrial targets. Gio was the tail gunner and a damn good one too. My dad used to brag that Gio had shot down a squadron of Messerschmitts. This never went down well with Jerry, the man Flower married just after my dad's eleventh birthday. He always called the new hubby Jerry, absolutely refused to call him Dad. Jerry got some revenge by never legally adopting Mario. And he'd stick in the knife by laughing when Mario would talk about Giovanni and tell him it was all bullshit since nobody could have shot down that many Nazis.

It wasn't until Mario joined up and they put him into Army Intelligence (a fuckin' oxymoron he used to say—Army and Intelligence) that he did some research and tracked down Giovanni's war record that confirmed he *had* that many confirmed kills. And another five unconfirmed . When he mailed the documents to Jerry, his salutation was:

Dear Husband No. 2 (#2 as in shit): Read it and weep. And not to put too fine a point on it: Next time you say my father was a fraud and that I'm a liar, I'll take your head off at the neck.

"Get my son a drink," my dad said to the bartender.

"Some shit, huh?" my dad said. "I'm sure Big Ben's having a coronary." A waitress with long honey-colored hair and cornflower-blue eyes passed by and gave my father a big smile. "Hey, Michelle," he said, returning her smile, only bigger.

Wade and I looked at each other and just shook our heads.

Women just love my old man. Yes, he's still a handsome dog, but he's sixty-nine years old. And it's not just women over fifty that are attracted to him -- this waitress, if she was in her twenties, she'd just had a birthday. And she was definitely sending signals to him.

He watched her go to the end of the bar and order drinks for her tables. Then he saw Wade watching him. "What?" he said. Wade nodded in Michelle's direction. "Michelle?" my dad said. "No, no." He took a hit on his drink. "In fact, I think I'm finally slowing down."

"Not a chance," Wade said.

"It's true," my dad said. "And it's a sad day too."

I knew there was some kind of story coming, so I just sipped my drink.

Not Wade, he couldn't wait. "What?" he said.

The bartender listened as he washed glasses near to us.

"You know how I always get takeout at Pedro's?" my dad said. "There's this cute new waitress just started there. Meagan. And she's always smiling at me, flirting, asking how I'm doing."

"Maybe she's just being nice to a dirty old man," I said.

"No way. Meagan is sending messages. I figure she's in her mid-twenties. So the other day I go in for some takeout and Meagan's nails are all done, and she's looking hot. So I asked her what's the big occasion?"

"'My senior prom,' she tells me. 'It's tomorrow night.'"

"She's seventeen?" Wade said.

"Seventeen, eighteen, I didn't ask," my dad said. "Because here's the depressing part. I was trying to figure out how it would have been if this had happened to me when I was eighteen. Say a woman fifty years older than me comes in and hits on me…wouldn't I have wondered what the hell she was thinking?"

"So no more flirting with little Meagan?" Wade asked.

"Nope," my dad said. "We're through before we even got started. It's sad."

"Yeah," I said. "But here's what's even sadder. When you were eighteen, that was 1968, right?"

"So what?"

"So that means the woman would have been born in 1918."

Wade bottled up his laugh, but I knew he was roaring inside.

"Shit, Pops, you'd have been hit on by someone who was born at the end of World War I."

My father chugged his drink and signaled for another. "You are…" he said, without looking my way, "…a cruel son."

"Here's the real question, regardless of age," I said.

"Go ahead, you're on a roll."

"Meagan's of consenting age, legally, if not morally. So somehow if you did get together with her, you know that somehow Pedro would get wind of it. And he'd eighty-six your ass from his restaurant."

"No, he…" my dad stopped. "Shit, he would."

The bartender poured directly from the bottle into my dad's glass. He wasn't going to miss any of this.

"See, that's definitely a sign I'm getting old. Because I'm actually thinking about it. God, how far I've fallen."

The bartender got so caught up he couldn't resist joining in, "So, it comes down to which is more important now in your golden years? Meagan's fuzzy taco? Or Pedro's *tacos al carbon*?"

We all looked at him.

"Hey, I'm sorry, I…shit."

"You're wanted at the other end of the bar," Wade said.

He couldn't go fill those drink orders fast enough.

"Well?" I said. "That was crude, but you do have a dilemma. Food or sex?"

"I'm not sure," my dad said, getting up and taking his drink to head for our table. "But, what the hell. There are other Mexican restaurants in Paraíso del Mar."

11

We sat down, and the waitress took our food and drink orders. Then Wade and I filled my dad in on what we'd learned about Stephen McDougal. We talked about it all through the salad, the steaks, and houses fries—giving him information, answering questions, trying to figure it all out—so that by the time we finally ordered coffee, we had covered it from every possible angle and had arrived at a conclusion: We were screwed. No commission, no sale, no chance to salvage anything out of this mess.

"He's guilty," my dad said.

"And you know this how?" I said.

"Because the husband always does it. Don't you watch TV?" He signaled for the check. "That's a joke. But statistically, husbands are far and away the culprits. I mean, ask yourself, who benefits from her death? Husband, right? The police check into the insurance angle?"

"Not yet, but he's already cashed in a boatload of money with his second wife."

"Abbey was a good-looking woman," my dad said. Of course, he would know that. "So maybe she's nearing forty, feeling a little insecure about her looks and hubby's not paying attention to her, so she has a little fling or two."

"Or ten or twenty," I said. I glanced at Wade but only for a moment.

"So he gets pissed off, kills her," my dad said.

"They were getting a divorce. Doesn't make sense," said Wade.

"It's got to be Stephen McDougal," my dad said.

"But he's got an airtight alibi," Wade said.

My dad grabbed the check before Wade or I could even get within sniffing range of it. He slipped his AmEx card into the invoice holder without bothering to check the amount.

Wade looked at me and gestured at the check. I shrugged my shoulders for an answer. When my dad grabs the check, he's paying, and don't even go there.

"So Agatha Christie lives," my dad said. "We have a dead body. We have the prime suspect, who statistically lines up as the killer, but supposedly has an airtight alibi, and the local cops are standing there with their thumbs up their asses. And people say nothing ever happens in Paraíso del Mar."

The waitress returned, and my dad signed the slip after adding I'm sure what was an overly generous tip and we headed for the door. Michelle waved good-bye to my dad, and we stepped into the cool ocean breezes of the night. From the restaurant's deck, which was jammed with people sitting at redwood tables, drinking, laughing waiting to get inside, we could hear the surf roll in and crash on the shore.

"Quick," Wade said, "before he sees us."

"What?" asked Dad. "Who...aw, shit."

Too late. "Hey!" a piercing, nasal voice called across the deck.

"Damn it, it's the professor," I said.

"God," Wade said. "Why doesn't somebody kick him in the asterisk?"

The professor uncoiled his lanky frame and hustled over to us before we could get down the stairs. "Ah," he said, "the living embodiment of heroic antitheses."

"Prof," my dad said, looking past him. "You left that little darling just to give us another lesson?"

"No, no," the professor said, not looking back at the woman, who chugged her drink and ducked away into the crowd. "Samantha will wait for me." He pushed his thick bifocals back up the bridge of his long nose. "I called you two" — indicating Wade and me — "the embodiment of heroic antitheses because I believe your reputation as Paraíso del Mar's super salesmen, a little onomatopoeia that — "he grinned at us " — is in the shitter."

"Bad news travels fast," I said.

"Yeah," said Wade, "right across the deck at Kincaid's."

"So, Hiram," my dad said, "what's your fuckin' point?"

The professor doesn't like being called Hiram. He thinks the five years he was at Harvard has moved him beyond such ordinary labels. He also doesn't like the lack of reverence my dad or Wade, and I have for him.

"My goodness, Mario," the professor said, but took a step back. "Nothing personal, I was just reflecting about Matt and Wade's involvement in the tragic news about a murder, right here in our sleepy little town. And what you think happened."

"The butler did it," I said.

"Yes, yes, very funny. But of course, there is no butler involved here."

"You never know. Appearances can be deceiving. But Prof, let me ask you a question. Can you turn two single syllable words into four syllables?"

"I'm sorry," he said, "I don't follow."

"Matt Singer's word magic. I turn two single syllables into four and by so doing accomplish two things at once. Make a point. And tell you how I really feel."

"Okay," he said. "Show me."

"Fu-ukk You-uuu."

12

"Always with the smart mouth," Chief Ben Black said.

"At least there's some smart in there," I said.

Just as I'd predicted, Ben had called Wade in for, as he put it, routine questioning, and then asked me to join the party.

We were sitting in his office in front of the Chief's massive desk. It's the biggest desk I've ever seen. Shiny, oiled walnut topped by an inch-thick glass with nothing on it except the Chief's impressive parade of model cars. Ben loves expensive automobiles—Lamborghinis, Aston-Martins, and his favorites, Ferraris. And whenever he buys another for his collection, he has a high-end model company build him an exact replica. Exact down to the precise shade of paint, the same leather seats, and interior, even the damn wheels and tires. And then it joins the motorcade.

What had happened between Wade and Abbey wasn't relevant, or at least that's what we'd decided, and Duncan had confirmed. "If they ask," Duncan had said, "then you tell the truth. But only if they ask."

And so far, Big Ben hadn't asked.

His last question had been, "You think somebody porkin' Abbey did this?"

"That's a piggish comment, Chief."

Which got me the smart-mouth comment.

He adjusted one of the model cars, a Lamborghini Aventador with the gullwing doors that pivoted up, so they were like twin batwings. "This bullshit private investigation license you've got doesn't pull any weight with the real law."

I nodded. No argument there. The Paraíso del Mar cops were legitimate, recognized by the State of California. And in Paraíso del Mar, the Chief was a law unto himself. Wade and I were just small-time investigators. Really small since we hadn't had a case in over four months.

After I'd left the force, I'd just drifted into the investigation business. But you get tired of the voyeur shit—taking photos or videos of one rich person screwing around with another rich person's wife or husband, so the alleged injured party can keep more of the money. Meanwhile, they're out screwing around too.

And as Wade had said about most of our cases, "Dey don't end with dey bang from a revolver o' dey slammin' of dey front door, dey end wit' dey bang-bang-banging o' dey headboard against dey wall."

I keep the license current. You never know when a crime wave will hit our shores like one of the monster waves we get every decade or, so that washes up over the end of the pier. And Wade and I want to be ready.

We also go to the shooting range, mostly to just feel the surge and power of our weapons and waste some time and ammunition when we're bored.

Ben shook his head, puffed out his cheeks, and exhaled a long exasperated breath.

"Just because I felt patriotic and hired your ass a long time ago doesn't mean you still get privileges," he said.

"I didn't expect any."

I'd never expected or wanted, *anything* from Ben. The fact that he hired me was a surprise. To me. And, ultimately, too late to him.

But he was right about the patriotic part.

In June '98, I'd graduated Paraíso del Mar High School and mostly being dumb and gung-ho and still remembering Oliver Stone's movie, *Platoon*, I drove twenty miles inland which was where the nearest U.S. Marine Recruiting Station was and enlisted.

By December of that year I was deep in Iraq and part of Operation Desert Storm. I got lucky, made it out alive and when my time was up, pulled a Roberto Duran and said, *"No mas."*

I came home to Paraíso del Mar and a bleepin' parade as a wartime hero. All pretty bogus to me. Because in between the insufferable desert heat and the cruise missle and bombing attacks, I'd jumped by parachute at night behind the lines and managed to save two Marines being held captive. Nothing heroic about it. The stars were aligned, the *I-Ching* came up in perfect combination, I was the luckiest jarhead on the planet. It happened. Some of the enemy got in the way of my bullets. It's hard to explain or talk about.

Go to a bar, and eventually if some guy's drunk enough, and pissed off at his wife or boss, or just pretty much his life, he'll tell you about some dude he'd like to waste. Some asshole that cut him off in traffic and how he'd like to just blow a fuckin' hole in the son of a bitch.

Thoreau said, *"Most men lead lives of quiet desperation."*

"All men lead lives of murderous fantasy," is what I say. It's in our DNA, back to our lizard brain beginnings—screw the guy up bad. Waste the prick and never look back.

That's every man's fantasy.

And no man's reality.

Because very few men ever go through with the deed. Sure, there will always be random acts of violence. Crimes of passion. Arguments got out of control, and somebody died. Some husband or boyfriend caught his wife or girlfriend humping some guy and blew the shit out of him. And sometimes the wife and girlfriend too. A father would kill to save his wife or children. A kid would empty a 16-shot Glock to save his mom.

But that wasn't being a killer, even though people died. That was an accident. And accidents were never like the fantasy. Because in the fantasy, the gunshot was never that loud. And there was never all that blood hemorrhaging from the hole that the bullet made, with the guy's best friend or brother or neighbor dying. No coming back. He was going-going-gone.

And now there he was the once angry man with the smoking gun literally in his hand, the hand of the killer. His life forever changed. His family's and friends' lives and anyone who ever had a passing acquaintance with him, their lives changed too. *Jesus, Larry shot him? No way. He shot him?*

The poor guy never got over it. He never understood it. He could barely remember his life B.T.S.—Before The Shooting.

I couldn't remember the last time it had happened in Paraíso del Mar, and Abbey's was the first in many years. But other cities, other perps? You'd talk to them, listen to their stories, which were always the same: total devastation and incomprehensible acceptance of the fact. Every one of them refused to face the truth of what they did until the judge's gavel came down and the guards led them out of the courtroom, their life, the lives of everyone they ever loved—wife, kids, family—annihilated forever.

Those enemy soldiers were the only men whose lives I've taken.

Unseen shapes in the night. There, then not there. I only saw one of them face-to-face. When he charged me, his rifle empty, the bayonet knife gleaming in the moonlight, somehow I'd managed to avoid most of the slash—if eighteen stitches in your side is avoidance—and countered and slammed my own blade deep into his throat, his hot blood erupting in a crimson shower.

When we were getting out of there, and I was carrying one Marine on my back and pulling the other by his arm, my uniform sticky with that enemy soldier's blood, because there wasn't time to clean up, the coppery stench was so intense, I retched my guts out on the light-brown sand.

Sometimes at night, that aroma comes to me in the dark, wrapping me in a suffocating cocoon of red and I wake up sweating, my heart thundering in my ears.

And none of the bullshit that the shrinks, both military and civilian tell you, *"Sometimes, just sometimes, war is justified, Matt,"* helps.

None of it.

As long as it was for God and country, then you were innocent. If it was under the stars 'n stripes, you could fire-bomb entire villages of innocent people who had no idea their country was at war. You could invade countries whose oil you needed or whose borders you needed to secure for that oil. If it was World War II, under the American flag you could give an enemy airplane "the whole nine yards" (that being the length of an ammo belt in a P-51 Mustang—twenty-seven feet of .45 caliber bullets, 475 of them, each five inches long—and sleep peacefully. Hell, in that war, if the "buck stopped" on your Harry Ass Truman desk back in August 1945, you could drop the Big One on Hiroshima, and then, just in case the Japanese didn't get the hint, do it again on Nagasaki.

But it's all bullshit to think you can accept it, much less justify it.

I never could. Even though I had no choice.

It still bothers me.

We are all killers.

It just depends on the circumstances.

My circumstances, the USMC decided, were worth a Navy Cross, a Purple Heart, plus a small rainbow of ribbons. Embarrassing as hell.

It only got more embarrassing when the good folk of Paraíso del Mar decided I needed to ride on top of the back seat of Justin Frye's brand new cream Cadillac convertible (Justin being Paraíso del Mar's hotshot car dealer) in a little parade. Since the main drag of town is only six blocks, "little" was the operative word. But it was definitely a big event for the town. Grammar school kids waving flags happy and smiling, mostly because they'd gotten out of school for the event. Some older folk clapping, also waving flags. A couple of crusty Korean War vets who'd donned their old hats (the rest of their uniforms either too tight to wear or too far gone) and saluted as I rode past.

My dad was waving and pumping his fist at the end of the parade at the little assembly of seats and the bunting-covered raised dais and guest platform. A high-ranking Marine officer spoke about bravery and honor. Some other city officials and rich citizens also spoke about America and the cost of freedom. But the audience really only listened to two speakers—Chief Ben Black then in his eleventh year, and His Honor Mayor Reed Lockhart, at that time running for a third consecutive term.

I mumbled and stumbled through the few paragraphs my dad and I had written together expressing my gratitude and humble thanks, and then slid away from the dais and through the city parking lot and got the hell out of there. I drove up the coast to Santa Barbara and surfed with a couple of locals.

When I came back, Big Ben summoned me to his office. Mayor Lockhart joined the meeting, and I was pretty much railroaded into becoming one of Paraíso del Mar's Blues. Since I only seem to do anything at full speed, the fact I made detective in record time and got partnered with Mike Gillette just seemed like part of the plan.

All of that seems like it happened to someone else.

"So can we see him?" I said.

"See him? What the hell for?"

"Support," I said.

"Chief," Wade said, "his wife's been murdered. He might need somebody to talk to."

"Yeah, right. Like fucking McDougal needs a shoulder to cry on."

"So?" I said.

"Okay," Ben said, "be back here at eleven-thirty. You'll get five minutes."

Wade and I muttered our thanks and went for the door, but it swung open and filling the doorway with his considerable bulk in his custom-made uniform was Purdy. But custom-made doesn't mean bespoke. Because he's so damn overweight that no standard uniform could contain his hulking form. He always looks like a slob. Wrinkled, rumpled, with permanent dark sweat circles under his armpits, and a ballooning belly that would shame a woman ten months pregnant.

He blocked the doorway, daring us to try and get past him.

We waited.

"Purdy, what the fuck you waiting for? Get in here," Ben barked.

And now in a little *jiu-jitsu* of life, Purdy had been reversed, because Wade and I stood shoulder to shoulder in front of him. You could almost see the thoughts rolling through his pea brain on whether to charge us, then his eyes flickering to the Chief, and finally his angry acceptance and resignation to step to his left and allow us through. "Assholes," he hissed as he passed by.

That made it even better.

Heh-heh.

13

Stephen McDougal wasn't smiling when we walked into his cell. He was still in his street clothes—black Hugo Boss sport coat, silk T-shirt and some French brand of jeans that must have cost eight hundred bucks. His long legs were stretched out into the cell and crossed at his bare ankles. He wasn't wearing any socks with his Ferragamo loafers.

"Shit, I was expecting Stillman."

"Attorneys have their own clock," I said.

McDougal uncrossed his ankles, crossed them the other way. "You have any idea when they'll let me out of here?" he said. "This is fuckin' boring."

I figured he was in shock. Or acting tough. Or maybe *did* kill Abbey. Because he didn't seem like a man whose wife had been brutally murdered.

"Yeah, must be tough," I said.

I guess I didn't hide my sarcasm too well.

"Look," he said, "I'm blown away by all of this. I still can't believe it's true. So if I'm not tearing my hair out over Abbey's death, or yelling and crying, it's because I'm...I'm still in shock. I'm numb."

Wade looked at him for several seconds, didn't say a word.

"I'm not acting like you think I should, so I'm guilty?" he said.

"We don't think you should act anyway," I said. "Emphasis on act."

"What the hell's that supposed to mean?"

"This is a traumatic event. There's no rule book on behavior."

"Right," said Wade. "And nobody can tell you what you're feeling or how you're acting is right or wrong. It just is."

McDougal seemed to accept that and agree with it, his head nodding slightly. "So, if you two can't get me out, what're you doing here? Jesus, this isn't about the house, is it?"

"No. We just came by to see if we could help in any way."

"Yeah, get me some breakfast. All I've had was a cup of day-old coffee and a biscuit that was hard as a rock."

There was a series of several electronic beeps, and the door to the jail opened, and a cop pointed down to McDougal's cell. Which seemed unnecessary. There are only three cells in Paraíso's jail, and only one of them was occupied.

We watched as Julian "Bags" Stillman backed into the room, his arms loaded with three briefcases, every one of them bulging.

That's why he's called "Bags"—in an era of the internet, thumb drives and cloud technology, Stillman remains a dinosaur and has hard copies of everything. And he lugs every one of his current files around in one of his dozen or so legal briefcases. How he remembers which files are in which briefcase is a mystery to all of us.

He lowered the briefcases to the floor and looked at us.

"Mr. McDougal isn't answering any more questions," he said. "And anything he may have said to you before this was privileged and therefore inadmissible."

"Relax, Bags, we're Stephen's real estate agents."

"We're the hired help too," Wade said. "Just like you."

Stillman weighed this, and you could tell he wasn't happy being referred to as just another hired gun. Especially considering who the other employees were. Then, of course, there was his diffidence about proper nouns.

"I don't know how many times I have asked you to *not* call me Bags. My name is Julian or Mister Stillman. But not *Bags*. It's rude and disrespectful."

"Geez, Bags, you're getting touchy," Wade said and gave him a long stare.

"So when you getting me out of here?" McDougal said.

Bags went into one of his bags and pulled out a blue folder. "We just need to go over a couple of things, and then I'll file the documents, and you'll be a free man." Bags looked at McDougal. "Well, free on bond."

"No way! I have to post a bond? That's bullshit. I haven't done anything. There's no evidence to tie me into this."

McDougal ranted off and on, Bags went through his "couple of things," which turned out to be a boatload of crap, and Wade and I never got to ask any more questions.

We went to lunch at Lucy's Restaurant. Probably the best place for breakfast and lunch in Paraíso del Mar. Or pretty much most of the beach towns within twenty miles up or down the shoreline. The food's terrific. And so are the waitresses. And not just because they're all named Lucy.

Not really. But that's what every waitress's name tag says in white script letters: *Lucy*. That way they don't get hit on by too many Romeos, and it keeps things fun and hassle-free.

"I don't like McDougal," Wade said in between bites of an egg-white omelet with broccoli and tomatoes, no cheese.

"Because he's an asshole? Or because he seems hinky?"

"Both."

Our Lucy came by and topped our coffees. Wade waited until she was out of range. "As my grandmamma Eurlene used to say about people like him, 'He thinks his shit don't stink, but his farts gave him away.'"

"I would have liked your grandmother."

"Hard not to."

"Okay, so he's a dickhead, and his alibi is bulletproof. But I agree." I took a big bite of pancake, followed with a full forkful of my own egg-white omelet. "So I think I'll drop by the Marriott, see if any of the maids or the nighttime staff might have another view of McDougal."

"You think Carlos the assistant manager was hiding something?" Wade said.

"Not intentionally. But Carlos does want to be *the* manager, so he might unconsciously be editing his information."

"Not want the hotel to look bad."

"Drop from four stars to three stars."

Wade signaled Lucy for the check. "While you're checking out the beds there, I'm going to be checking out the bed at my house. I need a little nap."

"A nap?" said Lucy. "At this time of day?"

"Yeah," said Wade. "Interested?"

She gathered up the check and the money. "My first name's Lucy," she said, with a big smile that definitely had some cheese in it, "but my last name isn't goosey."

14

"Gonzalez," I said. "Maria, hey."

She turned from her linen cart and looked at me. "Hello, Singer." She smiled, "How are you, Matt?"

Maria Gonzales could definitely be some lonely man's horndog hotel fantasy: She comes in to clean the room, thinks you're so hot, and within minutes you're between the sheets.

Of course, it will never happen. But Maria does have that quality. Even behind her minimalist makeup and her maid's uniform that she purposely wears a couple of sizes too big, she still gives men whiplash when she walks by.

Maria looked past my shoulder to see if anyone else was around and gave me a small kiss on the cheek. We did a favor for Maria a while back, and she's always been grateful. Not *that* grateful, but still very appreciative. Maria had some immigration issues with the government stiff-neck that was processing her green card application. Seems that he felt Maria shouldn't protest about being felt up, even as he claimed, it was inadvertent. Of course, he also told her, without any gloss, that if she wanted to stay put she had to put out.

I learned all this through Maria's cousin, Juanito. So Wade and I paid Immigration Supervisor Jonathan Hepburn a little visit as he walked out of the Federal Building. A week later Maria had all of her immigration papers. She didn't know who to thank until Juanito told her. "I owe you so much, Mister Singer," she'd said, with only the slightest, lilting accent. "And you too, Mister Wade."

Since then Maria has always gone out of her way to make sure any visits we had at the hotel or for our guests, which were usually buyers from out of town, got the very best service.

"So what can I do for you?"

"Oh, it's that obvious?"

"You don't usually see me here at the hotel, so I think there's something you need. Maybe some kind of trouble."

She wasn't just a pretty face.

"I'm checking on some facts about a case."

"Okay," she said. "Walk with me. I need to get this cart to the laundry."

"A man stayed in Room 1214 two nights ago," I said.

"Okay."

"Did you work in that room?"

We turned a corner and stopped in front of the elevator. "No, "she said. "That was Tuesday, right? And on Tuesdays, I am on the fourth floor." The doors opened, and she bumped the cart over the elevator door gap and when I was inside, punched the button for the basement. "But I can ask Cheryl, that's her floor on Tuesdays."

The doors opened, I stepped out and held the door for Maria. She pulled her cell phone, hit a button, and then in Spanish too rapid for me to follow she rattled off a series of questions, got answers, asked more questions, and then with a sweet, *"Gracias,"* hung up.

"Cheryl remembers he asked for four extra towels."

"Is that a lot?"

"Si," Maria said, slipping into Spanish because the question was so dumb she forgot to explain for us *gringos.* "The hotel gives six towels to start. Four big towels and two huge ones. So, yes, four extra is a lot."

"Maybe he's really into hygiene," I said.

"Maybe," Maria said. "Because when she went into the room, the shower was running and there was lots of steam coming out the door."

"Anything else?"

"Just the towels, Matt." She looked at me carefully. "What is this all about?"

"I'm not sure yet."

"Oh, no, wait," Maria said. "Is this about…about the woman who was killed?"

"Now how did you come up with that?"

"You come to the hotel for the first time in maybe a year. You ask about a particular room. If anything's connected to the people in that room. And since so little happens in Paraíso del Mar, a murder is definitely big news. So you come here, ask those questions, and it's easy to figure out."

"Maybe Wade and I should take you on as a partner. Yes, it is about that. And of course, I have to ask you not to mention our talk."

"Matt! Really?"

I held up my hands in surrender. "Sorry, just being cautious."

"How does this man figure into it?"

"He's the husband."

"*Madre de Dios!*"

She looked into the corner of the laundry where several men were tossing linens, towels, bedding, and the countless other things that hotels wash into a bank of huge, industrial washing machines. She didn't say anything for a few moments, thinking.

"So he is at a hotel, and his wife is murdered? And he was here all night?"

"Checked in 9:26, checked out 8:31 the next morning. So he has an alibi."

"Not an alibi. A reason."

"What?"

Maria looked at me like sometimes the professor looks at me when I get smartass on one of his pedantic lessons. "Matt, no man checks into a hotel, orders extra towels, and is there by himself."

"Hey, Maria!" one of the workers called out. "You going to bring that cart over or you want special service?"

"I have to go," she said and leaned into her cart. "Oh, and Matt," she said over her shoulder, "Happy Birthday."

"How'd you know that?"

"You think I'm just a pretty face?"

15

"Hey," Kincaid yelled as I approached the bar, "it's the birthday boy."

"Shhh," I said.

The fact that Pat was behind the bar tonight made me feel good. He doesn't tend bar anymore unless it's something special. Of course, I should have known something special didn't always mean something good. Or not embarrassing.

"Oh, getting sensitive in our dotage, huh?" Pat said. "Okay, first thing, give me your car keys."

"What? Nobody drives the Snake except me."

"I don't have issues about my penis size," he said. "And I don't want to drive it. I just don't want *you* to drive it. At least not tonight." He held out his meaty paw.

I fished the keys from my pocket and dropped them into his palm. "That must mean I'm getting a lot of free drinks tonight," I said.

"A lot for you," Wade said as he came up to the bar, "means maybe two." We shook hands. "Happy B.D."

"Thanks."

His left hand was behind his back, so I knew it was a present of some kind. Probably not good.

"I was going to wrap this," he said, "but it didn't seem appropriate."

His left hand came out with some rolled-up grey material. He took hold of it with his right hand and shook it out. "Ta-dah!"

It was a T-shirt. With my driver's license ID photo.

Above my head was printed: MATT-A-SAURUS

Below my face was: BELIEVED TO BE PAST FORTY YEARS OLD!

Kincaid and a few of the other bar patrons all had a great laugh. So did I. It was pretty funny.

I took the tee and held it at arm's length. "Where the hell'd you get my driver's license photo?"

"I lifted it from your wallet a few weeks ago while you were down getting coffee, snapped a photo of it with my phone, and there you are, emblazoned for all posterity."

"Thank you. I guess."

"You going to wear it tonight?"

"I don't think I'll ever wear it," I said. "It'd be like Justin Timberlake wearing a T-shirt with his own face on it."

That got even bigger laughs.

Kincaid put a tall *mojito* in front of me, and I took a long, cold sip.

"*Cento anni,*" my dad said as he came up and threw an arm around my shoulder.

"Hey, Pops," I said. "You don't have any surprises, do you?"

"Only that I'm buying."

"Not a chance," said Wade. "You picked up last time."

"I can't buy my boy a birthday dinner?"

"Hey!" Kincaid said. "Nobody's buying dinner, it's on the house. So shut up and drink up. You want to give this place a bad reputation?"

"Your reputation was ruined long before tonight," I said. "But I accept your hospitality quickly."

"What're you having, Mister S?" Kincaid asked my dad.

"One of those," he said. But Kincaid's attention was looking past us at the hostess stand. "Okay." He turned to one of the other bartenders, "Hey, Alan, get Mister Singer a *mojito*. Excuse me a minute, guys."

We watched Kincaid hustle to the hostess stand where Mayor Reed Lockhart was flashing his megawatt smile and shaking hands with several couples waiting for their tables.

"Fuckin' guy's a lock on his seventh consecutive term," my dad said, "and he's pressing flesh like he was a southern diplomat."

The Mayor shook Kincaid's hand vigorously when he came up, actually gave him one of those two-handed jobs. He and Kincaid exchanged a few words, the Mayor pointed toward the door like he was waiting for someone and Kincaid nodded. Then Kincaid said something to the hostess, and she immediately wrote something on her guest list.

"My guess is he didn't have an appointment," I said.

"Mayors don't need appointments," my dad said.

"Who do you think he's waiting for?" said Wade.

"Ask Kincaid when he comes back," I said.

But we didn't need to do that, because the door opened and in walked the Mayor's date. Well, actually his daughter, Leah Lockhart, the living dream girl of every Beach Boy song—tall, stunning, and the kind of blonde hair that Clairol used in their commercials. Leah was probably in her mid-thirties, but you couldn't tell that by her lithe, athletic figure and the way she carried herself. And when she smiled, her father's grin looked like it needed teeth-whitening.

Leah gave her father a hug and a quick kiss on the cheek. She waved to several people at tables, and then she and the Mayor went to sit down. Reed had to shake hands and slap customers on the back all the way to his table. Just before they got to their destination—a booth in the back— a good-looking woman in her late forties stood up from her chair and squeezed His Honor's arm. I saw a look flash across Leah's face that could have cut steel. But the Mayor patted the woman's husband on the arm and pushed onward.

A waitress was instantly at their table, looked like she asked about drinks, and got a request from the Mayor and a polite headshake from Leah. By the time the waitress got back to the bar, Kincaid had the drink waiting. He handed it to the waitress and came back to us.

"The Mayor always orders the same?" I asked.

"Double Cutty on the rocks," said Kincaid. "And probably a Merlot for dinner."

"Not the House Red, I'll bet," said Wade.

"Nothing wrong with our House Red," said Kincaid. "It comes from Sonoma."

"I drink it all the time," said Wade. "It's just that Reed doesn't strike me as a value menu kinda guy. I'm sure he's top-shelf, private reserve label on everything."

"Spottswood Cab," said Kincaid. "Two thousand and five. I give him a deal on it. A buck fifty a bottle. But if he's really putting the schmooze on somebody, he comes in the day before and wanders through the cellar."

"So what're we having?" I said.

"The two-dollar Night Train Special."

"Give me back my keys," I said. "I'm not drinking."

We headed for our table, which was near the Mayor's. As we passed, Leah looked up and gave us a big smile. I'm sure Wade, my dad, and I each took it personally.

"Your Honor," my dad said. "No, no, don't get up." He shook Reed's hand, smiled at Leah, and kept us moving toward our table.

"Okay," I said after we sat down, "thanks for the tee, but no birthday cake. I mean it."

"Don't worry about that," said Wade. "All those candles? Probably set off the fire alarm."

Which should have set off warning alarms in my head.

Wade and my dad love to screw everybody. And anybody.

So after we went through the salad, the main course, including two bottles of Kincaid's personal picks—an '02 Fiddlehead Cellar Pinot Noir followed by an '01 Bridgeview Merlot—it was time for coffee.

And the Screwing.

Because suddenly it looked like the entire staff of Kincaid's, including the damn cooks, dishwashers, hostess, waiters and waitresses, and of course, Pat himself who led them, and of course everyone else had to join in, in a goddamn loud, off-key songfest of "Happy Birthday."

I sat there, kept a big, embarrassed smile on my puss, and endured it. As they were hitting the last "to yooouuu," I glanced up and saw Leah looking at me. She shook her head slightly and mouthed, "I'm sorry."

So it wasn't all bad. At least I got the sympathy vote from the politician's table.

My dad threw a couple of twenties on the table.

"It's on the house, remember?" I said.

"Yeah, but the waitress still needs a tip."

Wade and I each matched hm.

"Big night for her," Wade said. "Hell, she probably wishes you had a birthday every night."

"This one was tough enough."

Sheila, our waitress, came by and when she saw the tip, confirmed what Wade had said. "Oh, wow. Thank you," she said. "I mean...wow, Happy Birthday."

As she picked up the cash, a big man jostled her.

Big Ben.

"Sorry," he grumbled. And slid his considerable bulk into the Mayor's booth.

A moment later, Leah blew a kiss to her father and excused herself. My dad and Wade headed for the door.

"Thanks, see you two thugs later," I said and followed Leah to the bar.

What the hell, I thought. It *is* my birthday.

16

You don't look very happy on your special day,"Leah said as I took a seat next to her at the bar.

"You mean my unbridled joy wasn't apparent?"

"Let me buy you a drink," she said. "Put a smile on your mug."

"I'm already smiling sitting next to you." She looked at me. "Sorry, was that too obvious?" I said.

Way to go, Singer.

"Perhaps I'm slipping in my advancing years."

"You could always claim you were drunk." She extended her hand.

"Leah Lockhart," I said before she could.

"What? Oh…?"

"I mean, you're Leah Lockhart, and I'm…"

"Matt Singer," she said. "So we both know each other."

"Of each other."

"That too." She beckoned the bartender with a long index finger, the nail glossy with shiny red polish, and he appeared almost instantly; obviously a fan of Leah's. "Give the birthday boy his fondest wish," she said and looked at me out of the corner of her eye.

"Another *mojito*?" the bartender asked, anxious to let us both know that he was both observant and smart because he remembered his customers by both name and drink. I nodded, and he went off to do his job.

"You don't like Big Ben?" I said.

"You mean my unbridled joy wasn't apparent?"

I laughed.

"He's always been around my family," she said. "My father says they were friends together on the force. Before I was born."

"Your dad was a cop?" That was news. And I thought I knew all the stories of the town's big players.

"Only for a couple of years," she said, "then he went back to school, got his law degree from SC, working as a real estate agent by day, taking classes at night."

"Pretty ambitious," I said.

"That's my dad."

"So why don't you like Big Ben?"

She looked at me, started to say something, and then changed her mind.

When my drink arrived, I picked it up, clinked glasses with Leah, and said, "Thank you and cheers. Next one's on me. And maybe the one after that."

She looked at me.

"It's okay," I said. "Kincaid took my keys. So I'll be taking a cab or calling Uber."

"Fortunately, my house isn't too far," she said.

Leah's house was just one door up from the Strand. It was a two-bedroom, one bath. Remodeled, but only about eighteen hundred square feet. Which meant it was worth six million, easy. Like I said, Reed doesn't own all of our town, just its most expensive parts.

"I can walk there," she said.

"I just got here, and we're already talking about leaving?" I said. "The night's still young."

"Even if you're not." And she laughed again, huskier, louder. "Sorry, sorry. Damn, I am getting sloshed."

I put my birthday T-shirt on the bar. Leah reached across me, pulled it over, and shook it out. She looked at the shirt photo and compared it to me. "Were you having a bad day when this was taken? "

"I'd been waiting three hours to renew my driver's license."

"That explains it."

"Ah, so there you are." Reed Lockhart came up and patted his daughter on the shoulder. "Hello, Matt," he said and shook my hand. "Happy Birthday."

"Thank you."

"I'll see you later," Ben Black said to Reed's back.

"Yeah," the Mayor said without turning around. Then *sotto voce* said, "That's what I'm afraid of."

Leah and I exchanged a look. I'm not sure what was signified in it, but it seemed to vindicate her dislike of Big Ben.

"Not to talk business on your birthday, but what a mess about the McDougals."

"It's horrible," Leah said. "Poor Abbey."

"What's that do to your listing?" Reed said.

I shrugged for my answer. Reed might be the Mayor, he might be friendly, but he was ruthless about real estate. And if there was a way to get the listing for his company, he'd do it.

"Don't worry, Matt. I'm not trying to steal it, I was just trying to figure out its long-range effect on the town."

"Dad! Can you stop worrying about property values? Just for once."

He looked at Leah, and his eyes flared. Then he smiled.

"Ah, you're right. So can I buy you a drink, seeing as it's your birthday? And for my *faux pas*?" Reed asked.

"Thanks, but the Lockharts have already done that once. Besides I should be heading home soon."

"Bartender," the Mayor called, "another round for my daughter and Matt. Even though he says, he's had enough." He slapped me on the back. "Hell, you're still young and so is the night."

Leah and I exchanged another look. We both smiled.

"So," I said, "I just learned that you were once a cop here in Paraíso del Mar."

Reed momentarily glanced at Leah, and then turned to me, "Just like you, brothers in blue."

"You and Ben worked together?"

A look of annoyance flashed across his face and was immediately replaced by his mayoralty smile. "No, no. Ben worked for *me*. I was a sergeant, he was a rookie."

"Sorry."

"Nothing to be sorry about. Ben loved busting people more than I did and I had…well, I had other things to do. Right, Leah?"

"Yes."

"Ben liked things done, bang-bang, results right now. I preferred the longer range view. Might not be as flashy, but in the long run, more effective. Because it lasts."

The bartender delivered our drinks.

"But make no mistake, Ben was and is a great policeman."

"Oh, c'mon, Dad, you made Ben's career. If it wasn't for you, he'd still be pounding the beat. Or maybe off the force entirely. For brutality."

"Shh, Leah. That's not polite. And not true."

"Okay, whatever you say. Be politically correct, fine," she said. "But you did everything for him." She finished her drink, picked up the new one that Wes had delivered. "And I mean *every*thing."

"I didn't give him his nickname."

"Oh, Dad, please, not again."

But he ignored her and stepped closer to me.

"It was one of Howard Hughes's little starlets. Ben did some off-the-clock security for old, weird Howard, so every once in a while Ben would get invited to one of Howard's little *soirees*. And one night, I guess things got a little crazy, and there was Ben with no pants on, and this little starlet comes running out of the room, yelling, 'No, no. That thing's so long it swings like a pendulum.' And from then on he was Big Ben. I don't think he minds it."

"I have always hated that story," Leah said.

"All right," he said, "my bad." He kissed her cheek again. "I've got some business."

Suddenly he started coughing. So violently, he doubled over from the severity.

"Daddy! Are you okay?"

I was going to slap Reed on the back, but the bartender appeared with a glass of water. Reed took a small swallow. "I'm fine, I'm fine," he said.

"Dad, maybe I should go with you," she said.

"Don't be silly. I'm not dying. I just had a coughing spell."

But he turned his head away from Leah, and I saw him spit into a handkerchief. And his spittle was mottled with red. He slipped it into his pocket and headed out.

"Good night, good night," he said, crossing the long ocean-blue carpet of Kincaid's restaurant, waving to the little table islands of people—once again the sleek politician, charming his constituents.

Leah watched him go. Her face was knotted in worry.

"What is it?" I said.

She shook her head.

"Is your dad sick?"

She waited before saying anything. "I don't know for sure. You saw what happened when I asked him. He just brushes it off like it's nothing. But you don't cough like that and not have something wrong."

"Has he gone to the doctors?"

"Yes. But he says they're all quacks. Even though they're from UCLA and Cedars. I mean, the doctors he sees are among the best in the country."

"Well, you could call them and see if they'd tell you anything."

"I tried. And they all invoked the doctor/patient confidentially clause. Assholes."

"I know a couple of people. An attorney. He might be able to help you."

"That's kind of you, Matt," she said. "I appreciate that. I know someone too. One of the nurses where he goes. I'm thinking maybe she and I should have lunch."

Spoken like a true politician's daughter—there's always a backdoor deal.

"I hate that story he tells about Ben," she said.

"More a guy thing," I said.

She looked at me, studied me for a long moment.

"I saw him...or *it* once," she said. "Why they call him Big Ben."

I waited. What the hell was I supposed to say?

"When I was thirteen. He and my dad had gone bodysurfing, and afterward, he came up and took a shower at our house. My dad was upstairs talking to somebody on the phone. And..." She stopped, clearly reliving an unpleasant memory.

"That's okay," I said, "you don't need to go on."

"No," she said. "I started, I'll finish." She took another swallow of her drink. "And the shower stops. The bathroom was right near my room. Technically it was *my* bathroom. And I hear the water stop, the shower door open, and then a moment later, my bedroom door opens, and there's Ben with his...with his *thing* dangling down, and he says, in this bullshit nonchalant way, as if everybody walks around nude with their schlong hanging down to their knees, 'Darling, I couldn't find any towels.'"

I didn't want this story to continue because it couldn't go very many good places.

"Sorry," I said.

"I just stood up," Leah said, "and I walked to the door, made sure I looked him right in his eyes, and only the eyes, and said, 'Try the cabinet under the sink.' And then I slammed the door—and if he didn't back up, it would have hit him in his dick and then his face."

"I'm assuming you've never told your dad."

"Oh my God, no. I've never told anybody that story, Matt," she said. She looked at me, curious, questioning. "I wonder why I told you."

17

I didn't have any answers for Leah that night.

I did have a lot of questions, though. For myself. About Leah. And me. Wondering if those beautiful blue eyes looking directly at me meant anything other than just my wishful thinking.

She'd drained her glass and then said good night. I offered to walk her home, but she patted my cheek and said, "Very gallant. But it's only a block and a half."

"Right. And besides, nothing bad ever happens around here."

"Except for Abbey McDougal."

Shit. I didn't know what to say to that.

"*Cherez la femme,*" she said. "*C'est toujours le mari.*"

"Sorry," I said, "I left all my French back at Paraíso del Mar High."

"'Look to the woman.' And, 'It's always the husband.'"

Leah took my hand, turned my palm over, and wrote her phone number in ink. "Don't be too hygienic," she said. "At least until you've transferred my number."

"I'll wear a glove," I said and watched her head for the door.

The bartender looked at me with a mixture of resentment and awe. Probably mostly resentment. "You want anything else?" he asked. When I shook my head, he said, "No tab, it's all on Kincaid."

I put another twenty on the bar and headed home. I could have called a cab, but it was a nice, warm night and my house is only twenty or so blocks, so I decided to walk.

I took a slight detour and walked on the Strand. Usually, it's pretty busy, even at eleven o'clock—owners taking their dogs out for a last poop before retiring; one or two couples lost in romance; and the occasional surfers riding their skateboards, smoking a doobie.

But tonight I was the only one down there. The air was soft, gentle, most of the houses dark. But one was ablaze with lights, the biggest and the most expensive house in town—Mayor Reed Lockhart's mansion. Two men were standing in the front patio area that faced the water, arguing loudly. They were pissed off and shouting at each other. As I came closer, I could see it was Reed and Ben. The wind was blowing south, so I really couldn't hear anything. I kept my head down as I passed within thirty feet of them, but I'm sure it didn't matter since they were in each other's face. As I cleared the house, I caught a couple of phrases on the wind:

"Go to hell..."

"Damn it, Ben, that's just..."

And finally, Ben shouting, *"You will absolutely not do..."*

I slowed down, hoping I'd hear more, but it got very quiet. I snuck a quick look back, but they'd gone inside the house.

Trouble in paradise? It sure as hell sounded like it.

I thought the walk home and the booze would have wiped me out, but I couldn't sleep. I flipped channels for a long time.

Late-night TV is extremely depressing. Not only are you a sorry son of a bitch with insomnia, you're part of the demographics that needs all kinds of body slimming, abdominal crunching, chin lifting, lose-three-dress- sizes-in-thirty-days, and all the other programs to get your life back to where you don't always hate yourself. And your life's been shit because you didn't have this magic blender that can do everything but wipe your ass, or a carpet cleaner invented by some superior intelligentsia (most likely aliens) that would take out stains embedded so deep they might require offshore drilling. Not to mention wonder foods, wonder drugs, and a series of amateur home videos of wonder women who promised to love you very much and be sure to email them for their astonishing all-nude, all-beautiful women tape.

I fell asleep with the TV on, and when I woke up the next morning, it was to *Scooby-doobie-dooo*! I switched off the tube, input Leah's phone number into my cell, saved it, and took a shower.

My office is right above a Starbuck's on one of the best corners of Paraíso del Mar. Right in the heart of our little downtown. It's a sweetheart deal, my office. If I angle my head just right I can see a glimpse of the Pacific. What bullshit real estate agents call a "peek-aboo" view. It's also a sweetheart deal because the rent's free. My dad owns the building. Bought it back in the mid-sixties. Over the years he's leased out the ground floor space to retailers, the top space to various small-time businesses. For a long time, the bottom was occupied by Patterson's Men's Clothing. Then Julian Patterson died of a heart attack, and since both of his boys were more interested in taking clothes off of women rather than putting clothes on men, the business failed. Over the years it's been a surf shop, a bikini shop, a woman's shoe store, a head shop where the owners smoked their products and profits, and for the last three years, a booming Starbucks.

My office was last used by a small insurance broker, Lawrence Garver. Larry probably insured half of Paraíso del Mar. He did so much business that eventually he needed a bigger space and moved into one of the bigger office buildings in the next city over.

I've been here since I got my private-eye license. Every time I try and pay my dad some kind of money, he threatens to throw me out. So I shut up and give thanks for being lucky. But what I have been doing is putting the equivalent rent into bonds, so that my dad has a secret trust fund. When he turns seventy in a few months, I'll give it to him as a birthday present.

In the summer with the window open and the fresh ocean breeze and the aroma of all those lattes and mochas, it's not a bad way to watch all those girls in their summer dresses and bikinis and nurse a hangover.

So that's what I did, between going downstairs and ordering a bold Venti, popping several aspirin, and drinking several glasses of water. I asked the barista for the intravenous size coffee, but he didn't get it either way: the joke or the coffee. About three o'clock I heard someone coming up the stairs for me. I knew it was for me because that's where the stairs end: small landing and the door to my office. I waited. Slow footsteps, heavy or weary footsteps. So I knew it wasn't Wade. Because in spite of his size, Wade is Fred Astaire on his feet.

There was a single rap on the pebbled glass front, and the door opened, and there was Mayor Reed Lockhart.

I got to my feet.

"No, no," he said. "Don't get up." He was wearing a light tan summer suit, crisp white shirt, and a red and white striped tie. He loosened the tie as he walked into my office.

"Your Honor," I said and extended my hand.

"C'mon, call me Reed." He shook my hand and sat down in one of the chairs in front of my desk. Actually collapsed was more like it. He looked beat.

"Can I get you something? I've got bottled water in the 'fridge there."

"No, thanks. I'm just a little tired. Haven't been getting my usual sleep."

I took my seat and waited.

He looked out through the window and watched all the people in the streets of his town.

"I love this town," he said. "People of Paraíso del Mar, they're some of the finest around."

"Yep," was all I could say.

"You grew up here, right, Matt?"

"Yep."

"So you've seen how our little town's grown, gotten a bit more sophisticated, how we've become even better."

I nodded. Better than another "yep."

"We've grown, but it's been a controlled growth. We didn't sell out." He shifted in the chair. "Hell, I remember when I had to fight the damn city council to stop them from putting in a McDonald's right down here near the water. Would've been four doors down."

"Where Hennigan's Bar is?" I said.

"Exactly. And it was a helluva fight too. They kept talking about all the tax revenues the city was going to get, all the additional tourist business, all that financial rationalization. But I wouldn't let them do it."

"But we have a Starbucks now," I said.

"Big difference," Reed said. "Big difference. Starbucks has a more upscale demographic, younger clientele."

"Younger? Isn't McDonald's a kid's place?"

He looked at me like I was being sacrilegious. "I'm talking about the paying customers. Their parents. People who are there for the Value Menu aren't Paraíso del Mar material. Hell, why do you think property values have gone up so dramatically?"

"Because of Starbucks?"

He stared at me for a moment. Pissing him off slightly I'm sure.

"Because of controlled expansion," he said. "We only let top cabin companies come in here. Hell, I'm sure your dad told you that when

Patterson's Men's Clothing had to close and your dad was looking for new renters."

"Yes," I said.

"So Starbucks downstairs and the new Fusion Sushi Bar, they attract upscale customers. Those customers see how great our town is, think they'd like to live here and…"

"And real estate business is booming." I tipped my cup to him. "Thank you."

"I bet your dad could get $3.5 million for this."

"3.9. But then I could be a little too enthusiastic."

"I don't see you as buying your listings, Matt."

Buying your listings is what other bullshit real estate agents do. They give the seller an ego-gratifying, overinflated figure of the owner's house just to get the poor sap to sign. Then a couple of weeks later, they start badgering him that the price was too high, that the market wasn't reflecting its value.

"I don't, Reed. If I were going to do that, I'd have said $4.5."

Reed undid the knot in his tie and pulled it out from his collar. "I don't like doing business that way."

I knew Reed didn't come here to discuss property values. So I decided to just wait and see why he'd showed up.

He carefully folded his tie, just like Julian Patterson used to do: gentle, so it wouldn't crease, keep its smooth texture.

"Leah is all I've got or all I truly value in this life, Matt."

I waited.

"She's more to me than all of this"—he waved his hand around, I think to include all of the Paraíso del Mar land that he owned—"more than my life actually."

I waited a little more.

"And maybe I'm a little overprotective, and I know she's thirty-four years old, I hope she won't mind my saying that and certainly has a mind of her own, but…you don't have children, do you?"

I shook my head. What an asshole, he already knew the answer. But what do you expect from an attorney? I was wrong. He wasn't a wolf in wolf's clothing; he was a shark in summer cotton poplin.

"Well, I ask that because only a parent can know how deep their love for a child really goes. Beyond, way beyond."

Okay, I'd had enough.

"If we decide to get married, I'll be sure to come ask you for her hand." I stood up. "But seeing as we've never had a date and last night was probably the first time I've talked to Leah except nearly twenty years ago at a surfing contest, I'm trying to figure out why you've come to see me. Your Honor."

"Get off your high horse and sit down."

"I was just leaving."

"Goddamn it, Matt. I'm trying to be civil here, and you aren't helping."

"Look! I don't know what the hell you think you need to tell me, or why for that matter. If you take this approach to every man that looks at Leah, it's a wonder you have any time to govern. But you're out of line here. Way out of line."

I headed for my door. "I'm going to get a coffee. Close the door after you leave."

He got up rather quickly considering how slowly he'd sat down, and tried to block my way.

"Okay, okay, I'm sorry. I'm an asshole." He searched my face. "Can I tell you something, Matt?"

"Sure."

"I'm sick. Maybe real sick. And I think Leah knows or suspects…"

"She does," I interrupted.

His face fell a little.

"Oh, well…of course. She wouldn't be Leah if she didn't. So all I am saying is that if something should happen to me, I was just wondering if you might kinda look out for her?"

"What are you talking about?"

He rubbed his face. "I'm not sure, really. But when I saw you two together at the bar last night, I got a funny feeling."

"Maybe it was the lobster." Bad joke, but this was getting uncomfortable.

"What I mean is, Leah, in spite of her brains and beauty and sophistication, can be a little too trusting. She gets that from Diane—that was Leah's mom. They look a lot alike. Especially now that Leah's about the same age her mom was when she passed away."

"Reed, I'm not sure what's going on here. I mean, Leah and I only had a drink or two. Nothing went on. I didn't feel like she saw fireworks or anything like that."

He looked at me again. "Yeah, you're right," he said.

"Can I buy you a latte or something?" I said.

"I'm good, thanks. Anyway, I'm sure this is all just a reaction to things that have been going on. Just a little too much stress lately. Nothing to worry about."

"It usually isn't," I said.

We headed for the stairs.

Reed looked at the steps. "You've got a couple of these that need replacing."

"Yeah, one right in the middle, and the first one at the bottom."

"I ever tell you about the guy tried robbing us and our stairs?"

"No."

"This was at one of my first homes in town. Over on Pacific. Sold it few years ago and they've put up a McMansion. But back then it was a dumpy old two-story. Had a set of rickety stairs going up the back. Termites had chewed most of them hollow, and dry rot had gotten the others."

Reed and I carefully stepped over the last step of my stairs.

"So this guy sneaks up the stairs about two in the morning, steps in the wrong place and crack, goes right through it. Snapped his tibia right in two. He's yelling and screaming, wakes up Diane and me—I think Leah was maybe a year old. Yelled so damn loud neighbors came, we called an ambulance. And the cops."

"Seems about right. Guy's on your stairs two a.m."

"Right. But then, week later I get a letter from his attorney, suing me for negligence on the upkeep of my home. Went after me on my homeowner's policy."

"You were an attorney, so you just defended yourself?"

"And I made sure that I ran up a big bill with his guy. Buried him in paperwork. Then, during the discovery phase, I put him through all the bullshit stuff—where he worked, his college, hometown, anything I could think of. His attorney was so dull he never once objected on grounds or relevance. Ran up the hours in deposition, ran up his bill. So we finally got to his defense, which was that he was visiting a friend, somebody named George Jones, and had mistaken the house. Of course, there was no George Jones in the neighborhood; in fact, there wasn't even a George Jones in all of Paraíso del Mar. But the best question was when I asked him if he was pissed off at George, going up to see him at two in the morning.

"'No!' he tells me, rather indigently, 'Why would you ask that?'

"'Because,'" I said, 'I was curious why you felt it was necessary to bring a crowbar and a satchel with you.'"

I laughed, partly to be polite, mostly because it was a funny story.

"Nice talking to you, Matt." He turned to go, then said, "And, when you asked if I visited all of the men that looked at Leah?"

"Yeah?"

"No. Just the dangerous ones."

18

"Well, danger's my middle name," I said after I'd told Wade everything about Leah and her father.

"You and Billie Joe Armstrong's son."

"Who?"

"Lead singer for Green Day. He and his wife had a son; his official middle name is Danger. With a capital D."

"Was that a *Jeopardy* question?"

"Being *au currant* has its advantages," he said. "Beats getting old, Mattasaurus."

We were having drinks at Hennigan's Bar, the place that could have been a McDonald's, except for Paraíso del Mar's own Knight of Templar, Sir Reed Lockhart.

"So where are we?" I said.

"The Mayor don't like you 'cause you doggin' his daughter. The poleece Chief don't like either of us because he thinks we coverin' up evidence or have screwed up his investigation. Stephen don't trust us. I'd say we be just where we suppos'd be."

"See, we're not totally useless as agents. We can be used as bad examples."

"And we be even worse examples as gumshoes."

"What're you talking about?"

"McDougal's guilty."

"And you know this how?"

"Ancient Fulani tribal instinct handed down through the generations."

"And not diluted by all these years of sedentary American living?"

"Sedentary, my ass. I still run three miles a day."

"Yeah, yeah. So why's he guilty?

"He was too cool 'bout not being totally fucked up over Abbey. Divorce or not, man doesn't just shrug off the slaughter of his wife."

"You aren't buying that he was in shock?"

"Are you?"

"No."

"So, you think there's a way to get into the crime scene?"

"You don't mean break the yellow tape?"

"What're you nuts? We go through a window."

"If this was December we could go down the chimney like Santa Claus."

Wade looked at his watch. "Another fifteen minutes, the new shift comes on."

"And they'll be a half hour going through duties, and there's still plenty of daylight left."

Wade put money on the bar, gulped his drink, and we were on our way. Paraíso del Mar's latent crime-stoppers heading out to be active crime-starters.

We cruised past Abbey's house. The yellow crime scene tape was festooned all across the front door, along with several warning bulletins. "Doesn't look like we can claim ignorance," Wade said.

"Oh, we can always claim that. In fact, I think that's a given."

I stopped the car several doors up. "Well," I said, "we're at the criminal equivalent of 'Texas Hold 'em."

"Meaning we're all in?"

I put the Ford in gear and headed up the street. Wade looked at me for an explanation. "I'm thinking we go in the backyard."

"Which means we've got to go through the neighbor's yard and then break in."

I turned the corner, went down the appropriate number of houses on the other street, and parked. We got out and tried to see through to McDougal's house. No luck. The neighbors on this street were nature lovers, so none of the trees or hedges had been trimmed back. I looked at several houses, narrowed it down. "It's either this one on the right or the one on the left."

"You counted how many houses from the corner, right?" Wade said.

"Yes."

"So how can it be either or?"

"Lots are little narrower on this street. Say ten feet. So ten houses, that's a hundred feet or so. Which could be two homes right or left."

"Damn, I'm impressed," Wade said. "You *do* know real estate."

"How's your tribal instinct?"

"Why?"

"I was hoping you'd get some kind of ancient feeling, which would save us from flipping a coin as to which house it is."

"Left one," Wade said.

We started for it. Then the front door opened and a muscular black Rottweiler trotted out, his lease trailing behind him. A second later, a man in his late forties picked up the leash and came out. He was wearing Under Armor running gear from the backward cap to his neon green shoes.

Wade and I did quick U-turns and headed for my car. The runner came jogging by, nodded to us, and kept going. The Rottweiler looked our way too. He didn't nod, just slid his tongue across his teeth. We watched them head up the street.

"You think he's got another dog in there?" Wade said.

"If so, I hope it likes dark meat."

"Right. Rottweilers don't be eatin' chicken."

We scooted along the jogger's side yard, cautiously opened the gate, and checked to make sure there weren't any more dogs. There weren't. But the yard had certainly gone to the dogs. My first step into the yard, I hit a land mine: a big pile of dog shit. What pet stores don't tell you is that the size of the dog equals the size of the dog poop. And that was a big Rottweiler. This poop was fresh too because it squirted up over the side of my shoe and hit my socks and my pants.

"Goddamn it," I said as quietly as I could, considering I would need to toss the shoes and drive home in my boxers.

"Whoa," said Wade. He stopped in mid-step. "Damn, we're going to have to maneuver carefully through this."

I wiped the bottom of my shoe on one of the few patches of grass that didn't have dog shit, angled my foot to get whatever I could off the side of my shoe.

"This can't be all from one dog," I said.

"Could be, if it's every dump he's ever taken in his life."

We went very carefully and finally made it to the back fence. Or where the back fence should be. Because in front of it were bushes and trees and weeds so damn thick you'd need a machete to whack through it.

"Maybe the gods are telling us something," said Wade. "Like we shouldn't be doing this."

I looked around the yard and saw an old redwood bench up against the fence, covered in leaves, half-hidden by the bushes. I managed to pull it free. I propped it against a low-hanging branch of a tree and made sure it was secure.

"We're going over that?" said Wade.

"Yeah, we just scoot up it, and then jump over the other side."

"Just like that?"

I put a foot on the bench. It was more slippery than I thought. "Well, maybe not the scooting part," I said. "But I don't want to go back through all that shit."

"You first," said Wade.

I put a foot up and grabbed the end of the bench, made it to the tree trunk, and eased out on a branch that stuck over the fence into McDougal's yard. There wasn't much room between all of the other branches, but there was no going back because I wasn't sure I could land upright in the jogger's yard. And that would be a genuinely shitty outcome. I eased further out on the branch, pushed away as many stray branches as I could…and jumped. It was a literal leap of faith. Because I really didn't know for sure what McDougal's yard contained.

I shot forward, crashed through branches, came clear, hit on my feet and then pitched forward. I did an involuntary somersault and bounced into a full prone layout. The judges would have given me a 9.6.

"It's grass," I called back to Wade. "Clean grass."

"No shit?"

"No shit."

A moment later Wade flew through the air, landed cleanly on both feet, a big smile on his face until his momentum took him forward and his feet went skyward, and he landed on his ass.

"You *stuck* the landing," I said.

McDougal's patio doors hadn't shut all the way, so with a little pressure, we were able to push one of the panels back and got inside.

"No breaking, but definitely entering," Wade said.

"You think that means a reduced sentence?" I said.

"I'm only worrying about that if I get caught," said Wade. "And I'm not getting caught."

We moved through the house as quickly as we could without disturbing anything but trying to not miss anything either.

The white tape outline of Abbey's body was still on the upstairs carpeting, blood everywhere. There were four circles of tape on the floor. I pointed at them, "Probably the shells," I said.

"He was moving toward her when he shot her," said Wade. "First circle's here, next one's few inches closer." He bent down and looked at the circles of tape. "These are almost a foot and a half closer."

"He shot her, waited a second to see the damage, and then moved in just to be sure?"

"Looks that way. What did the medical report say? Two in the abdomen—maybe those were the first two—then one in the heart and another in the right temple."

"Right temple because she's falling and he's still shooting?"

"And he's aiming for her heart, but her head drops into the line of fire."

"Pretty chilly shooter," I said.

"Yeah. But not a pro. He didn't pick up the shells."

I went into the bathroom but didn't find anything out of the ordinary. I came back out, and Wade was looking out the window. "Uh, oh," he said. "Patrol car."

I checked my watch. We hadn't been here more than five minutes. "They stopping?"

Wade waited a moment, "No. Kept going up the street."

"You seen enough?" I said.

He looked around the room one more time. "Yeah."

I turned for the door.

"Shit," Wade said.

"Yeah, I know. We didn't learn much."

"No, I mean shit. On the rug. From your shoe."

I looked back. Sure enough, there was a small brown smear on the light beige carpet. I went back, but Wade grabbed my arm.

"You can't try and clean it up. That'll just make it worse."

I took off my shitty shoe.

"We've got to get out of here before the patrol comes back."

"I thought you said they went up the street?"

"They did. But they turned around."

From outside we heard the thunk of two car doors closing.

I figured we had two minutes to get out the back door. I wasn't sure what we'd do then.

I was wrong. In less than thirty seconds, before we'd made it to the first floor, we heard the front door being shaken. It had been locked and remained that way. From a slight angle, I could see the patrolman check a couple of windows and peer through one of them. Wade and I held our breath.

Finally, we heard two car doors slam, followed by their engine starting up and driving off.

We both exhaled.

"You think the jogger called them?" Wade said.

"Don't know."

I moved through toward the kitchen and stopped and pulled a very expensive and nasty-looking butcher's knife from the wooden rack next to the oven.

"Uh, I don't think a knife's going to be much defense against a police .38 special," said Wade.

I took the knife and held out my pant leg. "I'm not fighting anybody. Except maybe this damn smelly stuff." I bunched some material just below my knee and made a slit. Then I worked the knife's edge into the opening and cut around. The seam at the back of the leg took a little effort, but when I'd cut all around, the loose bottom section dropped to the floor.

"You'd better do the other leg," Wade said. "Just in case you get stopped, and the cop asks you about your sartorial style."

I cut the other leg and stepped out of that.

"Damn, you need some sun, Matt. Your legs are reflective. Definitely Rottweiler chow, those chicken legs."

I picked up the pants bottoms, put the offensive shoe on top of the shit-covered leg, and rolled it all together. I gimp-stepped toward the back patio door then took the other shoe off. I would make better time this way and what the hell was I going to do with one good shoe? Wade went first and checked the street then I followed.

We walked all the way around the block and got to my car. Tomorrow was trash day on this block, and the street was lined with filled containers waiting for pickup. I pulled some trash bags from a can and wedged my pants and shoes down deep, then put the other bags back over them.

"You picked the wrong can," Wade said when we got in the car.

"What do you mean?"

"You put that crap in Recyclable."

19

My trash can was alongside my house, between my garage and my neighbor's house. So I slipped out of my now cutoffs and tossed them into the can. I went inside and took a long hot shower. Then I got a Heineken, put on some sweats and a tee, and walked down to the beach. You can do that in Paraíso del Mar, if you're careful—walk around with an open container.

The breeze was cool, and there were several groups of surfers still out, trying to catch the last wave of the day. I plopped on the sand and looked out at the horizon. Claire Singer, my mother, was out there. In the waves. When she'd passed away from a long, wasting battle with cancer, she'd wanted to be cremated and her ashes released in the Pacific along the beach at 26th Street.

So that's what we did, my father and I. Just the two of us one late August afternoon. We waded and then swam out about a quarter mile, my dad holding up the urn like it was a torch from the Statue of Liberty. Then we both treaded water, and he said some mangled kind prayer and how he'd always loved her, the words just pouring out of him in a bubbly, spit-flying torrent, tears running down his cheeks. Then he opened the urn and took my hand, and we both sprinkled her ashes on the ocean, her gray and soft white flakes mingling and dissolving in the blue water.

I had never seen my father cry before. Never have since. He held the urn under the surface, watched it fill, then emptied it back, making sure every last ounce of my mother was there in the ocean. Then he filled the urn one more time, put the cap back on and released it. The water was extra clear that day, so we were able to watch it for a while as it swayed back and forth so gently, drifting down, down until it vanished into the darker, deeper waters.

I used to come and sit on the beach and talk to my mom, telling her how much I missed her, complaining when my life wasn't going so well (mostly as a teenager), and sometimes just to ask her advice. I haven't done that in a long time.

I drained the last of the beer and looked north up the beach. Running right by the water, at a good clip too, her feet splashing in the small waves that rolled up in their last few thin drops, was a tall blonde, her hair flowing out behind her like a pennant. It was Leah. She was keeping pace with a beautiful black and white Siberian husky that she had on a leash.

I waved as she got closer. She didn't notice. So I yelled, "Leah!"

She turned, didn't slow down, and then when she figured out who it was, tugged a little on the leash and turned in my direction. She tracked right up through the soft sand, not slowing down, and stopped before me. The husky came up, sniffed me and stayed there, its tongue hanging out.

"Hey, Matt," she said, between light, unhurried deep breaths. "I was taking Tash out for some exercise."

"She's a pretty thing," I said and ruffled Tash's fur. Small tufts of black and white hair floated away in the breeze. "How long have you had her?"

"She's not mine. She's my dad's. He usually takes her for a walk, but lately..." She stopped, and I could see her worried look again, and just that quickly it vanished. "So I run with her. Huskies need a lot of exercise, tire them out. Otherwise, you leave the gate open and..."—she slapped her hands together—"bang, they're gone. And they don't usually come back."

"Like their freedom," I said.

"That. Or maybe they just don't remember where they live." She thumped Tash. "She's a good girl, huh, Tash?"

"Want to sit, take five?"

"Just for a few." She hunched down and then gently plopped her butt on the sand. Never put a hand out for balance. "So, you survived your birthday?"

"Piece of cake. Although, come to think of it, I didn't get any. Cake. I think I was too embarrassed to stick around and eat it." Tash paced a couple of times in front of us and then settled down, her belly on my feet.

"Nice and warm," I said.

"Take that as a compliment," Leah said. "She doesn't bestow her affections on just anybody." Leah looked at me. "That happen to you a lot?"

"What? Dogs pile on Matt?"

"No. I meant females just come up and throw themselves at you?" There was a long moment of silence. At least it felt long. "Like I did," she said.

"You threw yourself at me? How'd I miss that?"

"I gave you my phone number, without you even asking."

"I don't think that's a throw, more like a softball lob."

"Which you haven't followed up on yet."

"You mean calling you?"

"Yes."

"I didn't want to rush things."

"You don't think more than nineteen years is long enough?"

"What?"

She laughed. "Nineteen years ago. When I was fifteen. You gave out the awards for that surfing contest they had off the pier. Do you remember that?"

I thought of playing dumb, but that's not really playing, it's true. So I told the truth.

"Yeah, I do remember."

"God, I got the biggest crush on you that day," she said. "It was totally unrealistic. I mean there you were, I think you had won some big contest in Hawaii…"

"The Waimea Challenge."

"Right," Leah said. "And there I was, pretty damn lucky to have caught some great waves that I didn't really ride, just stayed up on them, and you gave me that trophy."

"Hey, staying up is what it's all about."

"The trophy and that little kiss."

I didn't remember the kiss. And then I did.

"And that did it? A kiss on the cheek?" I said.

"It was supposed to be on the cheek, but I moved and got your lips."

She laughed, embarrassed. "I didn't want to brush my teeth for a week." She threw sand over her feet. "My God, what a stereotypical teenage crush."

"Wow," I said. In fact, that's about all I could say for a moment. "Actually, I think it's pretty cute." I looked at her. "And I'm flattered."

Leah jumped to her feet.

"So what if instead of calling you for a date, I just asked you for it?" I said.

"You mean like now? Right here?"

"Yes. Like what about at eight tonight?"

"Wow, that's really something. You think just because I'm out running with the dog that I've got nothing better to do and can go out on a date just like that?"

"Not just like that. Think of it as a nineteen-year build-up. I mean, assuming you *don't* have anything *better* to do."

"I do have one thing," she said.

I'm sure my face fell with disappointment.

"But call me, and if I can postpone it, we're on." She gave a gentle tug on the leash. "C'mon, Tash, time we girls moved on."

As she started to run, I said, "Does that mean you've still got a crush?"

"After nineteen years? C'mon." She and Tash headed for the water's edge. She stopped and looked at me, "But I still have the trophy."

20

"You're kidding, right?" said Leah.

"I wish I was," I said. "Trust me, it's not by choice."

"Let's go, Singer," Purdy yelled. "This ain't no sorority party."

"Where are you?" Leah said.

"The beautiful Paraíso del Mar Police Department."

There was a long moment of silence where all I could hear was Leah's breathing.

"What the hell happened?"

"Typical police bullshit. And another screwup."

"Goddamn it, Singer!" Purdy yelled.

"I gotta go, but I wanted to call and let you know."

"Wait," she said. "You had one call, and you called me?"

"Yeah. To explain. And also ask if you could call—"

"Absolutely," she interrupted. "Who? Wade?"

"No, Wade's on a date. So I doubt if he'll answer his cell."

I looked up, and Purdy's ugly bulk was right next to me. He held up his fist and extended his index finger. "One," he said, loud enough for Leah to hear.

"I'll call your dad," she said quickly.

"Two," said Purdy. "Three."

"And Duncan Fitzgerald," I said. And just got the number in before Purdy broke the connection. He went to grab me, but I was out of the chair and his range before he figured it out. "Don't fucking touch me, Purdy."

He laughed and checked with the other two cops in the room. "Can you believe this asshole?" he said.

My war with Purdy has never stopped.

"Okay, hotshot," he said. "Get your ass down the hall. Annie will tuck you in."

Purdy motioned to the two cops. "You guys escort him. Never know, he might try to make a break for it."

"Oh, yeah," I said. "You don't have a legitimate charge, and I'm going to give you one. You always were good at figuring out the legal system, *Corporal* Purdy."

He wasn't sure if I'd just insulted him or was recognizing his rank, but covered it by yelling, "Your time's coming, Singer. Your time's coming."

"How ya doin', Matt?" said Annie. She opened the jail door, and I stepped inside. "Sorry about all this bullshit," she whispered.

"Thanks," I said.

And so for the second time in as many days, I was back in Paraíso del Mar's jail, this time as a suspect.

Annie shut the door, tapped in the electronic keyboard, and I was locked up. The other two cops went back to their other duties. Annie made sure they were out of sight and said, "Hey, I've got some fresh-brewed coffee. Italian roast. You want a cup?"

"Absolutely." I looked at her. "What about Purdy?"

"Screw Purdy. He won't be coming back here. Unless he forgets the last time, he visited you in a cell."

There was another reason Purdy wouldn't be coming back. He'd already spent enough time here as a scofflaw. At least three different occasions that I knew of, probably a lot more that the Chief had kept secret. But those three times were when Purdy had raised such a goddamn ruckus, been so drunk, and had assaulted a local that the Chief had no other choice than to toss his sorry ass into jail.

On one of those times I'd run into Annie outside the station. "It's just too bad we went electronic," she said.

"Why's that?" I'd asked.

"Because if we still had the old lock and key system, then somebody could lose the key."

Two cups of coffee later and a couple of hours of sitting on my ass on the bunk, the Chief had me brought into one of the small inner rooms where they grill people. Purdy was there too. The fact that it was the Chief doing the grilling and not one of his men meant he was really pissed off.

"We could wait for your lawyer," Ben said. "If you think you need one."

"Do I?"

"No, asshole, we just brought you in here because we like you," Purdy said.

Ben looked at him, and Purdy shut up. Ben sorted through some papers and looked at me. "Witness says he saw you going into McDougal's house."

"Witness?"

"A neighbor of McDougal's called in said he thought someone had broken into McDougal's house."

"Is that right? And this Good Samaritan neighbor saw this certain someone—someone you've somehow decided was me—actually ripping the police yellow tape and barging right into the house?"

"They didn't break the tape, asshole," Purdy snarled. "What a dumbass."

Ben's look at Purdy suggested that most likely that title would be awarded to Purdy. Because he'd blurted out, just like I'd been hoping, what they had and where they might be going. My guess was that the jogger had come back, somehow saw the bench leaned up against the tree, and believing he was Paraíso del Mar's best detective (goddamn interloper for my title), had put clues together and called the department.

"I didn't go by the house. But since it is my listing and the house is still for sale, I could have gone by and made sure the front lawn and everything else was shipshape."

Ben smirked at my bullshit line, but he couldn't really refute it. He closed the file. "You stepped in shit this time, Matt."

If he only knew.

"I don't follow," I said. "McDougal's alibi holds. From where I sit, I think I'm looking pretty good."

Purdy almost jumped in, but another look from Ben prevented that.

"I mean literally. I'm having a search warrant issued for your house."

"Oh, damn. And the place is a mess."

"Joke all you want." Purdy couldn't help himself. "But we find those sh..." He stopped before he gave away all the surprises.

"A search warrant? For what? The secret to the pyramids? C'mon, Ben, you're taking somebody's word that McDougal's house was broken into and that the perp was me? Just because somebody said they think they saw me?"

"Not just you," Purdy said. He caught himself, too late.

"Get out of here, Purdy. Now."

Purdy started to protest then saw Ben's face was crimson with rage. Purdy whipped out of his chair so fast it spun out, and he fell to his knees. He scrambled up, went toward the door for a couple of steps in a half-crawl, sprang up, flung open the door and was out of there .

Ben stared at the door and then turned his gaze on me. His brows were knitted together, a black storm warning, his face crowded with controlled hatred. "Where were you last night about six, six-thirty?"

"Probably at my house, or maybe taking a walk."

"We have a sworn statement that says that you and your buddy, Wade, were over on Clayton Court."

"Clayton Court?"

"Yes, the street behind Pacific, where McDougal lives."

"I know where Clayton Court is. I know all the damn streets in Paraíso del Mar. Remember, I grew up here? I was just trying to figure out when the last time I was actually *on* Clayton Court. Has to be a couple of years."

The door banged open, and Ben was about to yell at Purdy, but instead, it was the Mayor. And he didn't look any happier than the Chief of Police.

"We need to talk, Ben," said Reed.

"I'm conducting an interview," Ben said.

"Let it go," Reed said. "We have other more important things. Besides, I saw his attorney coming in the front door, so he'll have him out of here in ten minutes."

Big Ben stood up fast and glared at Reed. "Who do you...?"

"Gentlemen!" Duncan said loudly. "My client has nothing more to say." Duncan walked right past Reed and thrust a packet of documents on the table. "Here are all the necessary filings. Among which, Chief Black, you will find a motion of police harassment and abuse of power."

Ben didn't look at the papers, just took them and dropped them on the table. He was still looking at Reed. It was an exchange of hostilities without a word being said.

Duncan pulled me up. "Let's go, Matt. It appears the Mayor and the Chief have bigger fish to fry."

21

"Small potatoes," Duncan said as he dropped me off. "Don't worry about it."

I got out and was about to shut the door when he said, "I don't want to know the answer, and in fact, I am officially *not* asking the question. But, Matt, please don't let me discover later that you actually did break into that house."

"No worries, Duncan. I always watch my step."

"Good. Because it would undermine my confidence in your good judgment."

"Thanks for bailing me out. And the lift. Good night." I closed the car door.

But the passenger window slid down, and Duncan leaned toward me. "This is a rhetorical question, and only you can answer it, but what is the shelf life of a favor?"

"Duncan, how many times have I told you I will pay for your services? And every time you refuse. So send me a bill for this."

"Next one. But if you use your better judgment that won't be for some time."

He accelerated away before I could say anything.

Probably just as well.

Just as I got inside my house, my cell rang. It was Wade.

"Leah left me a message saying to call you," Wade said. "What's up?"

"Oh, nothing, partner, but while you were getting your nuts off, I was getting my nuts roasted by the Chief." Then I said, "Don't worry, I didn't give them your name."

"Whoa, somebody's whining."

I was about to curse him out and then realized he was right.

"You want me to come over?" he said.

"No, I just had to bitch."

"Why did they roust you?"

"Remember the jogger with the dogs?"

"The shitty-shitty-bang-bang dogs? That guy?"

"Yeah. I'm pretty sure he saw the bench we left against the tree, remembered seeing a large black man in his neighborhood, and called the station. They went back to McDougal's a second time, went inside and saw the shit stain and—"

"Bullshit," interrupted Wade. "They can't prove anything." Then I could tell he put his hand over the phone and said something to his date.

"I'll call you tomorrow," I said, and I hung up before he could say anything else. Hell, no sense both of us having a bad night.

I took a shower then microwaved the remaining half of a pizza that had been in the refrigerator and inhaled a *Negra Modelo* beer. I called Leah, got her voice mail, left my thanks, and asked her to call me.

I checked voice mail for the office. Three different agents had called asking the status of the McDougal residence. I called the first two agents, got their voice mails and left a message that it was currently for sale, no written offers, but several agents had said they were going to write an offer.

Going to and *did* are polar opposites in real estate. Fantasy and reality. Until you get it in writing, you've got nothing.

I called the third agent, one of my least favorite people in the business.

"Ronald Greenburg here."

"And Matt Singer here, returning your call."

"Ah, Matt…" There was a dramatic pause as if he had so many calls he just couldn't remember what home I was selling. If there was a more pompous, egotistical agent in town, I hadn't met him yet. Greenburg does extremely well. And he makes sure you know it. But then so do a lot of agents in Paraíso del Mar. Only they do it quietly. "I'm getting a listing," he said, "a few doors down from yours and…"

"Which one?" I said. I knew which one he meant, the McDougal's, since their neighbors, Lloyd and Melissa Hamilton, had asked me about the McDougal house the day we put up the sign. But I wanted to deliberately bust his balls. "We've got a few."

"Oh, right, right. Sorry. No offense, but I'd rather not say until it's official."

" Lloyd called you, huh?"

There was a sharp intake as Ron tried to cover that I already knew what listing he was supposedly getting. "Ah, yes. So…so how did you know that?"

"Oh, he'd asked us to list it, but we turned it down."

"Really?"

We hadn't officially turned it down because Lloyd had never asked us to list it.

But I knew he thought his five-bedroom, five-bath mansion wasn't *just* in the actual neighborhood, but in the financial one too. Not a chance. We'd listed the McDougal's home at fourteen-nine. We'd figured it would sell at fourteen-eight. But with the murder, all bets were off. It could go right into the toilet from all the notoriety, or it could blow past sixteen million for the same reason that the Los Angeles Clippers sold for two billion dollars because of Donald Sterling's racist comments. Lloyd had hinted that he thought his place would go in the eleven million range.

"Yeah," I said, "he thinks it's worth ten million. What a joke."

I'd deliberately underpriced what Lloyd was going to ask Ron to list it for because Ron is a blowhard asshole. Every real estate deal has issues. And in every deal, you can work out the issues. You want to make it a win/win for everybody, even if it means you don't win as much as you originally expected.

Not Ron. His only goal is win/kill you. If there is a dime left on the table in a deal, he'll chop your hand off if you reach for it. So anytime I could jam it to him, I did.

"Really?" he said again. "And you don't think it's worth that? I mean you've got McDougal's at fourteen-nine. And okay, it's a little bigger and a couple years earlier but…"

"A little bigger? It's twenty-seven hundred feet larger, the lot's two thousand feet bigger, and it's a decade newer."

"But the Lloyd's have done a lot of improvements."

"Hey, you can list it at any price you want, Ron. So what did you call me for?"

There was another pause. Obviously, he'd been outflanked on this. "Oh, sorry, I've got to take this call. I'll get back to you."

I hung up before he could finish with the bullshit.

So much for the real estate career.

How about the private investigation business? For openers, the Chief of Police was pissed at me. And our client, Stephen McDougal, had an airtight alibi, which meant the Chief's pissed-off level was going to rise and overflow. Because they were hunting a killer nobody saw, nobody heard, nobody knew.

I'm always tempted to say that things couldn't get any worse. But I never do, because too many times that's exactly what happens—things do get worse. Far worse than you can imagine. Because you can't imagine *that* happening.

Leah didn't call. I didn't come up with any brilliant ideas and about two in the morning, drifted off to sleep.

I woke up pissed off, thought about calling Wade and Leah, but took another shower and decided I'd earned a big breakfast. It was Friday so Kincaid's would be serving brunch in addition to his usual lunch and dinner. Brunch didn't officially start until ten-thirty, so I had three hours to kill, but I went over anyway.

I slipped into the restaurant, and while it was empty, it was still damn busy. The crew was setting up tables, and waiters and waitresses were back at the blackboard copying down the specials. A young brunette came running up, the hostess, "Oh, I'm sorry, sir, but we're not open yet."

Sir? Damn.

"It's okay," I said, "just tell Pat that Matt Singer's here." She looked at me like this was information beyond her job description, but before I had to think of another line, Pat walked out from the restroom area with a couple of what looked like maintenance guys and waved to me. "Hey, Matt." He said something to the two guys, and they headed for the rear of the restaurant. "It's okay, Hannah," he said. "Matt's a regular."

We shook hands. "You think it's possible to get a head start on the brunch menu?" I asked. "Nothing special, just some eggs and toast?"

"Sure," he said. "Everybody's doing the head start today." He pointed to the bar where the prof was slumped back in his chair.

"Oh, shit. I'll take a pass."

"Suit yourself."

"Heyyy, Matt," the prof called out. "Come, come, my friend, allow me to buy you a libation."

How the hell he saw me was hard to imagine.

"Sorry, Prof, I just stopped in to talk to Pat for a moment."

"No, I insist. You must let me buy you a drink. That is if Kincaid will deign to serve us."

"He's drunk, Pat."

"He came in that way," Pat said. "I gave him one drink. Watered way down."

"Matt!" the prof yelled. "Matt!"

Several of the crew looked at the prof, then at Pat. "Help me out here, Matt," he said. "Breakfast is on the house."

"That's not necessary." I headed for the bar.

The prof's hand wavered slightly as he held it out to shake mine. "Matthew," he said. "How goes the sleuthing business?"

"To use your vernacular, a paucity of clues, Prof."

"Ah, yes. But the case has just commenced, no?"

"Yes."

"So, as the investigation progresses, more clues should appear."

"In the fullness of time, Prof."

A waitress came up behind us. "Pat said you wanted some eggs and toast?"

I turned back to face her. "Yes. Scrambled egg-whites, sourdough, and coffee."

"Can you make that two, dear?" the prof said.

"Absolutely," she said and sped away toward the kitchen.

I turned back and saw the prof staring at me.

"You know, Matthew, when I saw you in profile just now, it struck me how matroclinous your looks are."

"Should I be offended at that word?"

"No, no. Matroclinous means that you have physical characteristics inherited from your mother. Patroclinous would mean from your father." He took a sip from his drink. "Shit, using dollar eighty-five words again when good fifty-centers would do."

A waiter came with our coffees. I took a sip.

"Did you know my mother?"

"Ah, one of Paradise's true beauties. No offense. "

"You tell me my mother's beautiful and I'm going to get upset?" I pushed his coffee cup to him. "Coffee's here."

He looked at it for a moment. "I am not unobservant, Matthew."

I started to say something, but he waved me off.

"I don't mean about the coffee, I mean about *me*. I see how people react to me, I hear what they say. That I'm a pompous asshole, always parading my vocabulary."

"Don't be too hard on yourself, Prof."

"Please, don't patronize me. You're of that tribe. When I called out to you when you were with Pat, I could tell instantly that I was the last person you wanted to see."

Busted, but I didn't say anything.

"But that's okay, Matthew. At least you're honest. Like right now, you didn't deny it with more bullshit. And I appreciate that."

We sipped our coffee for a while, neither of us having much to say.

The waitress delivered our orders. I just dug into my food. He watched me for a couple of bites and then ate a couple of forkfuls. "We are, all of us, affianced to doing good. But unfortunately, we carry inside of us a pattern, usually undetected, or if detected, unable to deprogram, of *automatically* doing the precise thing which we swear we don't want to do."

I ate a couple more bites of eggs and chewed some toast for my answer.

"You know, I went to Vietnam, came back, married, married another time, and used my position at the university to seduce young, willing college girls. They loved those big words. And I mistakenly believed they loved *me*. And that they were just fucking me for their grade. And even though I knew it was wrong, knew it would eventually cost me still another marriage, I couldn't stop. I didn't *want* to stop."

"We all have our crosses to bear, Prof," I said. I was getting uncomfortable with all of this discourse.

"I just forget that I'm no longer at Harvard."

"This is a beach town, Prof. Always has been, always will be, in spite of the prices of homes. Most people who live here just want to get a little sun, catch a wave or two, have a margarita, maybe have a surprise night between the sheets, and that's it."

"No shit. I just always hoped for more." He looked at me, smiled. "Ah, well, one's the pride of the herd on Monday, a Big Mac on

Saturday. Life chews you up, dumps you out. We're all just little turds in somebody's galaxy."

He picked up his glass and looked at the amber liquid in the light.

"And I'm stinking drunk..."—he drained the glass—"...as a skunk." He set the glass down hard, and a little burp escaped him. "Which, if you think of it, is an asinine expression. I mean what skunks drink? I mean can you imagine that sweet little skunk Flower from *Bambi* drinking?"

He stood up, swayed, and I caught him.

"I mean, the *Mephitis mephitica*, a perverse little mammal, yes, but a drinker? Not a chance."

I steered him toward the door. "Okay, Professor, I think it's time to say good afternoon." I got Kincaid's attention. "Hey, call a cab for the prof."

"I'm leaving?" he said. "But I haven't finished drinking."

"Yes, you have."

We reached the front door. Since it was still early, one of the bench seats there was empty. Usually, they're not. Because Kincaid's is always crowded, so you always wait.

"Did you ever think about that, Matt? About 'drunk as a skunk'?"

"I think maybe because it's one of the few words that rhyme with drunk."

He peered at me as if I was a great distance away. "There may be signs of intelligent life on the planet Singer yet." He patted the space next to him. "Sit down, my friend."

I did and looked at the hostess. She rolled her eyes and sought refuge in her reservation list.

"Or...or it could be," the prof said, gripped by another brilliant observation, "that nothing is as stinky as a skunk, so when you get stinking drunk..." He trailed off, his head swayed on the long stalk of his neck.

The waitress pointed outside. I looked and, thank you Speedy Cab Service for living up to your name, there was salvation on four wheels. I helped the prof stand up.

"What about when you skunk the competition?" I said. "You know, beat them so bad they don't score a point?"

"That's true," he said. "And if you're betting on the team that lost, for sure you'd have to have a drink. Or two. Which brings us back to being drunk as a skunk." He laughed like it was the funniest thing he'd ever heard.

I helped the prof into the cab and looked at the cab driver's name. "Mr. Orlando Ford," I said, "you are to drive the professor here directly home." Orlando nodded in agreement. "Give me your wallet," I said to the prof.

"My wallet? Do you need money?"

"No. But I want to show Mr. Ford your driver's license so he'll have your address."

22

"Number Two, Strand de Oro. Now that's an impressive address, Tash," I said. I had the Mayor's Siberian husky by the collar.

After I'd put the prof in the cab, I'd gone back, finished my breakfast, left a healthy tip, and decided to take a walk down by the ocean. I went down to the water's edge and walked in the wet, firm sand. I went to the pier, watched the surfers catch the few light rollers, and then headed back.

As I went up the concrete steps at the south end of the beach, I saw Tash, although I wasn't sure it was Tash just then, only that a Siberian husky was trotting north, her leash dragging behind her, and then turning around and trotting back. She was doing this right in front of Mayor Lockhart's house.

I made some kiss-kiss noises with my mouth and called to her, "Hey, Tash. Tash-girl, come here, baby." She turned and looked at me, those ice-blue eyes staring. "Atta girl, Tash. C'mere, girl." I squatted down, held out my hand, and wiggled my fingers. I made some more kiss-kiss noises, and she finally came over, skittish, ready to bolt. I gently moved my hand toward her and managed to snag the leash. She jumped back, clearly spooked by something. But I held tight to the leash, and she only made it to the end of it and was jerked back. She yelped in surprise, and I stood up.

"Okay, girl, it's okay," I said. I held out my hand and slowly moved for her. I figured, brilliant sleuth that I am, that it could only be Tash and that, just like

Leah had said, somebody had left the gate open and she'd made a break for it. I checked her collar, just to be sure, and gathered up the leash, so she was right at my heel.

"All right, girl, looks like you're going to be doing time back at the mansion. Pity I know."

We walked back to the Mayor's house and weaved our way through the impressive wrought-iron furniture on the patio facing the ocean. I moved for the side door, but Tash balked and let out a long, mournful whimper.

"What? It's okay, girl." I reached to knock on the door, but it was slightly open. "Ah, so that's how you made your break." I pushed open the door, and it gently swung back on its well-oiled hinges. "Hey, Reed," I said loudly. "Reed, it's Matt. And your escaped beauty, Tash."

Nothing.

"Reed?" We walked into the kitchen.

Tash let loose with a mournful yowl.

"Your Honor? Reed?"

I went around the corner into the lanai room, and Tash shied away so hard, I lost the leash. "Tash!" I yelled, but she headed for the door. Fortunately, it was closed. Then I heard a slight noise, like someone coughing, and I saw a pair of expensive shoes sticking out from the end of a sofa—shoes in a glistening pool of red on the deep-pile beige carpeting.

"Jesus!" I ran into the lanai room and there, between the sofa and an overturned glass table that had shattered into several nasty-looking jagged chunks and a thousand glistening shards, was Reed Lockhart.

Gasping for breath.

His right hand was pressed tight against a gaping hole in his left side, trying to stem the rolling tide of blood that poured through his fingers.

I bent down, my knees immediately soaked in his blood, and eased him to his right side so he could breathe easier and to at least get gravity working against losing more blood.

"Matt," he gasped, his eyes already dulling, fading from this life.

I reached for my cell.

In the plateglass window that looked out to easily the best view in Paraiso, I saw something move.

And then something hit me. And hit me hard.

23

"I'm having a hard time understanding this," I said. "Give me a minute or so."

"Take all the time you want," my father said. "There's no hurry, nothing to worry about." But that isn't what his face said, in spite of his words to the contrary. My dad *was* worried. In fact, he was beyond worried. He was in full parental mode: protective, anxious, scared, and trying to pretend that none of those feelings were true.

I looked at Wade. Nothing to read there, but then a blank look from him was a definite warning sign. When things get rough or dangerous, Wade goes into lockdown mode, buries his emotions, and gives off no warning signs to the enemy, so that whatever he does next is always a surprise. I wasn't his enemy, obviously, but I knew he was suppressing something.

"How bad am I?"

"I dunno," he said. "How bad are you?"

"I believe I still have my full cranial package."

"Which wasn't much," Wade said, "even before..." He gestured to the full bandage that was looped around my skull.

"Okay," I said, "once more from the top." I shifted slightly, my head swam a little. Got to do that slowly.

"Two days ago," my dad said. "The paramedics responded to a 911 call from some surfers who found you sprawled up against a stone bench they have at the south end of the Strand."

"Having taken a header off your skateboard," Wade said.

"Even though I don't own a skateboard and haven't been on one in twenty years."

"Surfers figured somebody stole it from you before they found you," Wade said.

"So they called the paramedics, they brought you in, doctors did x-rays, MRI, yesterday they did a CAT scan," my dad said. "They were worried." He looked at me for a moment. "We all were, Matt."

I moved my head, very gently, in agreement.

"Ah…" He waved his hand, his attempt at bravado. "The Signorelli clan tends to have *testa dura*." He pointed at his head. "Hard heads. I wasn't worried." Then he looked at me and shook his head slightly. "Well, not too much."

"That was Wednesday?" I said.

"And today's Saturday," my dad said.

"So I've been out of it for nearly three days?"

Wade nodded. "Okay, your turn—let's do the Mayor."

"His husky, Tash, had gotten loose. I got her and took her back to his house. Called for him a couple of times, the dog was freakin'out. We go into his Lanai room, she bolts, and I see Reed on the floor in a pool of blood, he's been shot, he's gasping for air and…"—I waited a moment to try and get the mental picture in sharper focus, but there was only a vague shifting in my mind's eye—"…and I saw something in the plateglass window, and somebody whacked me in the head."

"Shit," my dad said.

"Yeah, shit," Wade said.

"I know. So who did it? Any suspects yet? Obviously, whoever shot him conked me too. What's the Chief and his boys say?"

My dad and Wade looked at each other. It was some kind of signal.

"What?" I said.

"You haven't been awake to see any of the news," my dad said. "I know because I've been here watching you all this time."

"Dad…"

"And Wade too," my dad said.

"You guys didn't have to…" But then I looked at them. "Right, you had to."

"Just like *you* would have had to," Wade said.

I nodded. It was true. We didn't just have each other's backs. My life was your life. "So what am I missing?"

"The Mayor didn't die from a gunshot wound, Matt," Wade said.

"What?"

"He burned to death in a head-on car crash."

I shook my head in disbelief, but only for a second. Ouch. Shit, that hurt. My brain must have rattled around pretty hard from the blow because I was fuckin' sensitive. "What are you talking about? I saw him with all that blood. I kneeled down in it. Check my pants, they were soaked in it."

"You weren't wearing any pants," my dad said. "Just your boxers. And you reeked of booze. Like you'd been on a three-day bender." He looked at me, helpless.

"Stop. This is a shitty joke. And I don't think it's funny."

But something about Wade's face told me it wasn't a joke.

"Are you fucking kidding me? Really? This cannot be true. Jesus, I held Reed Lockhart in my arms, I heard him gasp for breath."

"I believe you, Matt," said my dad.

But he didn't sound all that convincing. He believed me because I was his son, his flesh and blood. But his cognitive powers were screaming *Bullshit! Bullshit!* Your boy's hit his melon, he's hallucinating, and we gotta keep this under wraps, inside this room.

"Let's say it's true," Wade said.

"It *is* true!"

"Just hear me out. Somebody shot Reed, you showed up at the wrong time, they whacked you and set you up."

"Yes."

"Who would want to do that?" Wade said. "And more importantly, why?"

"To cover up their tracks."

"Why not just whack you too?"

"I don't know. Maybe they panicked, maybe they didn't think of it until later. Maybe they didn't have enough time to take care of me and Reed too. Fuck, I mean, pick something, *anything*. I don't know what to say. Except what I saw."

"Matt," my dad said, "these are serious actions you're describing. Murder. A cover-up. A set-up. Shit like that doesn't just happen in here."

"So, what? I'm imagining this because it's too big for our little town?"

"No. It's just that…damn, Matt, what the…?" Wade was, for the first time I could remember, at a loss for words. He didn't know what to say. Or, more likely, what to think.

I didn't know what to think either.

"Either of you ever know me to make up shit like this?"

"Yeah, but maybe you did fall, Matt," my father said. "And maybe your memory tapes are all screwed up. Like in a dream where all kinds of events get jumbled together."

"Dad, c'mon. I was at Kincaid's for breakfast at seven-thirty that morning."

"Kincaid doesn't serve breakfast that early," my dad said.

"Jesus Christ, are you going to let me tell my story or are you going to just contradict everything I say? Goddamn it!" I slammed my fist into the bed. Ouch, another recoil to the old brain.

"Matt, slow down." My dad looked wounded. "We're on your side. This is just a lot of stuff to suddenly absorb."

I took a deep breath. "Okay, I think you guys should just go away for a while. Let me figure this shit out on my own. I'm assuming Reed's death is on the news?"

"Yeah," Wade said. "All over it."

"Great. I'll watch it, get the official version, and then we'll talk."

"Matt, I'm sorry," my dad said. "I just…"

"It's okay, Pops. Really. Maybe I *am* all messed up. Just let me sort this through on my own."

Wade shrugged his shoulders. He was uneasy too. He held out his hands in a gesture of futility. "Your dad and I are going to get some food, and then we'll come back and see you in a couple of hours."

"Sounds like the plan," I said.

24

The killer couldn't have planned this. It was too bizarre:

Kill the Mayor.

Whack me.

Kill the Mayor again.

Set me up with booze and a concussion and have a built-in denial framework for anything I claimed.

It was the stuff of bad melodrama. And raw power. The kind only two men in Paradise had. And now one of two was dead, probably killed by the other. And the fact that I'd seen the Chief arguing with the Mayor only added fuel to my fires. Fires I decided I was going to keep banked.

Because while I knew what I'd seen had actually happened, I wasn't so stupid that I didn't allow for the slenderest thread of possibility that I *had* imagined all of this, that to use the prof's lingo, I'd fallen into solipsistic vertigo.

This wasn't going to be easy. And it was definitely going to be dangerous because maybe setting me up wasn't enough. Maybe I needed to have my own accident. This time for real, and this time for keeps.

I turned on the TV and channel-surfed. In spite of Wade's declaration that the news of Reed's death "was all over," I didn't find anything for a good twenty minutes. Even on the all-news channels, the death of the Mayor of Paraíso del Mar in a head-on single-car crash wasn't headline stuff. So much for the parochial perspective. The one reporter that gave an update only said that our little "chic and very expensive seaside resort town" was planning memorial services on Friday.

Leah! What the hell must she be going through? I dialed her number but got the answering machine. "Leah, it's Matt. I am so sorry. Give me a call…if you're up to it."

Then I called Wade's cell. "I don't need two hours," I said. "We need to get going on this."

"You mind if we finish our lunch first?"

"Hey, I've been conked on the head. I could go nuts on ya."

"You didn't need a concussion for that."

"So you believe me?"

"Let's just say your pops, and I figure we owe you that much."

"Great."

"Hey, this ain't no Sally Field Oscar moment."

25

"You're sure you like the Chief for this?" Wade said.

"Absolutely."

"Just because you saw them arguing? That's stretching it."

"That's my guy. Who do you like? Somebody Reed screwed on a real estate deal? Can't be. You know one of his biggest selling points was that after ninety days if you didn't like the property, he'd buy it back from you at full price."

"He *was* a politician," my dad said.

"Yes. And he controlled the city council and passed more legislation here than LBJ did in Washington, but in the long run, it always seemed to be better for everyone. It's got to be the Chief."

"Why?" Wade said.

"I don't know yet."

"You don't think he's your automatic choice because he's always had a hard-on for you?"

That's my partner. If life doesn't bust your balls, he's good for it.

"And how the hell do you expect to prove it?" Wade said.

"The way we usually do…"

"No-no-no."

"Really?"

"Matt. Goddamnit, we sell real estate…"

"And do private investigations."

"…and we sucking on McDougal."

"So are the cops. But think how much business we'll get when we solve the two biggest mysteries to hit Paradise…"

"You ain't a mystery, Matt. Least not to anybody else in town outside this room."

Like I said, ball-buster.

"Humor me, I'm a concussed man." I looked at my dad. "Any big crime in town that you remember?"

He shrugged. "Nah, you know nothing happens…" He snapped his fingers. "Wait…yeah, right. But that was a long time ago."

"What was?"

"The disappearance of Miguel Santiago."

"Who the hell's that?"

"For a while, the hottest contractor in Paradise," my dad said. "He hit town right about when the boom hit, and prices started going through the roof. And Miguel was damn good too. His crews were tight, finished the job on time, and on budget. And always passed inspection."

"So what happened? Miguel disappears with everybody's up-front money?"

"Nope," Dad said. "Miguel was good at pounding nails, but also liked pounding the ladies too." My dad gave us his big shit-eating grin. He loves word games. I think that's the only reason he tolerates the professor. "Yeah, Miguel got more ass than a toilet seat, to use an expression that was old even when I was young."

"So what happened to Miguel?" I said.

"I told you, he disappeared."

"I know, but why?"

"This is my story, Matt. Let me tell it."

"Be my guest, Pops."

"They didn't have 'man love' back then, at least the way people talk about it nowadays, but Miguel was fuckin' handsome. No denying it. Even good-looking guys felt a little less confident around him. All the ladies loved Miguel. And Miguel loved all the ladies. Sometimes those ladies were single, and sometimes they weren't."

"Ah," Wade said. "Mikey liked it, and so maybe a husband convinced Miguel to move on?"

"Maybe a couple of husbands. Nobody really knows. One day Miguel had three jobs going at once, busting his crews' asses, and the next day he didn't show up on the job. And nobody ever saw him again."

"Was there ever an investigation?"

"For what? Back then, most of the locals had figured it was just a matter of time."

"You mean before some husband went after him?"

"No, before he just quit. Miguel being Mexican."

Wade and I looked at my dad.

"Hey, I didn't say that, and I sure as hell don't believe it. I'm just telling you what the locals thought back then. You know, Paraíso del Mar wasn't always paradise. Back in the forties and fifties, the people that moved here were shit-kickers from Oklahoma and know-it-alls from New York. You had GIs who'd passed through on their way to Guadalcanal decided to call this home. There were a few asthmatics that came for the clean air. And every one of them carried their prejudices with them just like they carried their suitcases. And a lot of hatred too. Shit, I don't think a black family even rented here until the mid-seventies."

Wade nodded in agreement, but so slightly that I don't think he even noticed he was doing it.

"So what's Miguel Santiago got to do with me?" I said.

"And why was that such a big crime?" Wade said.

"Other than Abbey McDougal, there hasn't been much in the way of crime here in a helluva long time. So back then, when somebody like Miguel disappeared, it was *something*."

"Let's say adios to Miguel, and concentrate on the Chief," I said.

"How about let's concentrate on verifying all of this first?" Wade said. "That might even lead us to the suspect." He held up his hand before I could protest. "Which could even be the Chief."

"Excuse me…" We all turned, and there was a stocky young man standing at the entrance to my hospital room. He was dressed in faded Levis and wore a Lakers tee that was stretched to its limits by his muscular frame. He stepped into the room like he belonged there. And he did. "Hi, I'm Doctor Jonas." He smiled at my dad and Wade and peered at me for a moment.

"Doctor?" my dad said.

"I know," Doctor Jonas said, gesturing at his tee, "I'm filling in for Doctor Pearson, and I didn't have time to put on scrubs. Although, since I'm not scheduled for surgery today, I wouldn't be wearing them anyway." He smirked at his own little joke and flipped open one of the manila folders he was carrying.

My dad looked and me and shrugged while Jonas reviewed what I assumed was my file. Wade looked at the doctor.

"So, how are you feeling today?" he asked without looking up.

"Good, I'm feeling really good. I'd like to go home."

Jonas closed the file and pursed his lips. "Usually when a patient has experienced a brain trauma like yours, one that keeps him insentient for three days, we like to keep them here for additional observation."

"He's been insentient a lot longer than three days," Wade said. "Probably since his birthday. The first one."

I flipped Wade the finger. "I'm doing great, really."

"Trust me, Doc," my dad said, "you make him stay here, he'll just be trouble."

Jonas smiled at this. "Look at my finger, Matt," he said.

Wade smirked at that.

Jonas held his right index finger straight up in front of his face, then slowly moved it right, then left, up, down, and back to center.

It wasn't hard to follow. And I guess I passed the test.

"All right," Jonas said, "that's not much of a test, but I'm of the opinion that once a patient has regained consciousness and all vital signs are good, no reason to occupy a hospital bed that someone else might need." He gave me the thumbs-up sign. "I'll tell the nurses' station that you can be released, and leave notes for Doctor Pearson." He turned for the door and stopped. "Take it easy," he said. "And no driving for at least three days."

Before I could protest, he was out the door dictating into a small handheld recorder.

"I don't know," Wade said, "maybe you should stay here."

"What?"

"You not being able to drive the Snake for three days might be dangerous for your health."

26

"Don't be doing any *Driving Miss Daisy* on me either," Wade said.

"Until I get in the back seat, you've got nothing to worry about. And just so you know, I don't like this any better than you."

"Right."

"And that's a racist comment."

"What?"

"If the situation was reversed, and I was driving you, would you have said it?"

"No."

"See?"

"But not because of our separate and distinct heritages. I wouldn't have said it because if the doctor told me to rest for three days, that's what I would do. Not be taking advantage of my best friend's good nature by making him schlep him all around town on fool errands."

"Make a left here," I said, just to piss him off. "And who said you were my best friend?"

Wade had volunteered to drive me around after I left the hospital, but now was definitely regretting it. I think going shopping for groceries had thrown him off. What the hell, I figured it was better to stock up and stay around the house than go out every night. The fact that he was following me around in Ralph's while I was pushing the grocery cart threw him off a little. Not that Wade's homophobic, but he just doesn't like the togetherness thing very much. No matter who's the couple.

After I'd gone up a couple of aisles, he said he needed a coffee and left me by the produce section. He was waiting at his car when I walked out carrying a full bag in each arm. He opened the rear door without saying a word, and I put the bags on the floor.

I eased into the front seat and adjusted the seat belt. "And about that chauffeur bit?"

"Yeah?" Wade said.

"If I was going to do it? I'd say, 'Home, James.'"

He chirped the tires a little getting out of the lot, and I smiled but made sure I was looking out the passenger window. Neither of us said much on the way to my house. It wasn't that far, but we were both uneasy.

When he pulled up in front of my place, I decided silence wasn't golden; it was painful.

"Look," I said, "I know this is asking way more than anyone has a right to ask. And it's not going to be easy. But, damn it, Jamal, I *know* the Chief's involved in this. Somehow, some way, he's responsible for Reed's death."

Wade looked out the window for a long moment.

"You ain't called me Jamal in a long time. I'd say a coon's age, but, well, you know." *Heh-heh.* "So when you do call me by that, I know you're serious." He turned and looked directly at me. "Taking down the Chief of Police is going to be a bitch."

"Not to mention hard."

"I hope you got Hagen-Dazs in one of those bags."

"Pralines and Cream."

"Well, shit, my man, as they say in those dumbass porno cartoons, 'Quick, before it melts!'"

27

"We're that Foreigner song," I said, *Cold As Ice."*

"And we're out of ice cream too."

We hadn't come up with a single reason or idea why Chief Black had taken out Mayor Lockhart. Lots of wild ideas, but nothing that made sense.

"Maybe it doesn't have to make sense," I said.

"It would help," Wade said. "Something makes sense, you at least have a way to track it. Otherwise, you've got nothing to keep you grounded, you're beyond the edge, and when shit starts happening, you have no reasonable expectation of the outcome."

"Since when has that ever worked for us?"

"It's a good theory."

"Okay, so maybe the reason comes out of the proving. You know, like the prof's always saying, 'cognitive dissonance.' "

"The prof says a lot of shit."

"So we start by finding out where the Chief was when the Mayor got shot."

"Hundred dollars says he wasn't anywhere near it."

"Well," I said and went to the computer, "we can check." I tapped on the keyboard. After a moment the Paraíso del Mar Police Department website came up.

"His schedule's not going to be on there."

"I know." I was very careful as I tapped the keys in a specific combination, and up popped the police department's private files.

Wade stared at the screen for a moment. "How the hell'd you get into those?" He looked at the screen a moment and then said, "Zak. You compromised or threatened him."

"I did neither. I simply invited him to speed up my computer and at the same time asked him all kinds of questions about how he set up the Department's files and worked back from there."

"I know the Chief was way too smart to use his birthday as the password."

"Of course. But it's good to know the Chief's a Taurus, born on April 30th, and some other special shit." I tapped keys for the Chief's files. "It took a little hit-and-miss, but I figured it out."

"You be a devious mutha," Wade said. "And Zak didn't put in any firewalls or send a reverse Trojan Horse file bomb for anyone who tried to hack into it?"

"I don't think the Chief wanted to spend that much."

"And Zak went back east and is teaching at M.I.T."

"So we're safe."

The Chief's calendar came up on the screen. I scrolled back through it to Wednesday.

"Departmental Conference, San Francisco," I read. "7 a.m. through 7 p.m. Departs 6:30 a.m., Southwest Airlines, Flight 232, arrives San Francisco 7:45 a.m. Return Southwest Airlines, Flight 1123, departs 7:10 p.m., arrives LAX 8:30 p.m."

"Good thing you didn't take that bet," Wade said. "He was nowhere near it. In fact, he wasn't even in town."

"Bullshit," I said.

"Maybe we should concentrate on who whacked you and go back from there."

"It's the Chief."

"Okay. Then who helped him?"

"Purdy," I said without even thinking about it. "He's the Chief's pooch. Fetch, Purdy. Sit, Purdy. Good dog, Purdy."

"So, the Chief shoots Reed, but nobody hears the shot?"

"I don't know," I said. "We haven't asked around yet. And maybe he used a silencer."

"He clobbers you," Wade started again, "then gets Purdy and they drag your limp ass twenty blocks away, douse you with booze, strip away your pants, and then position you on the Strand near a bench. That about how you're seeing it?"

"Sounds perfect to me."

"Jesus Christ, Matt, do you realize how damn far-fetched that is?"

"Cognitive dissonance."

"Do you know how that term started?"

"Can we stay on point?"

"Do you?"

"I don't need a lecture. I know it was coined by some guy named Leon Festinger."

"Not a lecture, just the facts, so you can relate. Festinger infiltrated this cult that said the earth was going to be destroyed on December 21st and that the cult members were the only ones who would be rescued by aliens. When the little green men didn't show up, and the world didn't end, so they wouldn't be thought stupid, they changed their prediction and said that the aliens admired the cult so much, they saved the world instead."

"So you're saying I'm making up facts to fit my story?"

Wade shrugged for his answer.

"How's that different from when shit happens, and the politicians or the cops or whoever's doing it makes up a story to fit the facts?"

"Because facts are facts."

"And history's written by the winners, who have a very different version of the facts. *Their* version. And their facts have been worked around to fit the story they want to tell."

"So how do you prove it?"

I tapped more keys and brought up Purdy's schedule. "Purdy was around. He was out in...patrol unit 435 from...looks like his entire shift."

"Who was his partner?"

"Purdy doesn't have a partner. Nobody wants to team up with him. Besides, if he has a partner, then he can't be at the Chief's command."

I minimized the police links and opened up information for the Police Chief's Conference. But I never found it. I went through at least twenty different pages of material, websites, blogs, and any possible link, and came up with a blank.

"Shit," Wade said. "Son of a bitch lied."

"Yeah."

"Still doesn't prove he killed the Mayor."

"Not yet. But why cover his ass on that day?"

"How'd you know it was only that day?"

"Right. But what's more interesting is why does he cover his ass at all? On any day? He doesn't just represent the law in Paradise, he *is* the law. He can do anything he wants." I looked at Wade. "Including getting away with murder."

28

"I just can't believe he's dead," Leah said. "And to die like that." She tried to stop the tears, but they cascaded down her cheeks. "I hope he died instantly." She gasped suddenly and looked at me horrified. "God, can you imagine saying that? That you hope someone dies quickly?"

"It's perfectly natural," I said. "You don't want anyone to suffer."

She blew her nose, sniffed back some more tears, and looked out at the ocean.

We were sitting in her living room at opposite ends of the sofa. Tash lay on the floor near Leah's feet. She was now Leah's. Tash looked at me and let out a long, mournful whine.

"What's wrong, girl?" Leah patted her, but Tash just kept staring at me with those soulful blue eyes.

I knew what was wrong. Tash associated me with Reed's death.

Just before Wade left, Leah had returned my call, and after again telling her how sorry I was, she asked me to come over. "I just need some company," she said.

Walking over to her house, I tried to figure out some way to see if she might have any idea of what went on in her father's life but didn't want to push it. There weren't many new details, just the grim summation: Single car crash, gas tank explosion, raging auto fire. Body burned beyond recognition. Identification only through dental records. According to the police report, Reed had lost control of his Acura CarTech NSX approaching a curve on *Vista del Paseo* and had gone straight into the only stand of palm trees along that road. The car had been highly modified and had twin turbos. The speculation was that perhaps the turbos had kicked in unexpectedly and launched the car through the apex of the turn, so he never had time to react.

"He was great driver, Matt," Leah said. "Years ago he went to the Skip Barber driving school, and he was so proud of his lap time. I think he said it was among the top three amateur times back then."

"And he raced his Porches for a while at Laguna Seca, right?"

"Yes. So I don't see how he could have plowed straight into the trees."

"They think the turbos kicked in without warning and the engine redlined."

"He'd just had it serviced last week."

She got up and went to the kitchen. I heard the refrigerator open, and she came back with two tall glasses of sparkling water. She handed me one and looked at me. "How are you doing? Your head?"

"I'm okay." I took a drink, the water was icy-cold and damn good. "Was your dad having any problems?"

"Problems? Like what? You know my father. He had the world by the *cajones*. I mean except for...except that he most likely had cancer."

"That's devastating news."

"Matt, you don't...you don't think he could have..." She shook her head.

"Took his own life because he was sick? No. Your father wasn't that kind of man."

That seemed to put her a little more at ease. "God, I don't know what to do first. There's the funeral arrangements, his attorneys—he must have three or four different firms, they've all called at least three times apiece. Some asshole insurance company attorney called and was implying that, well, you know...that he'd committed suicide."

"I hope you told him to buzz off."

"*Off* was one of the words I used."

"So," I began again, "your dad didn't...I mean, did he ever say he was worried about anybody? You know, sometimes the locals get really pissed about some of the zoning laws, some of the new regulations."

She looked at me like my concussion was more serious than she'd heard. "Matt, what are you talking about?"

"I don't know. I guess I'm just trying to..." I stopped and decided to try another direction. "Nothing, really, it's all just so strange. I can't imagine what it's like for you so I won't try."

She reached over and gripped my hand. "Thank you."

"Do you have a lot of things to do at your father's house?"

"I don't think so. The place is in great shape. He always kept it first cabin."

"Right."

I looked down at Tash. She'd finally settled down and was napping. Leah caught my glance and looked down at Tash.

"Good, she's sleeping. So now I have a roommate."

"When did you pick her up?"

"Just yesterday. A neighbor had found her outside the house, pacing back and forth, and poor baby and kept her for me. She was so skittish like she'd experienced some traumatic event." Leah looked at Tash, then at me. "They say pets are really attuned to their owners, so maybe she knew."

"I'm sure she did."

"I guess he was lucky if you want to say that, because the neighbor said the front door was wide open. Anybody could have come in and robbed him blind."

"Yeah. So nothing was taken? Nothing broken? No damage to anything?"

She peered at me again, and then said, "No. The place was immaculate."

<h1 style="text-align:center">29</h1>

You're a mess, Matt Singer.

Slipping into Reed's place after midnight?

But it was something I had to do.

I don't know why I expected there to be crime scene tape around it and chalk marks identifying where his body lay, and the dark dust of graphite that had been used to check for fingerprints.

Because there was no reason for any of it.

Only three people in Paraíso del Mar thought this was the scene of a crime, and two of them—Wade and my dad—were still on the fence about it.

Actually, it was more like five people. Number four being the killer, and five being whoever had helped him dump my ass—not just on the Strand, but into a world of hurt and shame.

Everybody else in town believed Reed didn't die here.

After I left Leah, I went home and fell asleep with my clothes on, pretty much as soon as my body touched the couch. When I woke up I could have sworn I'd been asleep for a day. But it was only for a couple of hours.

When I slipped through Reed's side gate, my radar was on high alert. This seemed too easy. I squatted down between two huge potted rare trees that framed his doorway. I had my lockpick kit with me but was hoping that even rich people were creatures of habit. There was no way a key would be under one of the plants; they must have weighed a couple hundred pounds each. I put down my Maglite flashlight, a souvenir from my days on the force, and swept my hand under the welcome mat, but came up empty. I looked around.

There was an ornate mailbox affixed to the stucco wall of the house that looked big enough to hold a crate. Apparently when you're rich *and* the Mayor, lots of people like to send you things. The box was filled with at least a dozen letters, handfuls of circulars, advertising flyers, and all the other postal detritus that accumulates in our lives.

Shit, no key, nothing but paper.

I ran my hands underneath the box and at the back of it, touched something: a sharp-edged little metal box held in place by magnets. I pulled it away from the mailbox. It was a Hide-a-Key from Pep Boys.

The key was a little rusty. Reed wasn't the kind of man who forgot his key so the Hide-a-Key may have been here for years. I worked it into the lock, turned it slowly, and went inside.

I waited until my eyes adjusted to the dark, but it didn't help much. The entire front of the house was all glass and faced the water, so if the moon had been out, I'd have been okay. But tonight it was cloudy and slightly foggy.

"All right," I whispered, and was startled to hear my voice in the stillness of the house. Jesus, talking to yourself. Way to go, Matt.

"Okay," I whispered, mostly to keep myself calm. "Hit the Maglite, but cover it up as much as you can."

I pulled my shirt out of my jeans and covered the lens with it, then turned it on. Damn, it was still bright. I aimed the beam ahead toward the lanai room and then turned it off. I'd seen enough to get there in the dark.

Three steps later I discovered I was wrong when my shin slammed into the edge of the wrought-iron coffee table, the one whose glass had been shattered when I found Reed.

Shit-shit-shit!

Goddamn, that hurt.

I inhaled deeply but didn't come up with any trace of the coppery smell of blood. All right, it had been several days.

I touched the table. New glass. Okay, seems reasonable.

I squatted down close to the carpet and hit the Maglite.

No blood. No stains. No nothing.

The carpet was brand new. I rubbed my hand across the fibers. They were crisp and rigid. I leaned closer and inhaled. Definitely new.

Somebody had come in, ripped out the bloody mess, disposed of it, and installed brand new carpeting. And nobody had seen it? That took power. But even so, somebody had to cooperate.

There were only three carpet stores in town. I knew where I'd be going tomorrow. I doused the flashlight and looked around. Through the wall of glass that faced the ocean, even without a moon, I could make out the white phosphorous glow of the wave's whitecaps as they gently rolled onto the beach. What an incredible view, even when you couldn't see much.

I was two steps from the front door when it opened, and the huge bulk of a man came through it. His flashlight snapped on, but before it came up, I had already started my kick.

Good thing all those years of training become instinctive because even as my left foot slammed into his flashlight and sent it flying, my equilibrium was screwed up. My momentum carried me forward, closer than they teach you, but I had no choice. I brought the Mag flashlight up from my knee and hit him right in the jaw.

In the aftermath, as I was running down the path, and my brain was processing, catching up, I'd heard his jaw go with a sickening *craaacckk!* and a yowl of pain, followed by two quieter grunts of shock as I buried my left fist into his solar plexus and hit him again with the butt end of the Maglite just below his left eye.

His body thundered into the door, but by then I was two steps gone and flying. My head pounded like somebody was hitting me each time my shoes hit the ground, but I had to get home.

And not just because I'd just had another fight with Purdy.

I could only hope he hadn't seen me.

Running home there wasn't anyone else on the streets, so unless he had somebody hiding in the shadows, it was his word against mine. My Maglite was dented from where the middle of it had connected with his jaw, so I knew he wouldn't be whining too much about fair or unfair. In fact, I didn't expect him to be able to talk much at all.

30

"Open up, it's the police."

I'm pretty sure that's what I heard, but I couldn't tell; the words were mushy.

I opened the door and stepped back.

"Jesus, Purdy, you fall off your skateboard too?"

His face looked like a bruised purple grape. "Up yours," Purdy snarled out of the side of his mouth. His jaw was wired, so his lips curled like a fat man's Billy Idol. "Get outta the way, asshole, we've got a search warrant."

"Let me see it."

Purdy jerked his head to the cop behind him and involuntarily winced.

I knew what he was feeling. When your brain gets rattled, sudden movements aren't good for your well-being or your balance.

The cop, "Watley," his brass ID pin said, thrust the search warrant at me. I took it and pretended to read it. "I don't know," I said.

"What?" Purdy growled.

"This is pretty vague."

"The hell it is." Purdy grabbed the paper and jabbed it without looking. "See, it says right here, 'Weapons utilized in the assault of a Paraíso…Paraíso del Mar police officer."

I'd hoped he would have a hard time with pronouncing the city name since Purdy's extent of Spanish is *si*, *tacos*, and *puta*, but his humiliation was even better, and funnier than expected. Even Watley had to hide a smirk.

"Geez, a Paradise officer got assaulted? Who?"

I moved back before Purdy could shove me. For an instant, I'd thought of messing him up just a little more, but saw that Watley's hand had never strayed from his baton. So I knew Purdy had primed him to strike. I bowed slightly and gestured them inside.

Watley marched back to the bedroom, Purdy went into the kitchen. I followed Purdy. He yanked out drawers, rifled through one with silverware, another with dish towels. When he'd come up empty, he'd slam the drawer back. He bent down to look under the sink and lost his balance slightly, his beefy shoulder banging into the cabinet hard. He put out his right hand for balance.

"Whoa, big fella," I said, purposely adding a cowboy twang. "Y'all don't wanna be jumpin' round like you're a youngster."

Purdy's eyes were small rivets of hate. He pulled open a cabinet door, yanking it so hard it slammed into the drawers and ricocheted back and hit him in the hand, and recoiled back into the drawers. "Shit, shit, shit."

I moved into the door's arc so he wouldn't retaliate and rip it off its hinges. "Want to tell me what you're looking for?"

"For a flashlight," came a voice from my living room. I turned, and Lieutenant Remington moved into the kitchen. "Matt," he said, and extended his hand.

I shook it. "Glenn, nice to see you." I turned back to Purdy. "A flashlight?"

Purdy started yanking shit out from beneath the sink—cleanser, a package of dishwashing pellets, various sponges, and a handheld vacuum cleaner.

"Stop!" Remington said. "Take a minute, Purdy."

Purdy got up, agonizingly slow, didn't say anything. He was definitely in pain.

There was banging from the back of my house.

"Go get Watley," Glenn said, "before he does some real damage."

"You mind if I put this stuff away?" I said.

"Go ahead," Remington said.

I bent down slowly, my head probably wasn't as bad as Purdy's, but I was still definitely shaky. And that little episode last night hadn't helped.

"You have a flashlight, Matt?" Remington said.

"Sure."

I got back up and went to one of the drawers Purdy hadn't gotten to yet and pulled out a small, one-battery penlight. "Here," I said and held it out. "It's small but really bright. It's an LCD."

"And this is your only flashlight?"

"Yes."

Purdy lumbered back, followed by Watley.

"Ask him where's his Maglite," Purdy said.

"I think you just did," Glenn said.

It took Purdy a moment to process this, then he looked at me. "Well?"

"I turned the Maglite in with my uniform. Jesus, that was years ago."

"You're telling me that's your only flashlight?" Purdy said.

"Yeah. I don't really have a need for one. Electricity's never gone out as long as I've lived here. And I've only got that because it was a gift. See?" I pointed at the barrel.

Purdy and Watley stretched their necks to get a better look as Glenn rotated the little light around so he could read the writing on it: "Lockhart Real Estate. Let Us Help You Find Your Way Home."

"So, *Corporal* Purdy," I said, emphasizing his rank again, "you think you're going to have to take that down to the station?"

Glenn knew I was busting chops, but he just smiled. He looked at Purdy, waited for an answer.

Purdy just stomped out, Watley in his wake.

"I guess that's a no," Remington said. He handed the flashlight back to me. "Probably want to hang onto that. Might be worth a little money someday."

"I'm not following."

"Reed Lockhart won't be making them anymore."

31

"How much more trouble you think you can make?" Wade said.

"I don't know, the day's still early."

"Yeah," Wade said, "that's what I was afraid of."

We had just finished breakfast at the Koffee Korner Kafe (the coffee and the food are much better than the name—bad spellers, great cooks) and I had spent most of it telling him what had happened and to work out my cover story for last night.

"It's just in case," I said.

"In case of what?"

"In case the Chief decides there's more to the story than meets the eye about Purdy's jaw."

"And his eye," Wade said and gave me a fake smile. He sipped some coffee and looked at me. Something was on his mind.

"Okay, what?"

"You know, it's been a few days since McDougal."

"Shit, I forgot all about him."

"Amnesia will do that."

"I don't have amnesia."

"No, but your brainpan got rattled, and it's easy for stuff to get jumbled around."

"I just forgot. It's not like I didn't have other things to do."

"Bruised ego then?"

"No. And don't say ED either."

He finished his coffee, pulled out his money clip, and paid the check.

"You keep working on the Mayor's demise, while I do some reconnoitering at the Marriot," Wade said.

"Would some of that recon include the fabulous Jacquelyn Thibideaux?"

"Abso-fuckin'-lutely. Emphasis on the middle syllables of the word."

"We've got all this crap going on, and all you can think of is sex?"

"It ain't all I think of. But the bigger question is why ain't you thinking of it?"

"Who says I'm not?"

"I never hear you say anything about Leah."

"Right. I'm probably the last guy who saw her father alive, only I can't tell her that. She's dealing with the sudden death of her father, only some insurance companies are pushing that it was suicide. The entire town, except for the few players involved, think Reed died in a car crash. The players and I know it was murder, only I have to prove it and then tell Leah."

"Leah and sex ain't going to be in the same context. At least for you."

"Anything else you can do to make me feel so good?"

Before he answered, my cell rang. "Girard LaMont," I said both as a hello and for Wade's benefit. "Changed your mind about doing the open house?"

"Well, I have changed my mind, but it's not about the open house."

Shit. Here comes trouble.

"Okay…"

"I was reading the contract, and it says we can cancel the listing anytime without owing you any commission, right?"

"I'm not worried about any commission, Girard. What's going on?"

"I can do that, right? Without any commission?"

"Right. But why are you going down this road?"

There was some muted rustling and some garbled talk that meant he'd put his hand over the phone and was talking to his wife. I waited ten seconds or so. "Girard?"

"Uh, well, I mean…this is…I've heard some rumors."

"Rumors? About what?"

Wade looked at me and frowned. I already knew about what.

"I heard you were in the hospital."

"That's not a rumor, that's a fact. Three days, I had a concussion that'd make an NFL player retire."

More rustling and muted talk as I'm sure he was either repeating what I'd just said or answering more questions from his wife.

"Matt!" Kelly LaMont had taken over the phone.

"Hi, Kelly."

"We're sorry, but these rumors about what happened to you, or more specifically *how* they happened, well, we just can't have that kind of negative fallout attached to us. I'm sorry."

"Whoa, wait a minute, Kelly. Let me understand this. The local gossip is that I was found at the north end of the Strand, drunk and in my boxers."

Kelly's sharp intake of breath told me she hadn't heard *all* of the details.

"That sound like the Matt Singer you know?"

"Uh…no. No, of course not, but…"

"Has another agent mentioned this to you?"

Now it was Kelly's turn to put her hand over the phone and talk *sotto voce.*

But I didn't wait.

"If they have, they are in violation of the ethics standard set by the California Department of Real Estate. And while they're definitely subject to a fine, they're also at risk for losing their license. And I don't really care who told you. But the question you have to ask yourself is this: Do I really want to work with a bottom-feeder? A rumor-monger who's not good enough to get a listing on their own talents and has to resort to mud-slinging tactics?"

"Gee, Matt…uh…" Kelly stopped, not sure where to go or what to say.

"Let me ask you this: If they can't sell you on their abilities, how do you think they're going to do when it comes crunch-time negotiating for you, getting you top dollar?"

Wade gave me a thumbs-up.

"I understand you're anxious about selling your home. It's always an emotional roller-coaster. But look at our track record together."

"Well, you've done a great job for us."

"This is the third home Wade, and I will have sold for you. And every time you always sold it for far, far more money than you paid for it, right?"

"That's for sure."

"So why don't we just let the rumors stay with those Chicken Little people who immediately think they need to run for cover when they think the sky's falling. And stick with the facts? And the facts are that we'll sell your home. For a lot of money."

There was more muted talk, and then Lloyd got on.

"Sorry, Matt. Kelly and I…"

"Don't worry about it. I'll be calling you soon. Hopefully with an offer."

I hung up and bumped my fist with Wade's massive paw that he'd offered over the table.

"I may have lost a few brain cells from the concussion, but not the important ones."

"That was brilliant, podnah. And right on the money."

"In every sense of the word."

"Okay, so the hotshot real estate team is back."

"Which means we can jump into a nearby phone booth and change into Paradise's best crime-fighting team outfits."

Wade checked his watch. "Actually, the only thing I'm hoping to slip into is between the sheets at the Marriott."

"Jacquelyn Thibideaux?"

Heh-heh.

"Nice. I'm worried about the LaMonts, and you're worried about your Johnson."

"Good to have the correct order of things in life."

We got up and headed for the door.

Outside, Wade went left, and I went right.

"My car's this way, Matt."

"I know, I'm going to take a walk. With a little luck, I won't see anybody."

32

"Hey, Matt."

I looked over at Gustav Butcher who was sitting on one of the few benches they have along the Strand. Gustav is Paradise's oldest living resident. "So far," as he always tells me. Gustav's pushing ninety. And for his age, he's doing great.

He waved me over, the cigar in his hand wafting little smoke clouds in the air. "Take a load off," he said. "Keep an old dog company."

We shook hands, and his grip wasn't just strong, it was fierce.

"Still got the firm handshake," I said.

"Yeah. That's from punching all those damn tickets on the S&P railroad." He took a puff on his cigar. "You knew I was a conductor, right?"

"Absolutely."

"Yeah, shit, I probably have told you that story a hundred times."

"No, Gus. I like hearing those stories. You started when you were fifteen..."

"Yeah..." He laughed. "Lied about my age."

"And," I said, "you worked for forty years."

"Damn, you have a good memory. Yep, forty years, so I retired at age fifty-five, although Southern Pacific thought I was fifty-eight."

He inhaled deeply on his cigar, exhaled slowly, and held it up for my inspection. "Once a week I have one of these, a *Tatuaje Noellas*. I know, stinkin' snob. Literally. That's what we so-called cigar connoisseurs are. My wife, Nell, won't let me smoke 'em in the house, so I come down here, sit on this bench, and watch the world go by."

"Not a bad way to spend the morning," I said.

"These aren't too bad, about eight bucks a stick. Every once in a while I fire up a *Cohiba Genios*. They're twenty bucks each. What the hell, I figure my age."

"Absolutely."

"But, I've got a special cigar stashed at home in a humidor. It's a *Gurka, His Majesty's Reserve*."

"Sounds expensive."

"Seven hundred and fifty dollars. Can you believe that? They dip it in Louis XIII de Rémy Martin, gives it a special flavor." Gus sucked deep on what I now realized was, comparatively, an inexpensive cigar, and blew out the smoke. "Seven hundred and fifty dollars for a stick of tobacco leaves," he said. "That's more money than construction workers used to make in an entire year back in the thirties." He tapped the long ash into the plants beside the bench. "One of my lifelong goals has been to receive more years of pension than the number of years I've worked."

"Sounds good."

"So come this December 3rd, we're dead even. That's my birthday, I hit ninety. Then on December 4th, I am firing up that sucker."

"Great, call me, I want to come down and inhale the aroma."

Gus laughed. "Shit, I almost thought of firing it up a couple of days ago."

"Why?"

"Celebrate one of the two funerals this town needs."

"Mayor Lockhart?"

"Hell, yes. The other funeral we need is Ben Black's. Goddamn Mayor and Police Chief supposed to be protecting us fellow citizens, and you'd have to go a long ways to find more evil sons of bitches than those two."

"Ben, I can understand, but Reed? Okay, he was a politician and a real estate wheeler-dealer, but I never heard anything bad about him. He seemed light years away from Ben."

"*Seemed*. But they were just opposite sides of the same crooked coin. They weren't Jekyll and Hyde, they were Hyde and Hyde. You just didn't see the menace behind Reed's thousand-watt smile."

"The town's booming," I said. "Real estate values are through the roof."

"Yeah. And they've built a new grammar school, and by the time they finish remodeling Paraíso High, it'll look like a goddamn state university. And we've got those purty streetlights in the so-called 'Gaslight Section,' and big stores in neighboring towns, so all we Paraísos can go there but not have to see them in our little slice of heaven."

"That doesn't sound terrible. Elitist probably, but not terrible."

"Right. And every one of those results, everyone, somehow benefited Reed Lockhart and most likely his asshole buddy Ben Black. They bought those positions years ago and have paid, and made sure their cronies paid too, to keep those power seats."

We looked out at the ocean for a few moments, Gus drawing deep on his cigar.

"I sound like an old fart, which I am," he said and laughed. "But this used to be a damn nice town back then. Yeah, the houses were small, and you had to drive to Santa Monica or L.A. if you wanted a fancy meal, but hell, the ocean was right there, the air was clean, some of the best beachfront in all of southern California. And now what've we got? Real estate prices that only the mega-rich can afford, which has driven out all of the locals—at least the ones that haven't died off, or the stubborn ones like me."

"There are more of us than you think, Gus."

He looked at me and smiled, the *Tatuaje Noellas* clenched between his teeth.

Gus sucked in a long draught of his cigar, held it a moment, then sent out three perfect smoke rings. "Yeah," he said and smiled at his little performance. "Take my advice, Matt, you keep clear of Black."

"I try to, Gus."

"He's a treacherous bastard. And most of the people around here are either too busy or too scared to call him on his shit. I mean, you heard about what he did on that body they found?"

"The set of bones? What?"

"Nobody's supposed to know it, but the skull? Cratered right in the center. Whoever the poor bastard was, somebody or something hit him hard enough to kill him."

So maybe Hal had talked to more than just Wade and me. Or, more likely his boss, Gerry Kelly, had spilled the beans during one of his drunken afternoons.

"How'd you find that out?"

"I still have a few brain cells left." Gus inhaled again and exhaled without showing off. "I stole that line, or the idea of it, from John Houston."

"What'd you mean?"

"Houston in *Chinatown*. Terrific movie. Houston plays Noah Cross, he's Faye Dunaway's father. So at one point when Nicolson's character, J.J. Gittes, is grilling him, Houston says something about still having his teeth. I always liked that line, so I borrow it every now and then and change it around to fit me." Gus looked off at the ocean.

"So, about the body they found?" I said.

"Oh, right. Shit, I was thinking about *Chinatown*. You know, I love that movie, but when you examine it, it falls apart."

"No," I said, "it's terrific. Right up to the end, one of the most memorable lines in movie history. "

"No doubt it's great writing and terrific acting. But think about it. If Noah Cross owns Los Angeles, the cops, the DA? Why the hell's he need to hire Gittes to track down the girl? Just put Escobar or some other cops on it."

"Maybe it's like *The Godfather*, and he wanted to have some layers between him and the crime."

Gus looked at the glowing end of the cigar. "Ah, well, that's entertainment. A little bit of illusion."

He got up slowly from the bench, I'm sure feeling every one of his years.

I stood up with him, put my hand on his arm. "What about the body, Gus?"

"Fucking Black had Gerry Kelly say the death was from 'natural causes.'"

"But..."

"What the Chief wants, the Chief gets." Gus turned to go, and then looked back at me. "At the right time and right place, they're capable of anything."

"What?"

"I was thinking about Ben, but hell could be anybody. Again from *Chinatown*...just before the shit hits the fan and Nicholson's character realizes he's just a paw and can be taken off the board any time, Houston tells him that most people haven't explored their dark side, mostly because they don't want to go there. He says, 'You see Mr. Gittes, most people never have to face the fact that, at the right time and right place, they're capable of...*anything!*'"

33

Why risk everything?

That was the question that was bothering me.

What the hell could Reed have known or done that would require such a renunciation of his life and everything he'd achieved? Because if I was right, Ben hadn't just murdered Reed. He had created such a deceptive scenario of his true death, the body so devastated by fire that proving he'd died from a bullet would be pretty much impossible. At least for the forensic talent of Paraíso del Mar. Especially talent that was so easily controlled by the Chief.

I knew Kelly was a lost cause, especially if I wanted the truth. So I waited for his assistant, Hal Bartkowski, just down from City Hall.

"I'm heading over to Chin's for lunch," he said and moved forward.

I walked with him. He didn't say anything for several yards. Hal's the silent type. And nervous too. His head kept swiveling around, checking everything out. Once he even turned back to look over his shoulder.

"Are you nervous about something?"

"No, why?"

I decided to table that idea. "So, what'd you make of those bones and the crushed skull?"

Hal practically leaped into the air. He stopped and grabbed my arm.

"Shit! You can't say anything about that." He let go of my arm and started walking again, only faster.

I moved to keep up. "What the hell's going on, Hal?"

"Nothing."

I put my arm in front of his chest and slightly blocked his progress. "Hal, c'mon. This is your surfing buddy here. What's gotten you so spooked?"

"I said nothing, Matt."

"Okay, so a set of bones turns up, the skull's got a dent in it looks like the Grand Canyon. Kelly's forensic examination, if he even knows how to spell it much less do it, determines that the poor bastard died of natural causes, and that's nothing?"

"How the hell do you know that?"

"I have a few friends left in town."

Okay, so I borrowed from Gus.

Hal checked behind us again and said, "Like I told you before, I'm just the bottom Indian on the totem pole. I just do what I'm told."

"And Kelly told you to run the tests, and you did, and you came up with something very different."

He didn't say anything for a while, then finally he nodded in agreement. "That body's been there a long, long time. Pretty much decomposed, disintegrated. No reason to really run any tests. You look at the skull, you know what happened."

"And Kelly didn't like what you said happened?"

"He didn't even care. He said run the tests and here's exactly the results I expect."

"He was following orders."

"Yeah."

Hal started walking again, and I stayed close so we could talk quietly.

"The guy's anterior fontanel, you know the baby's soft spot that's in the center of your head? It was caved in. I mean cratered." Hal then pointed to the back of his head. "And your occipital lobe? Had a crack there looked like a zigzag lightning bolt went clear across his skull. From the occipital lobe clear up into the left cerebral hemisphere."

"Somebody hit him with a hammer?"

"That would've been my initial conclusion. I kinda joked about it, and Kelly ripped me a new one. He says, 'How do you know he didn't have a heart attack first? Then fell off a second story and hit a concrete block?'"

Hal stopped in front of the Chinese takeout restaurant.

And then about had a heart attack himself.

Gerry Kelly came through the door.

"Matt Singer?" He looked at me and then at his assistant, and you could tell he wasn't too happy, for some reason, that we were together.

Hal gulped for air.

"Yeah," I said. "I'm trying to recruit Hal here for the slow-pitch league."

"You're yanking my chain, right?"

I gripped Hal's skinny arm. "Hal's got a real hose on him."

Kelly laughed. "You mean like Big Ben's?"

"No. You know, a hose of an arm? Like a baseball player. Like, say, Hunter Ryan?"

"Who?"

"Okay, Roberto Clemente in your time."

"He that spic that played for the Reds?"

"Clemente was Puerto Rican, and he played for the Pirates and is in Cooperstown. But my point was that Hal can bring it. I've seen him throw out a guy at home plate all the way from center field. And that's with a softball."

"Jesus," Kelly said. "Will wonders never cease." He held up his big bag of takeout and shook it. "I gotta go eat." He moved past us and said over his shoulder, "Don't take all damn day either, Hal."

We watched Kelly waddle his fat ass back to the car.

"Shit," Hal said. "That was close. I'm glad those bones will be history in a couple of days."

"What'd you mean?"

"Natural causes means no further investigation. And we're listing him as a John Doe, and that means no next of kin, so we'll cremate the bones."

"Why're they moving so fast?" I said.

"Don't know. It's all bullshit," Hal said. "There was a compound fracture on the radius bone." Hal held up his arm to demonstrate. "Right here" — he tapped his arm a few inches above his wrist — "nasty, jagged break. And the guy had an ID bracelet, and it slipped through the break and was around the ulna."

"They couldn't get anything off the bracelet to identify him?"

"They didn't even try. I mean it's rusty, but I think you could clean it up and at least get an idea. But Kelly says, 'He's a John Doe that died of natural causes. And I don't want to hear any more about it.'"

"They're burying this guy twice," I said.

"I don't see what's the big deal,"Hal said. "Why they have to lie. That body's been in the ground at least thirty years, probably closer to forty. They're going to be looking for his killer now? It isn't a cold case, it's frozen solid in the past."

Hal held the restaurant door open for me. "You coming in?"

"That's okay," I said. "I've got some things to do."

"And I don't think the weapon was a hammer," Hal said. "The impact area of the wound was too long."

34

"So that's the short version," I told my dad. "If anyone had any doubts about who runs this town, they shouldn't anymore."

We were having tacos at Pedro's, and our waitress was my dad's legal-but-wrong fantasy, Meagan.

"Ben was just following orders."

"You mean from Reed? He's reaching out from the grave? C'mon."

"Probably orders from before his…*accident*. Reed liked to keep things nice and peaceful here. What was his biggest concern? Real estate values. The more trouble goes down, the more property values go up."

"So they put the lid on this and everything's copacetic?"

"Absolutely. Reed Lockhart ran this town like the Godfather. And Ben was his Luca Brasi."

"Yeah, and that son of a bitch should sleep with the fishes."

"Luca Brat-si? I know that name."

We both turned, and there was Meagan. She smiled at my dad. Wrong or not, Meagan was definitely all things inappropriate: phat, hot, sex-bomb.

"I'm sorry, I wasn't eavesdropping, I just, well, that name seems familiar."

"*The Godfather*," my father said. "Luca Brasi is Vito Corleone's enforcer."

"Oh, right. My dad loves that movie, but it's old."

My dad smiled at Meagan, but the "wrong" part of his fantasy hit him hard just then.

"How are the tacos?" Meagan said.

"Irreplaceable," my dad said.

"I assume that means the fantasy's over?" I said after Meagan left us.

"*Niente non è libero. Anche il prete porta delle collezioni,*" he said without taking his eyes off her.

"What's that mean?"

"Nothing is free," my nana, Margherita, used to tell me. "Even the priest takes collections."

"So the price of Pedro's is a hundred fifteen pounds of mind-blowing sex?"

"Eat your taco."

Ever the obedient son, I did.

We both chewed quietly, and then my dad said, "Ah, it'd have never worked out. The age thing."

"There's always Viagra."

"Hey, I got all my hair, all my teeth, even though I have a lot of fillings. I've had the same waist size for thirty years, and I've never, ever needed Viagra." He took an angry mouthful of taco. He chomped for a moment, swallowed then said, "Shit."

"What?"

"Who am I kidding? It'd have never worked out, not because of the physical part, but the…ah, cultural part."

"I thought you just wanted to jump her bones?""

He gave me a look I remembered from fifth grade. It was a look of twin failures: his that he hadn't been able to teach me better, and mine because I was *idiota*. I remembered that look because it came the first, and only time, I'd cursed my mother. "Fuck you," I'd shouted before bursting into tears because she was sticking to her decision that since I hadn't mowed the yard or cleaned up my room—in spite of her dire warnings and heartfelt pleadings—that I wasn't going to Rob Chamber's birthday party.

But as devastating as the look was from my father, the hurt and shame that ran across my mother's face then was even worse.

"So," he said and waited a long moment before he continued, "to get back to the *buried* bones. Why are you so concerned with them?"

"I'm not really. But it's just another in-your-face act by Ben. Another fuckin' straw on the camel's back, or in Ben's case, another redwood log. It just pisses me off."

"I don't like this road you're going down, Matt. It's dangerous. Gus was right. Stay away from Ben."

"I'm not afraid of that bastard."

"Fear's got nothing to do with it." He finished a taco, drank some of his Corona beer. "Whatever the hell he's doing, for this town it's just business."

"It's not business. It's personal. Somebody whacked me, embarrassed me, and made me look like a fool."

"Oh," he said, "that's different. *Questo è l'azienda di famiglia.*"

That one I knew, only because he'd said it so many times before. "Yes, Dad, this *is* family business."

35

The warning signs were all over as I followed Nick, the young attendant, through rows of vehicles in the police auto yard.

"Well, at least they've blacktopped this dump," I said.

"What're you talking about? It's always been blacktopped," he said.

"What're you twenty?" I said.

"Nineteen, why?"

"Because back when you were five, this lot used to be all dirt."

Nick looked at me like I'd just told him contrary to what he'd learned in science class at Paraiso High, that the earth was, indeed, flat.

"F'sure?"

"F'sure, dude," I said. "Place was a dump. Oil and transmission leaks all over the place, looked like the La Brea Tar Pits, except without T-Rex. You hated to bring your patrol car down here because it automatically got covered in dust."

"Patrol car? Why didn't you say you were a cop?"

"Because I'm not. I was, a long time ago. Long time ago. Both in years and shit that went down."

"We still get some oil leaks," Nick said, I think to make conversation. "And sometimes a cracked tranny leaks fluid all over. But not too much."

Nick seemed like a nice enough kid. When I'd pulled into the lot, I could hear the rock music he was blasting from his stereo all the way at the entrance. I'd had to shout hello several times before he heard me and interrupted his air guitar performance, complete with Pete Townsend extended leg air leaps.

"It's back here," Nick said. "Hard to believe it used to be an NSX."

I had come here to see for myself and make sure.

"That bad?" I said.

"You tell me." He pointed at a ghastly, blackened mess of shattered and splintered and burned fiberglass and metal.

For an instant, I had a flashback of an M-41 Bulldog Tank disintegrating in a fireball.

"Everything blew out from the gas tank," Steve said, his voice rising a notch. "Must have gone up like a rocket. Ka-boom, whoosh." He slammed his hands together. "Yeah, it was..."

He looked at me and instantly shut up. "I'm sorry," he said. "Sometimes I'm...shit, I know, the Mayor died."

"Who brought it in?"

"Usual. Manny's Towing."

"You remember what time?"

"Had to be a few minutes after 6:30, because I had already locked up the shack and was just closing the gate when they came in and I had to re-open everything, start up the computer. Pain in the ass."

Six-thirty. I had put the professor into the cab around 8:15, discovered Reed maybe fifteen minutes later. So in about ten hours, the killer had clubbed me, dumped my booze-soaked ass at the other end of the Strand, gotten Reed into his NSX, dumped gasoline all over it, and plowed him into the trees.

Shit, maybe I *was* imagining all of this.

"Did you hear me?"

"What?" I said, coming back to see Steve staring at me.

"I said the fuckin' thing was still warm, you know? You could feel the heat waves coming off it."

"Right," I said, trying to cover my mental gap. "I was just thinking about the fire..."

I walked closer to the twisted mass that once was a very expensive car. The engine had come straight back through the firewall. The steering wheel column had speared Reed dead center. He wouldn't have survived the crash, much less the fire.

"You know much about cars? I mean, more than just storing them?"

"Hell, yes. I'm about to get my master mechanics certificate from ITT Tech."

"Great. So, how does a gas tank in the rear explode from a front-end collision?"

Nick looked at me, then at the remains of the car. He frowned, shook his head.

"Yeah, it is kinda weird." He thought on it for a moment. "Maybe some spark from the impact went down the fuel line back into the tank. I don't know."

"Could you tell if the gas tank was full?"

He shook his head. "Not really. It's completely destroyed. I'd say probably yeah. Must have been to blow up like that."

"Must have," I said.

We both stared at the grotesque hulk of steel for a few moments, and then Nick looked at me. "I should get back to the hut, you know, in case somebody comes in?"

"Yes," I said. "I've seen enough."

I shook Nick's hand and headed for my car. I dialed Zak. It was past eight back east, but I knew he'd still be working.

After we chatted for a while, I said, "Hey, Zak, I need a favor."

"Sure, Matt, what?"

"I need to see when Reed Lockhart last bought gasoline."

36

I burned fuel, rubber, and the road getting back to my house. But even though I covered the 4.6 miles in record time, Zak still beat me.

By the time I hit the computer mouse, and my email flashed on, the last thirty days of Reed Lockhart's credit card activity was right there—detailed rows of things he'd bought, restaurants where he'd dined, and only one entry for gasoline at the local Shell station, more than three weeks prior.

And while Reed had several cars, the Acura was his favorite, and he drove it all the time.

"It's bullshit," I said to Wade on my cell as I paced back and forth in my bedroom. "His model has an eighteen-gallon tank, they claim fifteen miles a gallon in the city."

"Which in reality is about ten," Wade said.

"Right. But even if you go with their claims, eighteen gallons at fifteen miles per gallon, comes to two hundred seventy miles. Divided by the twenty-eight days before the accident, is less than ten miles a day."

"And he was always in that damn car. So unless he paid cash to fill it up, his fuel gauge had to be into the red."

"And they said his gas tank exploded."

"Only thing blew up is their damn story. Shit, Matt, this *is* getting serious. We have to make sure when we go with this we haven't missed a thing. We're only going to get one shot at it."

"You gotta say shot?"

"You getting superstitious on me?"

"No, just saying we could use some luck. The good kind."

"Yeah. Well, I'll make sure a black cat doesn't cross my trail."

"That'll be the Chief's concern too," he said. "Making sure this black cat doesn't cross his trail."

And then he did a Jeff Beck air-guitar and sang, *"Ba-dada-da-dun-dun."*

"How was the recon mission?"

There was a moment of silence, and then Wade said, "Uh, it's still going on."

"Shit, Jacquelyn is at your place? I thought you were going to the Marriot?"

"She wanted to come here."

"Why didn't you say something?"

I heard some background noise through the phone, like a door opening, and Wade said, "Gotta go, stay lucky." And he hung up.

Lucky is right. Supposedly, when Napoleon was asked if he preferred courageous generals or brilliant generals, he replied, "Neither. I prefer lucky generals."

My phone rang. It was Wade.

"Hey, Jacquelyn heard me say lucky to you and told me this little bit of info, very arcane. If you have thirteen letters in your name, you will have the Devil's luck. Hell, you may even *be* the Devil. Listen to this. Jack the Ripper, Charles Manson, Jeffrey Dahmer, Theodore Bundy, and Albert DeSalvo. They all have thirteen letters in their names."

"Okay?"

"And, so does, count 'em on your fingers, Benjamin Black."

37

And not ten minutes later, Ben Black pushed my doorbell with his thick finger.

I was wary as hell when I opened the door. Maybe he had a weapon? Or that asshole Purdy with him. I wasn't ruling out any possibilities.

"Hiya, Matt. Sorry to barge in unexpected like this, but I was in the neighborhood and…"

"Really?"

"Yes," he said, biting down his anger that I had interrupted him. "This is off the clock, nothing official about it."

"Okay."

He didn't seem to know how to begin. "Uh…look…I know we've had our differences, but, even so, I still respect you. Hell, I might even like you…a little."

"Wow, I don't know what to say."

"And I wanted to make sure you were doing all right."

"I'm fine," I said and moved to close the door.

He put out a hand, which would have made it awkward for me to bang it shut in his face.

"I'd invite you in, Chief, but I was just leaving."

"Fine." He looked hard at me. "So…you are okay, right?"

"Absolutely."

"Headaches gone?"

"Yes."

"Not seeing things?"

What the hell?

"No," I said, probably a little harder than necessary. I hate to let my emotions show, especially with a barracuda-like him.

"Don't be offended. I know combat can seriously mess up a man. World War I they called it shell shock. World War II it was battle fatigue. Vietnam they had Agent Orange fallout. Hell, I don't know what they call the aftermath shit that vets get from combat over in Afghanistan."

"Me either."

"You know, I humped a bazooka during the Chosin battle. And Remington flew those Raptors. Fuckin' $361 million plane."

I waited. I couldn't figure out where he was going with this bullshit.

"Once a military man," he said, "always a military man. That's why I hire them. I've put a good half-dozen soldiers and Marines and Navy men on my force."

"And I'm probably the only one you court-martialed."

That set him back for a moment.

"Nah, nah. You had your principles, which was fine." He shifted his weight slightly. Ben may be up there in years, but he's got the physique and energy of a man twenty years his junior. He's still one tough bird.

"Being in battle like I was…like *you* were…you see things, experience things you wish to Christ you never had to see once, and certainly never want to see again. But sometimes, we *keep* seeing those things."

"Right."

"So, you having any flashbacks? Seeing things?"

Now he was really pissing me off. But I took a deep breath before I answered. "Nope," I said. "Right here in the present. Always have been, always will be."

"Good, good. I've heard that PTSD can be a real bitch."

"So I've seen on CNN."

"Great. No flashbacks, you aren't seeing things other people can't see?"

"What the hell's this all about?"

"Like I said, nothing, really. Just a friendly little off-the-record visit. Making sure everything's copacetic."

"I get it. If I'm seeing things, that could be a problem?"

"That's one way of looking at it. I'm glad we understand each other." He turned and headed toward an incredible showroom-condition Ferrari in the shiniest red paint I'd ever seen. I couldn't help but stare. He caught it and smiled. "C'mon," he said, "let me show off."

The last thing I wanted was to let this prick show off the newest addition to his penis compensation stable. Not that I really believe that psychobabble. Because if a man feels insecure about his Johnson and buys a flashy car as a way to compensate, Ben should have bought a Greyhound bus. But sometimes, vanity exposes our weaknesses. And like Doctor Sigmund said, "Sometimes a cigar is just a cigar."

And sometimes a Ferrari is just a Ferrari.

If there ever was *just* a Ferrari.

And this was *the* Ferrari.

"It's a 275 GTB/4," he said. "Not many of these left. Old Enzo only made about four hundred." He levered his body into the pleated leather seat. "Just got it a few days ago, drove it down from San Francisco."

He turned the key and blipped the accelerator. There's no other car engine sound like a Ferrari. And this one was tuned to perfection.

"God, I love that sound," he said.

"Yeah. You gotta be careful driving it though."

He looked at me, frowned. "What're you talking about?"

"You don't want to get a speeding ticket."

His smile was as empty as a vampire's soul. He eased the gearshift into first and then looked down toward the ocean. "I love our little town. The last thing I need in our little paradise is any little wave of trouble." He looked right at me. "I got enough waves right down there by the water."

38

"Sounded a little fishy to me," Tommie Shea Soh said. "But your house is clean, Matt. Top to bottom, inside and out."

"Great, thanks, Tommie."

I kissed Tommie's cheek and wondered if I should have tried for the lips. Tommie is a stunning six-foot Eurasian woman whose face used to beckon from *Vogue, Mademoiselle, Harper's* and a half-dozen European magazines devoted to high couture and other snobbish pastimes.

She quit modeling to have a child, father rumored to be an eastern European billionaire, with more rumors about *Rossiyskaya Mafiya*, illegal arms trading, and drug running. It didn't seem to affect Tommie. She might be the most confident woman I've ever met. Poised, calm, smart as hell, and never once shows off when it comes to her considerable talents. She just does the job and moves on.

Tommie is also flat-out the best electronics surveillance expert I've ever met. I think between the modeling and the child, she secretly did a brief stint at NSA. And she's always right.

Wade describes her conclusions in his best Ray Charles, "I guess if Tommie Shea Soh, you have to pack your things and go."

Of course, he's never hummed that in Tommie's presence.

I'd felt a little sheepish asking Tommie to come check things out, but I needed to know how the Chief was getting his information.

"So, how do you think he knew what I was saying?" I said.

"I don't think he does know. He was most likely trolling to see if you'd take the bait." She pushed back a shiny black wave of hair from her face. "Maybe he talked to the nurse at the hospital, or Purdy talked to her and reported back to the Chief. Could be a dozen ways. But bugging your house or phones isn't one of them."

"Great."

"What exactly are you saying that's got him pissed off?"

"It's probably better I don't tell you."

She looked at me for a long moment and then smiled. "You know I could just plant a device and find out myself."

"There is that," I said. "But why waste the time and equipment? When I get something concrete, you'll hear about it."

She chuckled. "I hope that pun was deliberate."

"Accidentally on purpose."

"Okay, I have to pick up Oren." She kissed me on the cheek.

"You'll send me a bill."

"I'll think about it."

After she'd gone, the subtle waft of her perfume lingered in the air of the living room. It was slightly intoxicating. Just like Tommie.

I picked up my now absolutely clean phone and dialed the first of the carpet companies in town. After a few minutes of hard sales talk, I was finally able to tell Karen Barkley what I needed. She laughed and said, "We're just a little ol' mom-and-pop operation. Kenny does the laying—the carpet that is, not our customers." Karen laughed at her own joke. "And I do the paying, making sure we get paid as well as paying our suppliers."

"You don't carry the brand?" I asked.

"Nope. It's way too expensive for our customers."

"Okay… "

"Jeannie, " Karen said. "That's who you should call, Jeannie Mercato. She's the high-end queen."

She laughed again at her own joke.

"You want a deal on a terrific, durable and *affordable* carpet, give me a call. Remind me we've talked and I'll give you a fifteen percent discount. How's that?"

"That's perfect, Karen."

Jeannie Mercato didn't carry that brand. Neither did the other carpet store or any of the other six in neighboring towns I also called. It seemed like someone had mysteriously appeared, removed 200 yards of deep-pile, ultra-fine grade wool carpeting—that just happened to be soaked in blood—then installed the exact same carpeting without anyone in Paraíso del Mar knowing anything about it.

"Maybe magical elves did it," Wade said.

This was several hours later, after Jacquelyn had gone back to the Marriott and Wade had gone to bed again, this time to rest.

"Whoever did it, he's too scared to say anything."

"Yes. But in the end, how important is that, really?"

"It destroyed valuable evidence."

"We find a way to prove he was there and pulled the trigger, all that other stuff either falls into place or falls by the wayside."

"Yeah, you're right. Okay, I've got ten minutes to get over to the station."

"What the hell you going to do there?"

"Start at the beginning."

39

"I was just finishing up for the day," Clarisse Townsend said.

"Sure, this will only take a minute," I said.

Clarisse is a Dolly Parton clone, platinum blonde hair, juicy, pouty lips, and a truly massive bust. She's also the Chief's personal assistant, and main squeeze, at least police-wise. She tries to cover it up by acting over-the-top professional, but it's one of the many exposed secrets around town. Everybody knows she and Ben do body cavity searches on each other.

Clarisse brushed back one of her chromium locks and said, "Chief Black left several hours ago. In fact, I thought he was going to see you."

"He already did."

"Oh?"

"I love his new Ferrari."

"Oh my God! Yes, it's just sex on wheels." She blushed appropriately.

I figured bullshit was the best maneuver with Clarisse.

"I forgot to ask him where he got it, you know, the company?"

Clarisse peered at me like that was the strangest request she'd heard in weeks, and no doubt the height of conceit—that *I* could afford a Ferrari. "Let me see," she said and tapped a few keys on her keyboard. "There it is, La Modena Motors, in San Francisco." She tapped a couple more keys, and the computer's printer hummed and delivered the information.

"Thanks," I said. I pretended to read the name and address, so didn't look up at Clarisse when I said, "Last Wednesday? I thought he said he was up at a police department conference."

That must have set off an alarm in Clarisse's little "take care of the Chief" mindset: Don't let anyone think he might be bending the rules. "Oh," she said and laughed. "You know Ben...I mean Chief Black, always maximizing his time."

"Absolutely," I said. "Thanks, Clarisse, you're obviously an asset to the Chief."

Actually *twin assets* I was thinking --hard to pretend you don't notice as my dad has said in his most inappropriate sexist analysis, those "big headlights on that small chassis."

"Why thank you, Matt. That's so nice."

I held up the sheet, nodded my gratitude, and turned for the door. "Oh," I said, in my best *Columbo* style, "He drove all the way down from San Francisco?"

"Yes. But you know the Chief, I'm sure he did it in record time."

40

"A time to weep and a time to laugh…" Father Russo said. He looked up briefly from his notes at the group of people gathered in the solemn quiet of Saint Teresa's church for Abbey McDougal's funeral.

While Father Russo continued with the rest of the Ecclesiastes scripture, Wade and I scanned the mourners. We had decided at the last minute to slip into the ceremony. Not because we believe in that old idea that a criminal returns to the scene of the crime or visits the funeral as one final cruel act against the victim, but because we felt we owed it to Abbey.

Her parents looked numb with grief. The financial genius brother, who looked like a power broker male model in a bespoke matte black suit, gleaming white shirt, and a Hermes tie that probably cost more than my entire outfit, held his mother upright by the elbow. No sagging permitted in the Titlebaum clan. The other family members who filled the left side pews ran the entire spectrum of ages from the newest tots to an ancient grandmother, who I assumed to be from the maternal side since she was clearly stooped with age and loss, and therefore most definitely *not* a Titlebaum.

There were only about six other people with Wade and me on the right side. Her husband Stephen wasn't one of us.

Father Russo concluded the ceremony with a prayer and everyone in the church stood up. Wade and I watched the others and the family file outside.

"Let's wait here," I said.

"Yeah," Wade said. "I don't think this was such a great idea."

We sat down. "Father Russo did a nice job," Wade said. "Considering."

"Considering he really didn't know her all that well?"

Wade nodded.

"Excuse me," a man's voice came to us from the entrance.

We turned, and the manly brother strode for us. I stood, Wade didn't.

"I am Denis Titlebaum." Moses coming down from Mount Sinai with the Ten Commandments couldn't have sounded more self-anointed. He didn't offer his hand, so I kept mine by my side.

"I shall try to maintain some degree of civility, considering where we are." He indicated Saint Teresa's wood-paneled interior and the refracted light coming through the stained glass windows. "But you two have some nerve."

Uh-oh.

"I'm sorry," I said, trying to delay the explosion. "Is there a problem?"

"Is it true that you work for *him*?"

"By him, I'm assuming you mean Stephen McDougal? And yes and no."

Denis sneered at me. Actually fucking sneered.

So I decided to hit back.

"Yes, that Stephen McDougal., Your brother-in-law, Abbey's widower husband."

Denis sucked in a huge deep breath and glared at me. He was about to snarl something when Wade stood up.

"You really want to be discussing this here? And now?" Wade said in that low, direct voice he uses when he gets serious. A voice that even he who was Denis Titlebaum reacted to, as in, *Oops, this man could be trouble*. But it was only for an instant, and Denis came on again. "My plane leaves in four hours. So, yes, we will be discussing this here. And now." He turned back to look at me.

"We work for Stephen and for Abbey," I said. "They owned the house together, so we represented both of them. And we are here because we are sorry for Abbey's death and to convey our sorrow for your family's tremendous loss."

"Thank you, I'm sure," Denis said.

That must be the tone he uses when he's taking a stockbroker over the coals for missing a quarter percentage point of arbitrage.

But before he could continue, Wade moved out of the pew. Denis could have tried to stand his ground, but while he was impeccable, he certainly wasn't impenetrable.

"Let's take this outside," Wade said and moved past Denis. I followed in his wake.

"Don't you dare turn your back on me," Denis snapped.

Wade did a spin move that Derek Rose would have envied and was past me and in Denis's face before I could register the slight breeze of his moving bulk.

"My family isn't Catholic," Wade said, "but a House of the Lord is a House. Of. The. Lord. And you, sir, will respect that." He stared at Denis for a moment. "Now if you still feel you want to confront us on a trivial matter such as our employment, instead of being with your family, we will be waiting for you outside."

Wade turned back and flowed past me. I could see the fire in his eyes.

I'm sure if we had been outside, that Hermes tie might have gotten very tight around the Titlebaum neck.

Denis must have taken a moment to gather his forces because Wade and I waited almost a minute before he came through the doors. I saw him put his cell back inside his suit. He stared at us, and then walked over, not as strong this time, maybe Moses light.

"This was a private ceremony. For family members and a very select group of people only. You two were not invited."

"That's already been established," Wade said. "I thought you were prepared to move forward on the case. If not, then we will be going."

"Wait a minute. What are you talking about?"

"You knew your sister better than anyone," I said. "Who, besides Stephen, would want her dead?"

I think the word *dead*, in spite of being at her funeral, hit him hard. It always does. *Passed* is gentler, less final, although they describe the same terrible loss.

"I…I don't know of anybody. Abbey was…"

His eyes grew bright, and he snapped his head away from us. He took several deep breath, and I saw his hand quickly move up and brush away the telltale tears.

Why the hell he felt he needed to hide his honesty from us, his pain didn't make sense. But then I guess you don't marshal those kinds of dollars by being "sensitive."

I don't like crying. Most men don't, at least those who aren't in Broadway shows and still adore Madonna (and I say that in the best "don't ask, don't tell" way). But when the tears come, I don't fight them. I can't. And the opening to *Up*, showing Carl and Ellie's wonderful life together doesn't count. Neither does the bedtime scene in *Despicable Me* (and those are just the cartoons). Wade has his own sniffle series.

When Denis turned back to face us, he had obviously turned on the steely resolve machine. His face was stern, just like his voice. "I believe that considering anyone but Stephen is nonproductive. Therefore, the fact that you two …gentlemen …were or still are employed by him, precludes us having any further conversation."

"We could always talk about the Yankees," I said.

His face went crimson.

"Oh, shit," I said, "you're a Red Sox fan?"

41

"The double-header continues tomorrow," Wade said.

"Back-to-back funerals," I said. "But tomorrow's is SRO."

"That's why it's good you're friends with Leah," Wade said and took a long hit on his drink. "You talked to her today?"

We were sitting at Leonard's Bar & Grill, although almost no one ever went there for the grill. Lenny had already owned the bar for a long time back when I was about seventeen and a couple of surfing buddies, and I used to sneak in for a beer. We always thought we were so cool. It took us a long time to figure out that Lenny knew our age. He just figured no one was going to drop the dime on him. And if he got busted, it would only be a warning since the city council members drank there too. In all those years before I went into Leonard's and the years since Lenny's still yet to fire up the grill to even make a hot dog.

"You want food?" he would say. "Go to a restaurant. This is a drinking establishment."

"But why," a tourist once asked him, "does it say 'Bar & Grill' if you don't grill?"

"For the same reason it says 'Leonard's, but nobody ever calls me that. Because that's the way I want it."

"You'd never get away with that back in Omaha."

"Yeah?" Lenny said. "Well, why don't you get back to Omaha while you still can? The drinks are on the house."

I drank back some of my beer. "No," I finally answered Wade. "I haven't called Leah. I will though."

"You know, you aren't required to tell her your suspicions."

"You mean turn in my Boy Scout Honor badge?"

"You were never in the Boy Scouts."

"Bullshit. Paradise Troop 47, Scoutmaster Sam Mallory."

"How many merit badges you get? God, I bet it was a lot."

"No. Only two."

"What?"

"Yeah. I got two right away, then we went on our first camping trip, and I got a severe case of poison oak, decided I didn't like being out in the trees…"

"Which pretty much 86'd the whole Boy Scouts idea," Wade interrupted.

"Yeah," I said. "You don't like being out in the woods, you're probably not going to be much of a Boy Scout."

"Like zero scouting."

"I said no to the trees and yes to the ocean. That's right when I really got into surfing."

"You sure it wasn't Scoutmaster Mallory didn't want to do some scouting in your short pants?"

"Not Sam. He was a terrific guy. His son Raymond made Eagle Scout, had one of those sashes goes across your chest like a bandolier, completely filled with merit badges and pins and medals. I think he was California Scout of the Year or some shit."

Wade took another long hit on his drink. "You can keep your badge and not tell Leah. In fact, it's probably better you don't tell her anything right now."

"Because of the state she's in?"

"That too. But more because we don't want to do this until we've got all our ducks in a row. Suspecting the Chief did it, which is here"—Wade held out his right hand—"and proving he did it"—he held out his left hand—"which is here." He swiveled his head between his two hands. They were far apart. "That's a lot of ducks."

"Fuckin' squadron," I said.

"And each duck gots to be lined up with no squawkin.'"

"Is that an ancient *Zuwir* warrior tradition?"

"We hunts lions, sahib. We don't screw wit ducks."

I finished my drink. "I had the feeling you were going to do some damage to Denis."

"Thought about giving him a bitch slap for disrespecting the church."

"So why'd you give him a pass?"

"Rich asshole or not, the man's lost a sister. That can make you act funny."

42

"I don't know what to say," Leah moaned. "I don't know what to do. I'm just numb."

"That's understandable," I said.

"I'm supposed to be making all of these decisions about the funeral and…and I just can't. So I'm just letting the people at Atkinson's do it all."

"Anything I can do?"

"Help me pick out a suit."

We were at her father's house. I had called her after Wade, and I left Leonard's, and she'd asked to meet me at Reed's mansion.

I couldn't help staring at the spot where I'd seen him lying there, his blood and life leaking out.

"New carpet?"

Leah looked at the pristine carpeting and shrugged. "I don't remember. Maybe."

She walked back toward the bedroom and into her father's enormous closet. Calling it a "walk-in" didn't do it justice. More like a "drive-in." It was easily the biggest damn space just for clothes I'd ever seen. All of it organized and designed to perfection.

"This looks like it could be in *Architectural Digest*," I said.

"It was. Four, five years ago. They did a huge spread on the house. I think the view was on the cover. I'm sure my dad has twenty copies of the magazine in his files someplace." She went to the row of suits, which had to be twenty feet long. "God, what am I going to do with all these clothes?"

I knew she really didn't want an answer just yet, so I went to the black suits. "Maybe this one." I held the sleeve out, the fabric felt buttery smooth and soft.

Leah took it down from the pole, looked at it, and then put it back. "That wasn't one of his favorites." She flipped through several suits and stopped on a muted black with the most subtle silver threads. "This one." She held it up, appraised it. "Yes. Thanks, Matt, for helping."

"Sure, but I didn't do anything."

"It's just nice having someone with me…in the house."

She went to the opposite wall, pulled a snow-white shirt, and selected a soft burgundy tie that would have given Denis Titlebaum's Hermes beauty a run for the money. "I guess he'll need shoes…" she said.

"And socks. And probably underwear."

Leah looked at me like I'd uttered a blasphemous phrase in church. "I mean…"

"Yes, you're right." She went to a built-in dresser snugged against the back wall, opened a drawer, extracted a pair of white boxers, opened another and retrieved black, calf-length socks. "This seems so bizarre," she said. "To have to dress him up in these expensive clothes when his body's…"

And then the impact of it all hit her. Tears blossomed bright in her eyes and rolled down her cheeks, taking the mascara she was wearing with them.

She hadn't gone down to identify the charred remains of what was left of her father. At least Ben had saved her from that. She couldn't have taken it. I doubt if most people could. According to Hal, when they'd put out the fire, Reed's body was a smoldering charcoal skeleton, his fingers clutched in a Black Death grip, his mouth petrified in a ghoulish rictus.

I took the handkerchief that was peeking out of the breast pocket of the suit. Leah's arms were full with clothes, so I dabbed her cheeks.

"Thanks," she said, her voice thick from crying.

I looked into her eyes. Damn, she was absolutely beautiful. Even now when she probably looked her worst.

"Matt…" she said, "let me see something." She held the suit up to my chest. "You and Dad were about the same size. I bet you could wear these, maybe just have the waist taken in."

"Oh, no, no. Thanks, really, but the last time I wore a suit was when I..." I stopped because I didn't want to say a funeral—Abbey's. "I'm just not the suit kind of guy anymore."

"Please, just try it on."

Crap.

"But not this one, since he's going to...wear it."

Awkward moment.

I took a suit jacket at random and put it on. Damn, it fit perfectly.

"I knew it," Leah said. "It's terrific on you. Take a look." She pointed behind me at a wide, full-length mirror reflected the lights and suits and shirts and...me.

They say clothes make the man. Reed's made me look like somebody I wasn't: suave, slick, totally professional – and a dead man walking.

"Thanks," I said. "It's absolutely terrific." In my nervousness, I stuffed my hands into the side pockets, and my right hand touched something—a card. I held it out to Leah.

"Garland's Flowers," she said. "Out in Burbank? That's odd."

"Maybe somebody gave him the card, and he forgot about it." I took off the jacket. "You want the card?"

She shook her head and put the jacket back on the hanger. "Think about the clothes, will you?"

I nodded and followed Leah as she carried the suit and his other clothes out to the living room and put everything on a sofa. "I could use a drink," she said. "And a walk down by the water." She picked up her purse. "So could Tash. I've been neglecting her the last few days. Would you mind if we stopped by my house first and picked her up and then took her on a walk?"

"Sounds like a good idea. I like Tash."

43

"Tash definitely doesn't like me," I said.

"I wonder what's bothering her," Leah said. We had walked into Leah's house, and Tash had gotten one whiff of me and started that mournful husky howl again.

I bent down at her eye level, held out my hand, and got a growl from her.

"Tash!" Leah stepped in-between us. "You get over there. Now!"

I wasn't sure whether she meant me or Tash, but I held my ground.

Tash slinked over to her doggie bed.

"No, it's okay," I said. "She's probably spooked from all the things that have happened."

Tash had lain down but kept letting out those sad, ear-piercing yowls.

"God, I don't know what's gotten into her."

"I better go," I said.

Leah looked at me and then at Tash. "Okay, I do have to take her on a walk, she's been cooped up inside all day."

"We'll take a rain check on that drink."

"Yes," she said and stepped closer to me. "Tomorrow, after…after."

"No rush. Whenever it's right. I know where you live."

She smiled, more out of politeness than anything. And then her arm slipped around my neck, and she kissed me. And it wasn't just a good-bye kiss, more like "Hello, look at what the future might bring."

The future may have arrived that very moment, but Tash let out a howl that might have broken the sound barrier.

We broke the kiss and moved apart.

"That's my exit cue," I said.

"We enter this life from darkness," Pastor Timothy O'Bannon said. "And it is into darkness that we return."

Father Tim is more Irish than any Catholic priest I know and presides over the only nondenominational church in Paraíso del Mar.

"And in-between those two black voids from which no one really remembers or knows"—he looked out over the huge assembly of people there for Reed Lockhart's funeral—"we try and make our lives bright with shining examples of goodness."

There was a soft murmur of approval from the crowd gathered at the gravesite.

"At least we try and do it with goodness," Father Tim said. "And certainly, no one tried harder or succeeded more than my good friend Reed Lockhart."

He continued his kind words, but I stopped really listening. I was trying to check out the mourners without being a bobblehead and keep an eye out for Leah, to make sure she was going to make it through this.

While the local L.A. media hadn't devoted much to Reed's death, they were out in full force for the funeral. Probably because some Hollywood actors and actresses were in the audience, as well as many of L.A.'s more visible politicians, some Los Angeles heavyweight police department officials, and a parade of rich businessmen. Reed knew a lot of prominent people. And obviously, a lot of people knew Reed, or they were here claiming they did.

Leah's hand gripped mine tightly as if she let go, she'd float away or scream like a wild, crazed woman. Which she might be for now, in the grip of her pain and loss. Coming over in one of the funeral cars, she had lost all control and raged against God, fate, life and every other belief system she could think of, and ended in a howling, primal scream that ripped up from the depths of her soul.

Now she just stared straight ahead, her eyes looking at Father O'Bannon, but not really seeing him.

The Chief was sitting on her other side, looking at the pages of his speech that I'm sure Clarisse had typed and maybe helped write.

My cell phone buzzed in my inside suit pocket. I slipped it out as surreptitiously as I could—a text message from Zak: ***Call me re: Reed's credit cards.***

What the hell? Damnit, I hadn't told him to search his records. This wasn't like Zak. I was pissed and curious at the same time. It wasn't like him to wildcat a request. I typed a "K' for my answer and put the phone back into my pocket.

Chief Black shook Father O'Bannon's hand and settled behind the podium. I looked at Leah. The Chief rattled his speech, adjusted the mic.

"Leah," I whispered, "I've got to do something. It'll only be a minute or so."

Panic streaked through her eyes, then she took a deep breath and nodded okay.

I bent down low and slipped in front of the others gathered in the front row. I glanced back and saw the Chief incredulous that someone would dare leave during *his* speech.

Screw him and the Ferrari he drove in on.

I went up the aisle, avoiding people's rude looks, saw Wade looking at me to see what was up, but I shook my head and kept going and found a quiet spot away from everyone and dialed Zak.

"Hey, Matt," he said before I said hello. Obviously, his caller ID was working. "Something odd came up on Reed's credit report."

"Zak, why were you doing a credit report? All I wanted was the last time he bought gasoline."

"Because when I ran this program, Z-18RamJet, that's one of my own algorithm programs that…"

"Zak!"

"Sorry, sorry. That was how I was able to get his gasoline purchases, but a by-product of that search was it kicks out any sequence of regular purchases. I didn't even know it had done it except when I was going to wipe the results from the computer, it kinda popped out."

"Doesn't everybody have regular spending habits?"

"Absolutely, but usually not in a business that's thirty, forty miles away."

"What are you talking about?"

"Once a week, like clockwork, Reed's Black American Express card *kachings* $85 to a Swanson's Florists in Burbank."

"Burbank?" I had repeated it, but I was already making the connection. That was the business card I'd found in Reed's suit.

"Seemed a little odd, so I linked the Z-18RamJet to my Z-360Geo program and was able to track down where Swanson's sent the flowers."

"Okay."

"A Mrs. Mayleen Santiago. Lives out in Pacoima, wherever the hell that is."

"It's out in the San Fernando Valley, probably half hour from Burbank."

Santiago…I knew that name from someplace.

"Did you get anything on Mrs. Santiago?"

"Uh, no, no. I didn't think I should take it any deeper without talking to you about it." He sniffed. "Although…"

Okay, here it comes.

"I ran a historical trace? He's been doing this for several decades."

"Holy shit."

"And…aw, shit, I'm sorry, but you know me and data. Once I get a sniff, I'm like a short dog in tall grass."

"What did you do, Zak?"

"Don't be mad, okay? But I leapfrogged over to his other cards, and he's been sending flowers to Mrs. Santiago for more than thirty years. Maybe longer. Thirty-three years is as far back as the records go."

"Okay, thanks."

"And…" He hesitated, somehow I knew that hidden beneath Zak's statements to me was another series of statements known only to him. "And," he began again, "for just about the same number of years, he's been taking cash withdrawals once a month. Started out at a thousand and over the years has blown up to ten grand."

"Reed did like to have a good time," I said.

"I guess, but he used his credit cards for everything, and I mean everything; so I'm just trying to figure out what the hell he does with that cash."

I was a little pissed that Zak had taken the search way out beyond the initial request, but this information might be valuable. It certainly sparked a lot of questions. So I decided to let it ride.

"Zak, thanks. You aren't still running the search, are you?"

"Do you want me to?"

"No, I just don't want you to get caught."

"Dude, there's no freakin' way any government spook nerd could trace my searches. Hell, I'd know they were doing it before they'd finish their programming."

"How could you do that?"

"Those types of investigations take specific sequencing programming. I've got a search engine set up to sniff out anything starts to get assembled in that way, total pattern recognition in the formative stages."

"Zak, how many millions of computers are there? That's impossible."

"I'm not worried about millions, just a few thousand in a very special place in Washington."

"Shit, Zak." And then I thought and said, "This telephone call?"

"Dude, the scrambler was running before your ID popped up." He chuckled across the miles. "You want a complete profile on Mrs. Santiago, just ring me up."

"I don't think so for now."

"Great, I'll text you the florist's address."

"I already have it."

"What?"

"I've still got a few teeth left in my head."

Sorry, John Houston.

Damn, I'm going to have to get some new material.

45

"Amen, is one of the oldest words we know," said Father O'Bannon. "It says 'The End,' and yet it also seems to say 'The Beginning.' A beginning of our new life that we must now live without our friend Reed Lockhart."

Shit, that meant I'd missed all of the Chief's speech. Guess he didn't' have much to say about his lifelong friend.

But whatever the length, it must have been too important to miss, judging by the steely glare the Chief gave me as I sat down next to Leah.

"Sorry," I said. "That took longer than I thought."

"No problem." She looked over her shoulder to make sure the Chief couldn't hear and put her lips close to my ear. Her breath was soft and warm as she whispered, "You just missed the biggest bullshit speech in history. I didn't think I could hate him any more than I did, but I was wrong."

There was movement all around us as people started getting up. The Chief leaned over to Leah, put his arm around her shoulders. I could swear she grimaced at his touch, but that might have just been wishful thinking.

"You need anything, Leah, *anything*! You call me."

"Yes," she said, then bolted up, shrugging off his arm and leaving the Chief and me eyeball to eyeball.

"Nice speech," I said, gave him my best "up yours" smile, and got up and walked away with Leah before he could say anything.

She and I didn't get far before the first of the mourners came up to her with their condolences and best wishes.

"I'll be at the back," I said quickly and headed that way to meet up with Wade.

"Who'd you call?" he said when we were apart from the stream of people who couldn't wait to get back to their luxury cars and a drink to affirm *they* were still alive.

I was going to ask how he knew I was on the phone, but left it alone.

"Zak. He uncovered some more stuff on Reed."

"What kind of stuff?"

"I'm not sure yet. But once a week for the last thirty-three years, Reed was sending an expensive bouquet of flowers to a Mrs. Mayleen Santiago."

"Santiago?" Wade said. "As in Miguel?"

"Unless we know any more Santiagos."

"Shit," Wade said. "What the hell's this mean?"

"Means we're taking a drive out to Pacoima tomorrow." Wade looked at me. "That's where she lives."

We saw Leah getting closer.

"You better stay with Leah," Wade said. "I'll go look for your dad, see if he can tell us any more about Miguel."

Wade set sail for the opposite side of the mourners where my dad had been sitting. And setting sail was the only way to describe Wade on a mission. He just parts the waters of humanity, easily, smoothly without a ripple, so that people never realize they've been moved aside.

An aromatic smell of cigar smoke drifted my way. I turned, and there was Gustav Butcher, a huge powerhouse of a cigar clenched between his teeth.

"Look at this sumbitch," he said. "Nine point two inches long. " He blew out a long plume of smoke. "Now that's a fuckin' powerhouse. Whether you're talkin' cigars or dicks." He chuckled to himself as two middle-aged women who'd obviously overheard, looked at him. "An *Arturo Fuente Opus X/A*."

"What happened to the *Gurka*?"

"Still have it. But I decided that for Reed I needed to smoke something rare, if not exorbitantly expensive."

He held it up so I could admire its beauty. "Hard to find these. Which is why it's hard to believe they're only about eighty bucks a stick."

Gus inhaled deeply, held the smoke, and let out a tiny funnel through his lips, rounded as for a kiss.

"I hate funerals. Even Reed's."

"Yes."

"They're all bad, no matter how beautiful the words." His eyes were suddenly glistening, and he pretended to wave smoke away as if it had caused his eyes to water.

"Worst funeral I ever went to was for Cameron. That was my boy."

I remembered. Cameron was a wild, hell-raising kid. Probably the best athlete and certainly the best football player in Paraíso del Mar High School history. He had a full ride to at least twenty different universities and was set to go to SC, be their next great running back, and follow in Marcus Allen's and Charlie White's quick footsteps. And the talk from all the scouts, both college and the pros, was that Cam was better than both of those two.

"You remember Cam, right? What happened to him?" Gus said.

"I do. That was a tragedy, Gus. Incredibly sad."

"I still don't think he took those pills on purpose. I mean, why would he? He had everything to live for. Football scholarship, hell, girls were callin' and comin' over to the house all hours, and I mean way after midnight." Gus took a light puff on his cigar, but I think the zest had gone out of it for him.

I didn't know what to say, so just patted his back.

"They say time heals all wounds. Bullshit. You never get over it. A parent isn't supposed to outlive his child. It's just not right. It's not natural."

"I know. There's no understanding it."

"Sometimes I think it's like you broke your leg, compound fracture. But the bones never get set. So when they finally mend, they're never right. And yeah, you can walk. But you limp. And you sure as hell never run or jump again. Or dance. For the rest of your life. You're always...*broken*."

"I'm sorry, Gus. I..."

I'm sure he didn't hear me.

"You know, we all get caught up in the day-to-day shit, the crap we believe is so fucking important—more money, more women, beating out the other guy. But in the end, what was it all about? Nothing. What matters is your family, the people you love. And if you lose them...? You've lost everything."

Gus took out a cigar clipper and snipped off the glowing end of the *Arturo Fuente.* "I think I'll finish this later." He looked down at the ashy red tip of the cigar in the grass and ground it out with the toe of his shoe. He tried smiling. "See you around, Matt."

I checked to see how much progress up the aisle Leah had made and then looked back at Gus who was slowly making his way through the departing crowd.

If you lose a spouse, like Stephen McDougal, you're a widower. Lose a husband, and you're a widow. Lose a brother or sister, and you're the surviving sibling.

But there is no word for a parent who loses a child.

Except, maybe, like Gus said, *broken.*

It's a living hell to outlive your child. And when you live as long as Gus has, it must be a double-edged sword of pain.

Like he said, there are no good funerals.

46

"Now *that* was a funeral," Mike Gillette said. "I tell ya, the Chief's got a way with words."

Yeah, I thought, like police brutality, falsified evidence, miscarriage of justice, and the whole panoply of illegal acts he's perpetrated behind the badge.

It's like my dad said, "There are three kinds of criminals. Those that make the law. Those that break the law. And those that enforce the law."

"A helluva guy," Mike said.

"Yes, Reed was that."

Mike was about to protest.

I knew he was still talking about Ben, and that's why I said it, but he decided, that it was best to not speak ill of the dead in even the smallest way.

"So who do you think is going to take his place?" Mike said. "I mean, this puts the whole election in the crapper."

"Mel Shoemaker's the other opponent," I said.

"Jesus on the cross," Mike said.

"And Mary on the donkey, and Joseph in the woodshop."

"C'mon, Matt, you don't think Mel's got a shot? How many times has he run against Reed and got his ass handed to him? Gotta be sixteen years."

"Except he's no longer running against Reed. And unless we get a write-in candidate, Mel's now running unopposed."

"Shit," Mike said. "Goddamn, I think we better get somebody thinking about this." He patted my back. "Mel Shoemaker as Mayor.

What the hell," he said. "Can you imagine?" Then he headed off to find the smarter heads that needed to do the crucial thinking.

Politics and business and the wheels of progress don't stop for anyone. Reed's closed coffin was still aboveground, and already conniving bastards like Mike Gillette were scheming how they could get ahead. Which meant the Chief had probably already selected his candidate. So maybe my write-in idea wasn't that far off. Politics makes for strange dead fellows.

Leah was shaking hands with a very slick-looking man in an expensive suit and looked over at me. She mouthed the word, "Help." But I wasn't sure what I could do.

I was watching her and stepped back, right into a brick wall. Actually, two of them—Alan Bartley and Jim Tucker.

"Sorry," I said, "I'm not assaulting an officer, or two."

Bartley and Tucker are two King Kong sized cops. They're both 6'5" and an easy 250 pounds of steroid-enhanced muscle. They both wear tailored uniforms that are tight on their ham-sized arms, emphasizing their massive chests. They ride Harleys and make them look like trikes.

"Yeah, like you could," Bartley said, giving me his "I'm the Law" stare.

The Law. Right.

As if I don't know better. Or remember better.

Because Bartley and Tucker and I all joined the force together. We used to share beers and joke and talk about tickets and crazy civilians. But once I left the force, it was as if I'd dropped off the planet, much less Paradise.

They're physical and mental cousins to Purdy—tons of years on the force, tons of beef on the hoof, and diddly-squat for advancement. They're both still fucking patrolmen.

They continued talking like I wasn't there.

"Shit," Tucker said, "I gotta get back to town, write some tickets."

"Wait, I thought you hit a five-in-one the other day," said Bartley.

"I did. Legit too. Asshole's going north on Sullivan..."

"What? That's a fucking one-way," Bartley said.

"No shit. Doing thirty-five in a twenty-five. Plus his tags are expired, so's his license. And he's driving a twin-axle vehicle in a residential area."

"Jackpot."

"Yeah, but I had to let him go."

"Why?"

"Just as I'm finished writing it up and about to hand it to him, goddamned driver tells me he's got this expensive sports car, fuckin' million dollar Ferrari under the tarp for somebody named Black."

"So you let him pass?"

"Like you wouldn't."

"No, you're right. Even a five-in-one ain't worth having the Chief up your ass."

"You see him around?" Tucker said.

"He's way back there, talking to some dudes. They look like money guys."

"Oh, yeah," Tucker said. "And I see Miss World's Biggest Tits is right next to him."

Bartley said. "Man, just a half-hour with those ta-tas."

"Don't get me thinking," Tucker said. "Shit, I guess I'll just have to kiss the Chief's ass later, tell him how terrific his speech was when I see him at the station." Bartley shouldered his way toward the exit.

"I pity anybody you stop today," Bartley said.

"Yeah," Tucker said, looking back, "Horny. And pissed off."

47

"You're not mad at me, I hope," Leah said.

"About what?"

"Those people, everybody talking to me as if we were the best of friends. Some of them I bet never even met my father. They're just here because the damn media showed up."

We were in the black limo heading toward the reception.

"Peter," Leah said to our driver, "your services are already paid for, right?"

Peter looked at Leah in his rearview mirror. "Yes."

"Day rate or hourly?"

"Day rate."

"So the sooner you dump us, the quicker you can get another assignment?"

I looked at Leah. I couldn't figure out where she was going with this.

"Yes. But, actually, I don't have another assignment after this."

"You do now."

"Ma'am?"

Leah looked at me and mouthed the word, "Ma'am?"

"I'm hiring you right now for the rest of the day, or evening, or however long we decide."

Peter hesitated, not sure how to respond.

"This is your car, right?"

"Soon's I pay the bank, yes."

"Great, so you're your own boss."

He nodded into the rearview mirror.

"So whatever your rate is, I just doubled it." Leah turned to me and giggled. "I can do things like this now, Matt, I…"

And the tears just erupted from her eyes, and she buried her face in my shoulder and sobbed and sobbed.

"Okay, Peter," I said, "let's head toward Malibu. You know any great restaurants there?"

"The Beaurivage is my favorite," Peter said. He glanced at me in the mirror. "I mean, a lot of my clients go there."

"Sounds like a plan."

The soft music stopped coming from the speakers, and I heard the rapid dialing of a phone. "I'm calling ahead for reservations," Peter said.

On speed dial? I'd say a *lot* of his clients go there, or he gets a little monetary favor from the owners.

After a few miles, Leah had regained her composure and refreshed her face. "I just couldn't talk to any more people," she said. "Thanks for doing this."

We drove along in silence. Peter was an excellent driver, moving us swiftly through the late afternoon traffic on the coast highway without any sudden bursts of speed or fast lane changes.

"Matt, do you think my father killed himself?"

"No. Impossible. You can't listen to dumbass people who have nothing better to do than shoot their mouths off for no good reason except to prove to themselves they think they're smart. Just stop listening to rumormongers and the attorney-ghouls."

"I wouldn't blame him if he did." She stared out the window. "Who wants to go through all that pain and suffering?" She turned back to me. "Maybe he did it for me. You know, so I wouldn't have to see him…go through all that."

My cell phone rang. Saved by the bell. I checked the caller ID.

"Wade. What's up?"

"Lots of people here wonderin' where Leah be."

"Leah be in the car here with me. We headin' fo' Malibu, have a late lunch."

"Why're you talking like a black sharecropper?"

"*Quid pro quo*? Tit for tat? Shit, you started it."

"Whatever. So, I finally cornered your pops. He was putting the moves on some blonde reporter for one of the cable stations."

"So what else is new?"

"The man got style, that's for sure. Just too bad it wasn't passed on."

"Leah thinks I have style."

She smiled at me, not sure what the hell was going on.

"Yeah, well, she has been under a lot of strain."

"So what did my dad say about the flowers and Santiago."

"He said we were trying to shoehorn everything we come across into making a case."

"Everybody's channeling Leon Festinger. My dad should stick to hustling."

"He does have a small point. I mean, things are getting wacko."

"Curiouser and curiouser."

"Right, Alice. We certainly down the rabbit hole on Abbey."

"Just when I thought I was out of it, they drag me back into it," I said in my best Al Pacino voice.

"Who's that supposed to be?

"We'll talk tonight," I said.

48

"Tonight became tomorrow, huh?" Wade said the next morning as I picked him up to drive out to Pacoima.

"Something came up."

"Like yo Johnson."

"You know, someday that attitude's going to cause trouble."

"What attitude? Talkin' slang?"

"No. Talking disrespectful about me and women."

"Oh, shit. You like her. Damn, I'm sorry."

I didn't answer, just got in the car, fired up, and we drove off.

"Aw, man, you not going to be sullen for forty-two point six miles, are you?"

"Forty-two point? You did MapQuest."

"You Italians not known for being, ah, geographically astute. Goes back to Columbus. *Mama Mia, I'm looka for India and I bumpa into Amedica.*"

"Italians found America, and they named the country after an Italian. Amerigo Vespucci."

"A history lesson too? I'll take the silence for the forty-two point six."

"Actually," I said, determined to stick it to him, "the name America was first used by the famous cartographer, Martin Waldseemüller. He was German."

"I said I was sorry."

I pulled into a parking lot at Denny's just before the entrance to the 405 North.

"Oh," Wade said, "that's why you're really cranky. You was expectin' Wade's famous homebrew. The ideal road trip, stakeout, and generally good health and well-being coffee."

"Needing caffeine has nothing to do with needing good manners."

"Shit, so you *really* sweet on her."

"Stop it. Nothing happened."

"Then you gonna need more than just coffee."

"I'll be right back."

"You gonna buy me a cup?"

"Not a chance.

49

We beat the odds getting to Mayleen Santiago's house. The freeway was pretty clear, the GPS was spot on, and there was parking right in front of her house. Shit, maybe we were in a Hollywood movie and didn't know it.

Wade looked around the street. "Mid three hundreds to low fours."

"You check Realist for that?"

"Naw, man, I can do raw data on my own."

It was a very hot day, well into the 90s, so the front door to Mayleen Santiago's house was wide open. A sweet, musky aroma drifted out to us through the screen door.

"Did Zak say what kind of buds the florist was delivering?" Wade said.

I rapped on the screen door.

"Yeah?" a male voice said from inside the darkened room. About thirty seconds later a very stoned, very overweight man in his early thirties shuffled to the door. He was definitely Hispanic, but some Caucasian too. He looked at us through red-rimmed eyes, a purple bong in his hand.

"We're looking for Mrs. Santiago," I said.

"You guys can't be the dudes from the cable company?"

"No," I said. "We're looking for Mrs. Santiago."

He started to say something, maybe "Oh," and instead turned and went back to the couch. Wade and I looked at each other then Wade tried the door—it was open, so we invited ourselves inside.

He was too stoned to notice we were right behind him until he plopped on the couch and almost dropped his bong when he realized we were right there.

"What the hell? You guys can't just come in here."

"You invited us in," Wade said. And before the stoner could react, Wade had snatched the bong from his hand.

"Goddamn. What the…? Look, man, I told Ramón I'd have the money by Friday."

"What's your name?" I said.

"Ritchie. What the hell, man? You don't know my name, and you're here to take my money?"

"Look, Ritchie," Wade said, looking right at him, "the reason we're here has nothing to do with this"—he held up the bong—"or being late on payments for the shit that's in it."

Ritchie actually shook his head, like some poor dog in a cartoon that's just run into a frying pan. All that was missing was Ritchie peeling his flattened face off the pan and back on his head.

"Ramón didn't send you?"

"No. And we're not from the insurance company. We just need to know where we can find Mrs. Santiago."

"Where she is every morning," Ritchie said. "At the church."

It took a few more circuitous questions and answers before we could get Ritchie to give us directions to Our Lady of The Angels Catholic Church.

And what a small beautiful church it was, more like a chapel built when the people would have arrived on horseback or in a buckboard. It was small, with whitewashed adobe walls, a modest dark-stained oak door with black metal braces, and a tiny cross on the roof.

And some of the most beautiful stained glass windows Wade and I had ever seen. The sunlight coming through them bathed the darkened interior in a soft rainbow of colors that shone like small lakes of light on the Spanish tile floor.

We stood at the entrance and waited until our eyes adjusted to the dark.

Up in one of the pews near the front, a woman was kneeling, her bowed head covered by a brilliant white shawl. She was the only other person in the church besides me and Wade. He looked at me and shrugged and sat down in one of the pews. It seemed like we'd suddenly gotten religion in the last few days.

I sat in the pew on the other side of the aisle.

There was a small confessional booth to my left. Its door opened and a tiny, wizened old man who had to be older than Gus, or maybe just looked that way, shuffled toward the exit. After a few moments, a priest came out the other door of the confessional booth. He looked around and when he saw us, squinted, I think more to look into his memory to see if he remembered us, rather than to see us.

"Good morning," he said. "I am Father Damien. You are here for confession?"

"No, I'm…I'm not Catholic."

He smiled, understanding. "The Lord listens to all of his children."

"We are here to see Mrs. Santiago."

"And may I inquire as to the nature of your visit with *Señora* Santiago?"

"Ah…it's personal."

"And what could be more personal than God?"

Wade smiled at the father. "There is a mutual friend we all have, and he recently passed away and…"

"You mean Reed Lockhart?" Father Damien said.

Our faces must have shown total surprise. "Oh, it is no secret that Mr. Lockhart is a most generous man. Both to the *Señora* and to our humble church…" He gestured at us. "Please, make yourselves comfortable. You may sit here without praying. Catholics do it all the time."

He went towards the confessional booth and then through another door near it.

Maybe I can speed things up, I thought. I walked up past the kneeling woman and looked at the crucifixion. I checked out the woman who was kneeling.

"It is always the sons that seem to suffer, no?" a woman's voice said behind me.

I turned to see a kindly, silver-haired Mexican woman in her late sixties or early seventies. She was wearing a long-skirted white dress, lots of silver and turquoise jewelry, and a Spanish shawl over her shoulders.

"Father Damien said you wanted to see me?"

I almost did a double-take to the woman in the pew but was saved by Father Damien.

"One of the altar boys is making tea."

"Oh, please, don't bother," I said.

"It is no bother," he said. "And this particular altar boy needs to do some minor penance."

The kneeling woman rose slowly to her feet, crossed herself, and smiled at me. She smiled at *Señora* Santiago and whispered, *"Hola. Dios te bendiga."* She walked slowly up the aisle for the front door.

Wade got up and opened it for her.

"You and your friend seem very kind, mister…?"

"I'm sorry. I'm Matt Singer. And that's my partner, Jamal Wade."

"Partner?"

"We're real estate agents."

"Oh, I am not interested in selling."

"No, we're not here about that."

She waited.

"Uh, we also do private investigation. Legally."

"Private detectives? Like *Columbo* and *Matlock?*"

Obviously, 70s and 80s TV had impressed her.

"Oh, we're not that good."

She laughed, and it was like a small, tinkling silver bell—clear and high.

"Do you mind if we sit down?" she asked. "My bones get tired sometimes."

I gestured for her to precede me and we sat in the pew where her friend had been. She waited for me to begin.

Which wasn't that easy, I discovered. I mean, how do you pry into a nice older woman's life about issues that really don't concern you except that you think it's part of a complicated, almost cabal-like, death of a man?

"So," I said, and then couldn't think of what to say next.

"Please. You have driven all the way from Paraíso del mar,"—and when she said it, the town's namesake seemed to come alive with meaning—"all the way to Pacoima to ask me something. So please, ask."

"We are checking into the death of Reed."

"What is there to check? He lost control of his car and"—she crossed herself—"he crashed, and his car exploded, and he was…"

She stopped and couldn't finish the outcome of the explosion.

"We're not sure about the accidental part of the crash."

She looked at me for a long moment, her dark eyes searching mine. "I do not understand. If there was a man who was more loved and respected than *Señor* Lockhart, he would have to be a saint."

I had no reply to that.

"Oh, *Madre de Dios!* Is this about the insurance?"

"What insurance?"

"*Señor* Lockhart's policy for Ritchie and me. The four million dollars."

Wade had sat down in the pew behind us. He and I had to look stupefied.

"Okay, now I'm the one that doesn't understand. Reed Lockhart had a four million dollar policy on his life and Ritchie, and you are the beneficiaries?"

"*Si, si.*"

"Why?"

"Because that's what a father does for his son and..." she added softly, "...the son's mother."

50

Guess what, Leah? You're not alone in this world.

Somehow I didn't see myself telling her that.

"Shit," Wade said, as he watched the traffic on the 405 freeway. "You're pretty much obligated to tell her."

"Right. And by the way, your father's hidden this from you all of your life."

"Maybe have Duncan tell her."

"Duncan? What's he got to do with this?"

"Well, if I'm Ritchie? I'm thinking that if I get four million dollars for openers. And because my daddy's very rich and I can prove I am an heir, I've got money to go after the other money and hire a nasty attorney."

"I can't believe *Señora* Santiago would allow that."

"But she's not going to live forever. And who can say what little Ritchie might want a few years from now."

"From what I know about Reed, I'm sure he's thought of that and put some conditions on the deal."

"Just hope she speaks louder than Ben Franklin...in Spanish or English."

I checked the rearview, hit my blinker, and changed lanes.

Wade and I had gone through two pots of Father Damien's tea, with some excellent almond cakes he said came from his *abuela* back in Madrid. The good father had lent us the use of his small private office at the rear of the church, and she had told us her and Reed's story.

"My brother Miguel"—she made the sign of the cross again—"only God knows what happened to him; although I have my ideas, but that is for later."

"Yes," I said.

"So Miguel is working in Paraíso del mar, driving all that way, so early in the mornings he has to leave, and he has the crews working so hard. And on Fridays, as a special treat to his men, I would make a lunch for them, usually my *empanadas criollas*, they seemed to like those the best."

She looked at one of the stained glass windows-- Jesus with a lamb, gathering her thoughts in memory.

"So one Friday I am at the site of one of the houses they are building and *Señor* Reed is there and he is so charming. Remember that I am barely nineteen and very naïve, and the trips to Paraíso del mar are such exciting journeys for me, the farthest I have ever been. Like going to a foreign country. So when Reed is there with words sweeter than the *dulces* I also make, I am, how they say in those romantic books, smitten."

Father Damien poked his head in the door. "Excuse me, *perdón*, *Señora*, but I need to get something from my desk.

"*Si, si*, come in," *Señora* Santiago said, waving him in and pulling back his chair from his desk. "We are sorry to inconvenience you."

"No, no," he said. He opened a bottom drawer and pulled out a small black ledger book. "I need to give Carlos, he is the altar boy who made the tea, credit for his penances." Father Damien tucked the book under his arm. "I know," he said, "in today's age, why not on the computer? But there is a certain gravitas in seeing your name written out by a fountain pen and finally seeing a check mark next to your name releasing you from your burdens."

Mayleen waited until Father Damien was gone.

"I do not need to give account of how Reed and I became lovers, or the joy and excitement." She stopped and let out a long sigh. "And of course, later, my shame when he said he could not marry me. Those hurts are best left behind."

I did some rapid calculations. And came to the conclusion that Reed had been a prick all his life. When he'd gotten Mayleen pregnant he wasn't married. Which meant Mayleen, being Hispanic, no matter how beautiful, how wonderful, would not do for a man looking to advance in life.

"Of course, Miguel was crazy when he found out. He and Reed had a fight. And Miguel beat him up so badly, I thought he had killed him." *Señora* Santiago took another deep breath. "That evil *policía*..."

"Ben Black?" I said.

"*Si, si*. Black, just like his heart. He was going to arrest Miguel for assaulting a *policía* because Reed was still on the force, but Reed would not press charges. He told everyone that *he* had started the fight. But even so, Black drove all those miles and came to our house and was like a mad man. I think would have beaten Miguel, but as soon as I saw him, I called our *policía*. Fortunately, back then, one of our neighbors was on the force, and he came right away and calmed everybody down."

She took a sip of tea.

I could see her eyes glistening with tears.

"It was a day or two after the fight and Black's visit that Miguel disappeared."

She looked at me and Wade.

"Do you think he had something to do with that?" I said.

"For Reed? No. For Ben Black? *Todo es posible*."

"That's a sad story," Wade said.

"*Si*," she said, "but not without its good parts. Reed certainly took care of me and Ritchie."

"Did you see much of him after...?" I shrugged, not sure how to continue.

"After Ritchie was born? Oh, yes, I think he loved Ritchie very much. I remember he would come over in the late afternoon when I had just bathed Ritchie and Reed would kiss him and tell me what a wonderful mother I was."

She shrugged, and this time a couple of tears slipped from the corner of her eyes that she quickly wiped away.

"But then, when politics entered his life, and he married Diane, our visits were fewer, and once he was going to become a father," she stopped for a moment, "an *official* father, that was the end of it. He sent me money and the flowers, and he bought this house for Ritchie and me. And of course the insurance policy. So, I cannot complain. Most women never have it as good."

Wade started to say something, thought better of it.

"I was young and foolish. A dreamer. And I know it's hard to imagine back then, but the things I so desperately wanted back then, to marry the man that I loved, who I thought loved me...well, for a

Mexican girl to marry a rich and successful white man? That just did not happen. They are, like in that story, the things that dreams are made of."

She set her teacup down with a brisk click.

"As they say in the Bible, 'I put away my foolish things.'"

51

"You're serious about this?" Wade said.

"Yeah, besides, you started it."

"How'd I do that?"

"You said Ritchie might shake the money tree."

"Yeah?"

"So maybe he wanted to uproot it."

We pulled up in front of the Santiago's, walked up, and knocked again.

"Shit," Ritchie's voice came from the darkness of the interior. "You guys again?"

We waited, nothing.

I was going to knock again when Ritchie slouched to the door, waved us away, and opened the door and walked outside.

"What?"

His eyes were even redder than before, and he was even more stoned.

"You couldn't find the church?"

"We did."

"My moms wasn't there?"

"She was."

"So…?"

"We have to ask you some questions about your father."

That knocked him back a little. Then a look of confusion, followed by a hard look of resentment.

"My father?" he said finally. "Oh, you mean that old white dude that sends us money?" Ritchie pulled another joint out of his shirt pocket, fired up a disposable lighterr, and inhaled deeply.

Wade and I waited him out, although I think Wade wanted to snatch the doobie from his mouth and replace it with his fist.

"Yeah," Ritchie said and exhaled a long plume of fragrant smoke away from us. "I heard he bought it driving his NSX. What a loss."

Wade and I looked at each other. What?

"Yeah, that NSX is a great car."

Ritchie took another deep toke, held it a brief time, and exhaled again. He held the joint out to us, smiling like he knew we wouldn't take it.

But Wade surprised him and took the joint, looked at it, then flicked it away into the street, where it sparked and went out.

"Hey, man!" Ritchie yelled.

"Look, asshole," Wade said, and Ritchie was suddenly not as stoned. "We are going to ask you some questions about your father. Your father. The man who's put a roof over your head put food in this…" and Wade slapped Ritchie in the stomach hard enough, so Ritchie exhaled suddenly and took a big gasp to get some air back.

"Okay, okay. Jesus, just be cool, bro."

"Don't bro me if you don't know me," Wade said.

"When's the last time you saw your father?" I said quickly before this escalated, and Ritchie got hurt.

"I don't know. Shit, gotta be ten, fifteen years at least."

"So you didn't see him last week?"

"Last week?" Ritchie looked at me like I was beyond stupid.

"Yeah," Wade said. "Last week Wednesday."

Ritchie's mind whirled a little bit, I'm sure, and he finally made the connections.

"C'mon, man. Last Wednesday? Shit, that was the day he died, man. Shit. You think I had something to do with that?"

Ritchie put out his chest, which still didn't come anywhere near matching the projection of his enormous belly, but it was a testosterone moment. *¿Quién es un hombre duro?*

"This is bullshit, man."

"So you didn't see your father last Wednesday? Where were you that day?"

"Ask my attorney."

He turned to go back inside, but Wade put his hand firmly against the screen door, so there was no way for Ritchie to open it without an incident.

"Don't get cute, Ritchie," Wade said.

"I ain't. I mean it, ask my attorney, Raphael Morales, biggest Mexican attorney around. He'll tell you that from last Tuesday morning until Thursday around 8:00, I was in jail." He looked at both of us and shrugged, a man resigned to his sorry lot in life. "I'll get you his card," Ritchie said. He looked at Wade. "It's inside."

Wade stepped back from the door just as a totally restored, cream puff 1960 Chevy Impala, in the original salmon-and-white two-tone paint job rolled to a stop behind my car.

"*Mierda!*" Ritchie said. "You guys better roll."

The Impala's doors opened, and four young men unfolded from the interior. They were all Hispanic, clearly thugs, and definitely pissed off about something.

No doubt about the money Ritchie owed them.

"Hey, Ramón," Ritchie called out, way over-the-top friendly.

The four beefs walked up across the lawn, one dark guy with jailhouse tats on his neck and arms, stepped right on *Señora* Santiago's tea roses, snapping several stalks coming through.

Wade and I stepped out a little wider, so all four thugs were between us.

"Who the hell are you guys?" one of the thugs said.

"You gotta be Ramón," Wade said.

Ramón was a little confused that someone he'd ever seen before knew his name.

"What's it to you?"

"Absolutely…" Wade said, "…nothing."

Ramón paused, thinking about it, trying to figure out if he'd just been dissed, then passed on it.

"Yeah," Ramón said. "That's me." He nodded to the thug next to him. "Pablo."

And Pablo could have been Pavlov because he instantly put on his hard face and took three fast steps for Ritchie.

Wade and I stepped in front of Ritchie.

"What the…?" Pablo said, and his hand went behind his flowery Hawaiian shirt for the small of his back where I'm sure he had his piece.

When your hand's reaching back, that side of your face is vulnerable.

Extremely vulnerable.

Wade hit him an amazing shot that pole-axed Pablo so his head went straight down to his left and his feet came straight out to his right. So he was horizontal for a brief moment. And then hit the ground with a loud thud.

"I give him an 8.9 on his landing," I said.

By the time Ramón and his two remaining buddies had figured out what had just happened, Wade and I had our automatics trained on them. For some reason, we'd decided to carry that day. Maybe because we were going to Pacoima, which has had gangbanger trouble since the 1940s with gangs like Dead End Boys, Pacas, Brown Stoners. And like the old adage, *Better to have a gun and not need it, then to need it and not have it*.

"Here's how it goes," I said.

"No, shit, man, no," Ritchie said behind us. "Man, you can't."

"Shut up, Ritchie," I said without taking my eyes off Ramón and friends.

Ritchie kind of moaned as if his life was over.

"How much does Ritchie owe you?" I said.

It took Ramón a few beats to figure that out, and of course, he upped the total.

"Three thousand."

"No way, man. C'mon, Ramón, you know it's only twenty-eight hundred."

"I'm adding travel and collection fees," Ramón said and laughed. And his two buddies laughed. What was amazing was that none of them even bothered to check out Pablo, who was so quiet that if I hadn't seen him breathing, I'd have sworn Wade killed him.

"Three it is," I said. "And just to show you he's cool about it and understands the importance of paying one's debts, you come back next Monday and Ritchie will pay you four thousand."

"What?" Ritchie yelled. "No, no."

Without turning around, Wade backhanded Ritchie in the chest and knocked all the wind out of him so hard, Ritchie's legs gave out, and he dropped to his fat ass on the porch.

It must have looked funny because Ramón and his dudes all smiled.

"And who the hell's going to guarantee that?" Ramón asked.

"I will," I said.

"And me," Wade said.

"But most important of all, Ritchie's going to guarantee it."

Ramón considered all this, mostly because with two black holes of automatics pointing at him, he had no choice. "Okay. But if this is a stall, or you guys screwing with me, I'm going to come get you."

"Fine." I reached into my wallet where I keep the PI cards. "Here's my card with all my information. You don't need to call for an appointment."

Ramón read it. "Private investigations? You mean like Sam Spade?"

Sam Spade? Ramón's literary references were older and more classic than *Señora* Santiago's.

"Something like that. How do you know Sam Spade? No offense."

For a second Ramón did take offense but then decided to show off. "Hey, man, *Maltese Falcon*, one of the best detective movies ever made. 'You killed Miles, and you're going over for it,'" he said in a weird Bogie imitation since it had a definite *salsa* flavor.

"Ah, now you're dangerous," I said.

Ramón looked at me, trying to remember.

"It's what he tells Brigid O'Shaughnessy."

"Right, the broad. Yeah. Okay, we're cool, let's go."

He turned back for the Impala.

"Hey," Wade said, and they all turned back.

"Aren't you forgetting something?" He pointed down to where Pablo was finally coming around.

"Pick up the trash," Ramón said to the other two and walked to the car without ever turning back.

"Shit," Ritchie said, "why'd you mess me up like that, man? Where'm I gonna get that kind of money?"

"Trust me, I think by next week you'll be okay." I fished in my wallet and pulled out one of Duncan's cards. "Call this guy soon as you get inside. And don't screw around. You go see him as fast as you can."

"Why am I gonna need another attorney?"

"To give you legal advice, and financial advice."

"Yeah," Wade said, "and after you pay Ramón, you are going to move."

Ritchie actually shook his head at this last statement, as if he'd been bopped between the eyes. "Move, man? No way, my moms would never leave this place."

"I didn't say your mother was moving," Wade said. "Just you."

"Man, you *loco*. I ain't moving, and even if I wanted to, where the fuck would I get the money?"

"First National Dad," Wade said.

52

"Sins of the father, huh?" Wade said.

We were heading back to the beach and traffic was a bitch.

"Must have been tough for Ritchie, growing up illegitimate," he said.

"Yeah. Especially with that term. *Illegitimate.*"

"Definitely pejorative." Wade adjusted his back against the seat. "Out of wedlock isn't too good either."

"Right. The kid's always coming out as damaged goods, somehow not worthy."

"It's better than what most people think—bastard."

"Why can't people just say the mother has a child but not a husband?"

"If they have to say anything at all," Wade said.

I nodded and tucked in behind an older model Chevy Suburban.

"You think Ritchie will stay away?"

"From Reed's money? Most likely. He's too stoned most of the time to try anything else. Or until he realizes he might be able to chip away some of it."

"If Duncan can't get the insurance money right away, then Ritchie's guarantee is worthless."

"So maybe Ramón will come and see us."

"I'd like that," Wade said. "I'd truly like that."

It took us another hour and twenty minutes to finally get home.

Wade had called Duncan from the car and set everything up, but Duncan wasn't guaranteeing anything.

"There are limits," he said.

"Even for you?" Wade said.

"When you're dealing with insurance companies parting with money, think glacial speed."

"Well, you be the icebreaker."

Even I could hear Duncan sigh over Wade's cell just before he hung up.

"Okay," Wade said. "Reed gets Mayleen pregnant, won't marry her, and Miguel beats his ass."

"Few days later," I said, "Miguel's never seen again."

"We've been in over our heads before, but never like this. How the hell we going to prove any of this? That Reed was murdered? That most likely so was Miguel, forty years earlier?"

"I can make the connections easy. In spite of all his smooth-talking bullshit, Reed was a deadly man. You didn't cross him without bearing the scars."

"So you think he took out Miguel?"

"Or had somebody do it for him."

"Like Ben Black."

"My Chief suspect."

I pulled up in front of Wade's place.

"I'm going to need a ride about midnight."

"Besides that being a song, what are you talking about?"

"I'm going to break into the morgue."

Wade snapped around and stared at me.

"Most sane folks break *out* of jail," Wade said, "they don't break *into* it."

"It's not really jail, just the morgue."

"Which is part of the jail."

"In and out in fifteen minutes," I said.

"To check those bones?"

"Yep."

"This has got to be the craziest thing you've ever done. And there's no good reason for it."

"Sure there is."

"What?"

"Reduction of possibilities."

"More like reduction of your license, reduction of freedom for breaking and entering."

"It won't be breaking, but it will be entering."

"You've said that before. What're you talking about?"

"There's that side doorway in the back where they store the traffic barriers and the cones and shit."

"Yeah?"

"When I first joined the force, they'd give me some of those shit assignments. Go out and reroute traffic on Paseo del mar, rookie. So they gave me a key to that entrance."

"All those years and you never turned it in," Wade said.

"I would have if they'd asked for it."

"Shit," Wade said. "I can't let you do this alone."

"You aren't. You're driving me there."

"And I'm waiting."

"No. Me slipping in and out is one thing, them seeing your car is another."

He looked at me. "How do you even know the key works?"

"See? There's your out. The key doesn't work, I can't get inside, and we avoid any risk."

"Shit," he said, "I hope it is open. Otherwise, I've got to listen to you come up with some other wild-ass idea."

I checked my weapon.

"You ain't going to need that," Wade said. "The people in the morgue already be dead.

"It's the living ones I'm worried about." Wade opened the door. His cell rang. He checked the ID and looked back at me. "Stephen McDougal."

"Don't answer it."

53

"Hello, Leah," I said as my cell rang. "How are you?"

"Sore."

"As in angry?"

She laughed. "As in *sore*. Down there."

"Ah," I said, trying to not let my male ego get in the way. "Is that a good thing or a bad thing?"

"What do you think?"

"Maybe a little bit of both."

"I was a little crazy last night," Leah said. "But in a good way."

"The best," I said, trying to maintain agreeable neutrality.

"I thought you might agree."

"What man wouldn't?"

She laughed for a reply.

I shifted my cell to my left ear and sat down on the couch. I was somewhat ambivalent about this conversation, trying to balance the memory of last night when Leah had, indeed, been nasty, and quite vocal and encouraging for me to be an equally nasty companion against the incredible weight of my knowledge of her personal life.

I definitely wanted to see her again. As soon as possible. But with that visit, wouldn't I be required to tell her what I'd learned? Yes, I could hold off until I proved the truth about Reed's death, but this recent revelation from Mayleen had become my responsibility, if not simple common decency to tell Leah. But pillow talk can be dangerous.

"So, do you want to see me tonight?" Leah said.

"In the worst way."

That sent her off into another low-throated laugh.

"Good. But it will have to be much later. I'm having dinner with a girlfriend that flew in from New York. Angeline, she was at the funeral. Tall brunette. You couldn't have missed her, absolutely stunning. She works for Sendlier and Kotch, one of the slicker Wall Street firms."

I wasn't sure what to say.

"We should be done by ten or eleven. I can come by your place."

Still unsure. After a few moments of silence, Leah said, "Matt, don't you want me to come by?"

"I do, I do. But I've got plans."

"Oh." I could sense the chill through the cell. "Never mind, we can do it some other time."

"No, Leah, it's not anyone else."

"Then what?"

"Wade and I have some work to do."

"At ten at night?"

"Actually about midnight."

"Really?"

"That's when we do our best sleuthing."

Another long silence and then she said, "What time will you be done?"

"One o'clock, I hope."

"So call me then."

"Really?"

"I'll be up. I'm not much for sleeping these days."

<h1 style="text-align:center">54</h1>

"You were asleep sitting up," I said to Wade.

"How you know I wasn't praying?"

"I didn't hear any 'Amen.'"

"That's because I wasn't done."

I had changed plans and decided to go over to Wade's place instead of having him pick me up. But when I knocked on his door, there wasn't any answer. I tried the handle, the door opened, and I went inside, and he was sitting up in his big, comfortable chair. One of the ESPN guys was yelling about some spectacular play, and Wade wasn't hearing any of it.

I took two steps into the room, and his eyes snapped open. He was automatically moving for me until he realized who it was.

"So what were you praying for?" I said later as his car made the turn down Spinnaker Street behind the police station.

"That's between a man and his Savior."

He cut the headlights and we coasted to about fifty yards from the building.

"Well, at least you weren't praying for a new partner," I said.

"How you know that?"

"Because who else could be this much fun?"

I looked back at him before I closed the door.

"You sure you don't want me to wait?" he asked.

"Nope. In case this goes into the toilet, no sense both of us being flushed down together."

Spinnaker was one of Paradise's older streets, so it had a canopy of trees from back in the day when the founding fathers had been Arbor Day enthusiasts. So when Wade cut his lights, the street went very dark, and even if there had been a moon, I doubt it could have cut through the high arch of green above. The only light was a single bulb that shone over the door.

Once I stepped into the circle of light, and up the steps, it felt like I was in the center ring under the big top with the spotlight shining down on me. If this went haywire in any manner, I was the clown who not only caught a pie in the face but got shot out of the cannon straight into the tiger's cage. Definitely dead meat.

I had put graphite on the old key, so when I lined it up with the slot, it easily slipped into the lock. So far, so good. I pushed, very cautiously, and slowly, oh so slowly, the deadbolt eased out of its strike plate with a lot of rusty scraping and grating.

I stepped inside, closed the door, snapped on my Maglite, and shined it into the room. It was just as I remembered, except a lot dustier. Black and white traffic barricades, warning signs, and several tall poles set in circles of concrete that had been used probably back in the sixties for the hometown fair.

I moved forward. No alarms went off, except the klaxons blaring in my head. I moved through the room, eased open the door, and checked the hallway. There were recessed ceiling lights every five feet, so it was damn bright. I moved to the medical examination room, opened the door just enough to slip into the darkness, and waited with my back against the wall.

I swept the flashlight across the room. There were three tables, each with a stark white cloth draped over it, but only one had a form underneath the cloth.

I quietly moved to the table, keeping the Maglite centered on it. I eased back the cloth and was looking into the eyeless sockets of a skull. It was stark white, all traces of the dirt from its burial site removed. It is eerie to stare at someone's bones, and soul-wrenching to look at all that's left of them, all that ever was.

"*Alas, poor Yorick,*" and the image of Mel Gibson playing Hamlet and looking at Yorick's skull and talking to Horatio blipped across my mind. I was hyperventilating, and my heart was pounding.

I maneuvered the skull and looked at the crown. Just as Hal had said, the center section, the anterior fontanel, was cratered. It had fallen into itself like a sinkhole. I looked at the back of the skull, and from the occipital lobe at the skull's base, the crack zigzagged across the crown. I put the Maglite under my armpit, pulled my .45 and put the butt end against the center cavity. It was a perfect fit. A hammer hadn't killed this man, it was an automatic weapon.

Maybe used as a club first and then putting a bullet into it.

I moved the cloth down and looked at the torso for any nicks on the ribs that might indicate a .45 slug had violated the body.

I heard a door bang down the hall. I covered the bones with the cloth and cut the Maglite. I waited in the blackness. Footsteps that sounded uneven and awkward were coming closer, along with some off-key whistling. I moved to the head of the examining table and crouched down at the end furthest away from the door.

Suddenly the door banged open, and the overhead fluorescents flickered and then flashed to life. And because it was an examination room, every inch of the space was illuminated.

He took a few steps into the room, letting the door bang shut.

"Shit, Roscoe," the man said. "You make enough noise to wake the dead." And Roscoe laughed, so damn pleased with himself.

Roscoe Charles. Jesus, he was old when *I* was on the force. He was still here? Roscoe had caught a bullet in the femur many years ago. The bones never healed quite right, and Roscoe had a pronounced limp and a rolling, lurching gait. That would have accounted for the uneven footsteps. There was no accounting for his awful whistling.

Roscoe had been rehabilitated, supposedly, but couldn't have caught a toddler who'd nipped a Tootsie Pop. Eric Painter, who was Chief before Ben, had assigned Roscoe to the midnight patrol at the station house. Nobody expected him to actually patrol since walking wasn't exactly Roscoe's strongest asset, but the damn fool did every night, two or three excursions around the perimeter, all through the station. Fortunately the station isn't that large, but still, you had to admire Roscoe's dedication.

The two rear walls were stacked rows of stainless steel drawers where the cadavers were stored under refrigeration. I'm not sure when or why the city thought that it needed a wall of containers for the dead. Maybe the city fathers thought Paradise was Chicago in Capone's time. A windy city by the sea with crime waves to match the Pacific's waves. I doubted if all of the people that died in Paradise in six months would fill all of the drawers. Talk about overkill for underkill.

By easing around just a bit, I could see Roscoe's wavy shape reflected in the stainless steel cabinets as he moved.

He went to the first table and flipped back the cloth and looked underneath.

Apparently, all of the tables had a second platform underneath the first. Roscoe was looking for an intruder.

I hated to think I'd have to whack poor old Roscoe, but I couldn't get caught. And the odds were that since Roscoe carried a little hip flask filled with "Old Grandad" tucked into his police-issue Sam Browne belt, he could be set up.

Shit, just like I was.

Wow, the significance of that hit me. Here I was trying to prove I'd been ambushed and set up as the patsy and was going to do the very same dirty tricks they'd done to me.

I wasn't liking myself. Not only because I would do it if I had to, but because I knew I could get away with it. Because like Wade said, who the hell breaks *into* a police station?

Roscoe went to the second table and ripped back the cloth and checked the second shelf.

I ran through my options.

Whack him. Hated to do that.

Leap for the lights, slam them off and be out the door before he could do anything. Might give him a heart attack.

I did option three.

As Roscoe ka-thumped toward my table, I crawled around the opposite side, hidden by the cloth that draped nearly to the floor. So when he got to the table and made ready to snatch up the cloth, I was flat on the concrete, below the metal platform. Then, as Roscoe stood next to the cart, I slowly scooched *under* it.

Shit, was this a preview for my life? Laying there in the refrigerated air of the city morgue, all thought and memory gone?

"Sleeping the Big Sleep," like Marlowe said. Only I wouldn't be in some dirty sump or in a marble tower on top of a high hill. I'd be, at least top-shelf on a stainless steel cart.

"Okay," Roscoe said and flipped the cloth.

"Jesus. Goddamn."

He wasn't expecting to see a pile of bones.

There was some rustling around, and then Roscoe said, "Holy shit, brother, that was some headache you must have had."

I couldn't see anything tucked under the cart, but I could tell Roscoe was handling the bones. "Let's see who you were, mister."

More metallic sounds, Roscoe moving. "Crap, too rusty."

Then total silence and the other side of the cloth made a whooshing sound as Roscoe threw it back. "Okay!" he yelled, "now I got you..."

Of course, there was nothing to see. I held my breath and hoped he wouldn't look to his left on the floor where my shoes stuck out from the end of the table.

"What the hell?" Roscoe said. His bones popped and creaked in the dead silence of the room as he stood up straight. "Damn, I am getting jumpy." He brought the cloth back over the body and limped for the door.

I waited, my flashlight ready, but sincerely hoped I wouldn't have to use it. Just a minute or so more.

"Hell, Roscoe," he said, "this is a dead-end job." And he laughed hard as he shut the lights. He opened the door, and I saw him silhouetted against the light from the hall. "Damn, I should be on Jimmy Kimmel. Dead-end job."

He laughed and ka-thumped down the corridor. I didn't snap on the Maglite until I heard the back door into the main building slam shut.

I went to the table to look for whatever had intrigued Roscoe.

On the skeleton's right arm there was an ID bracelet, rusted with age. The ulna looked like it had a crack along most of its length; and the radius was completely broken so that the bracelet had fallen down in-between the two bones of the forearm.

I eased the bracelet up through the gap between the bones and got it free.

I didn't bother to look at it. It was too rusty to reveal anything right now. But once I got it home, I'm sure there would be a story to tell.

Dead man talking.

55

"Hola," said Miguel Santiago across the years.

It had taken nearly an hour to get off the encrusted layers of rust. One of my grandmother Flower's remedies for removing rust and other stains was to mix baking soda and vinegar and apply the concoction to whatever article had been blemished.

I'd poured a half-cup of vinegar into a measuring cup, added several generous shakes of baking soda, and dropped in the ID bracelet. It foamed instantly, like some volcanic brew. I watched it for a few moments, then went and had a beer while the other brew did its thing.

Not that I didn't want to take out the bracelet and scour it and clean it right away, but back when I was nine or ten, I'd learned about the virtues of patience the hard way. Flower had put a couple of inches of the mixture into a cast-iron skillet that had gotten rusty from lack of use. After about two minutes of watching it, I got a Brillo pad and started scrubbing away. And that industrious help got me a whack on the head and a long lecture from my nana about letting things take their time and how I was too impatient.

I finished the beer, started scraping and scrubbing, and after a while, a few letters began to emerge: an "M"... some middle letters that were gone...then "el"... a gap and then "Sa"...these middle letters also gone...and the final "o".

"That's not much to go on," Wade had said when I'd called him.

"It's a start," I said. "It's not that hard to fill in the missing letters."

"You're playing a game of 'Hangman' for real."

"The timeline fits. Miguel's been gone more than forty years. Hal said that was his estimation of how long the bones had been there."

"Hold on a minute," Wade said.

I heard him tapping keys. "What're you doing?"

"Trying to find out who owns the property where they found the bones."

"What good's that going to do?"

He didn't answer, just tapped some more. "Paradise Enterprises LLC. Least that's the most recent owner. Looks like it's been sold a few times. Lighthouse Corp was the prior owner."

"So we find the owners, how's that going to help us?"

"We gotta start someplace. At the beginning usually works. "

"Okay," I said, "maybe that was one of his projects."

"Finding the owners might be the first loose thread we can pull to unravel this mystery."

"How far back do the records go?"

"Ten years. So maybe you need to call Zak."

"I'll email him. It's only five in the morning where he is."

"And you think a techno geek ain't up crunching numbers, doing his voyeuristic internet shit?"

I went with email and talked to Wade while I waited for Zak. "You still think I'm out there on this?"

"You're getting back into earth's orbit. If this really is Miguel, there's got to be another link to Reed."

"You were right," I said. "Zak is awake."

I sent my message and ten seconds later Zak responded: *That's a 3-cushion bank shot. I'm right in the middle of a big project, have something for you later.*

"No way of knowing if the owners back then are still alive," I said.

"So it's a dead end in every sense," Wade said. "But even if they are alive, how we going to prove they, whoever in the hell they are, were involved in Miguel's death?"

"The bones were discovered under the middle of the house. Somebody knew something."

"I guess it's lucky that back then construction was raised foundation and not concrete slabs like nowadays. And I won't say 'raising the dead,' although it'd be a good line."

"Holy shit!" I said. "I've got to make an emergency call to Duncan."

"Duncan?"

"Yeah, tomorrow they're scheduled to cremate the bones. They do that, there's no way to prove any DNA match."

And I'd been the straight man one too many times, because Wade said, "Then this whole thing would really turn to ashes."

56

"The fire's gone out already?"

Leah looked at me as we lay together in my bed, naked under the covers.

I'd called her, and she'd made it to my place in less than ten minutes, and we'd attacked each other. Consumed was a better description, just like in those overblown commercials or soft porn flicks, where the two lovers make their way from the front door to the bedroom, lip, and bodies locked together, shedding clothes all the way, and end it with an arcing dive onto the bed.

And then things had come to a screeching halt.

Leah had started crying.

And I'd started thinking.

Both of us because of the same subject—her father.

But each of us with such totally polarized viewpoints: Leah's idealized, mine compromised.

She thought he was a wonderful, loving man, filled with great and high ideals and total love for her.

I thought he was the worst kind of manipulative bastard, who knew no right or wrong, only desire, lust and pride.

Given that perspective, in which I was the only one who knew the truth, the idea of sex, especially supercharged, *I'm sore down there* sex, was beyond the scope of the few hours left to us before morning.

"No," I said, finally. "The heat's still there. I've just got so much whirling in my head."

"Oh," Leah said and snuggled closer, slipping into the crook of my arm. "I know. And I'm...I just can't help thinking about..."

And the tears came again.

We fell asleep that way, and when my cell phone trilled by my head, it was hard to believe it was 7:30 in the morning.

"I assume," Duncan's precise and obviously pissed-off voice said, "that leaving an emergency message on the service at 3:34 a.m. is not the result of a late-night bout at Hankins Bar?"

"No. Of course not." I checked Leah; she was coming around, but still in that twilight just before awakening. "Hold on," I said. I got out of bed, closed the bedroom door behind me, and went into the kitchen.

I started the conversation with Duncan telling him that the debt had been paid and that he should bill me for this. Still, it took me at least five minutes of hard negotiating to convince Duncan that I was serious about getting a court order to stop the cremation.

"Do you know how expensive this is going to be, Matthew?"

"We already covered your bill, Duncan."

Duncan said nothing for several long moments.

Finally, he cleared his throat slightly and said, "I will disregard that tone and the content of its message and proceed accordingly. Do you have Mrs. Santiago's information?"

I gave it to him and hung up. Tailored suits, exotic cars, a financial portfolio to rival Wall Street and secretaries that would satisfy your wildest dreams, in the end, Duncan was, like all of us, just another hired hand. Like Dylan sang, *"You got to serve somebody."*

I heard the shower going, so I picked up my Levis and shirt and slipped into them, gathered up Leah's clothes along the way, folded them neatly, and put them at the foot of the bed. Then I went into the kitchen and made coffee. I checked my email, but no message from Zak. I called Mrs. Santiago and decided not to give her any false hopes and just said we needed a signature for some documentation. She thought it was about the insurance and I didn't correct her thinking. I felt creepy. It's not nice duping a woman like that, but if this worked out like I thought it might, I think she'd give me a pass.

Leah came into the kitchen, her blonde hair darkened from still being wet, and looking like she'd just walked out of a shampoo commercial: Think visual crack for the ocular junkie.

"That smells good," she said and gave me a small kiss on the cheek on her way to the coffee machine.

I got up to get the cups, but she opened a cabinet and found them on her own. She took two down, filled them, and handed one to me.

"So…?" I said.

"So thanks for your valet services," she said. "Saved a girl from being embarrassed."

I clinked my cup against hers.

She took a sip, savored it, and said, "I'm sorry about last night."

"Nothing to be sorry about. It's a life-changing event, give yourself some room and take your time."

She nodded, took another longer sip, and set the cup down. "God, I need to take Tash for a walk, and I've got…" She stopped and looked at me.

I got up, put my arms around her, and held her for a moment.

"We'll do this another time…the right way."

"I'd like that." She kissed me—nice, soft, but nothing like the ones just a few hours earlier.

And then she was gone.

57

"You can't come here and do that!" Gerry Kelly yelled.

"We can and we will," Duncan said, never taking his eyes from Gerry's florid face. "It is clearly defined in the document."

"I already read the goddamn thing. What I'm saying is, who the hell do you think you are? You've got no rights in this town."

"Paraíso del mar ," Duncan said, "was incorporated on June 1, 1910, and as a city within the confines of Los Angeles County, it is, irrespective of its own municipal laws and ordinances, still subject to the laws of the county; moreover, and even more importantly, the laws of the State of California. Therefore, Mr. Kelly, we most certainly *do* have rights. And one of those is the order you see in front of you—to cease and desist any plans to cremate the skeletal remains in your morgue currently on table three."

Gerry blinked hard several times, sputtered once, and tried again. "Look, you've got no proof that those bones are related to..."—he make a pretense of reading the document again, but knew the names since he'd already read them three or four times—"... a Mrs. Mayleen and Richard Santiago. They married?"

"No," I said. "It's a mother and her son."

"Well, shit, so what? I'm supposed to just stop my plans and let you take those bones, which are really city property now, and run some goddamn tests?"

"Yes," Duncan said. "And not to put too fine a point on it, that is not what you are supposed to do, but what you are compelled to do."

"Hal!" Gerry bellowed. "Get your ass in here."

Hal Bartkowski burst into Gerry's office an instant later. My guess was he was standing right outside the door listening. Hal looked like he'd just swallowed a load of castor oil and it was bombarding his large intestine.

Gerry thrust the court order at Hal. "Read that goddamn thing and tell me if it's right."

Hal was either a *suma cum laude* graduate of the Evelyn Wood Speed Reading School, or, as I suspected, was listening and already knew the play because in what had to be less than ten seconds he looked at Gerry and nodded his head. "It's accurate."

"Shit, shit, shit." Gerry motioned for Hal to give him back the document. "You know what the hell the Chief's going to say about this? He'll blow a gasket. And then he'll kick your ass so far up into your shoulders you'll be shitting through your ears."

Gerry waited for us to laugh at that.

None of us did.

"And why would Chief Black be so predisposed to violence?" Duncan asked. "I am confident once he's made aware, perhaps from someone like you, Mr. Kelly, of the enormous public relations potential of this event, that he will be grateful for our help. Think of it. A poor soul, indeed a brother lost 'lo these many, many years, finally, through the coordinated efforts of the police force and medical examiner's department of the city of Paraíso del Mar , is once again reunited and resting in the bosom of his family. It'll make a helluva story."

Wade and I glanced at each other and turned away. Duncan had spun such a sugarcoated load of bullshit, it was all we could do to not laugh. I glanced at Hal, and even he was smirking.

But not Gerry. He thought about it for a moment and then said, "Well, hell. I mean, goddamn, I think you are right. I never thought of it that way."

"I'm sure you would have, given time to reflect upon it," Duncan said.

Yeah, like maybe a thousand years.

"All right. Hal, you see that Mr. Fitzgerald gets what he needs."

"Excellent," Duncan said, standing. "I believe our medical transfer team is parked outside."

"Wait, Jesus," Gerry said, "you're going to do this now? I haven't told the Chief."

"The court order will explain everything."

"So you think I should call the networks?" Gerry asked, transforming from blocking our investigation to a media addict in ten seconds.

"Certainly not until we have the results."

Gerry's eyes kind of became unfocused and his head nodded slightly. I'm sure he'd been imagining his mug on the flat screens of everyone in town and all over L.A., and was disappointed at having to wait for his fifteen seconds of fame.

"When will you have the results?" Gerry said.

"You'll be the first one we call," Duncan said over his shoulder.

Wade and I followed Duncan out. I nodded slightly at Hal. I hoped he understood that we shared an indignant rage at what the Chief had tried to do.

"I need to talk to you," he whispered as I passed him. "Outside."

58

"Somebody got inside the morgue," Hal said when he walked up to us.

"A body missing?"

"No, but this set of bones that's got Kelly's ass in an uproar? There was an ID bracelet on the forearm, and it's gone."

"Think it was important?" Wade said.

"Don't know. It was so rusty, I don't think you could get anything off of it."

"Maybe it'll turn up," I said.

Hal shrugged. He automatically checked back at the building, I guess to see if Kelly might be coming. "You won't believe the shit they're pulling now."

"What?"

"They're saying Reed Lockhart had a heart attack and that's why he went into the palm trees."

"How the hell can they do that?" Wade said. "I thought his body was burned beyond recognition."

"Exactly. There's no possible way any medical examiner could determine he had a heart attack first. Unless it's on CSI, and that's a TV show which has nothing to do with reality."

"Heart attack means…?" I said.

"They'll list it as 'death by natural causes.'"

"Kelly know there are other ways people die?" Wade said.

I didn't say anything, just started back for Kelly's office.

"Matt," Hal said. "Wait, where're you going?"

"Don't worry," I said over my shoulder. "He won't know how I found out."

"Shit!" Hal yelled.

Wade caught up to me at the door.

"You sure you want to do this?" he said.

I nodded my head and kept walking.

We burst in on Kelly when he was on the phone. He looked at us for a moment and then said into the phone, "I'll have to call you back." He hung up and stared at us. "What?"

"Just curious about Mayor Lockhart's death."

"What about it?"

"I heard you're listing his death as from natural causes."

"How the hell do you know that?"

"A birdie told me."

Kelly sat down at his desk. "Reed had a heart attack. That's a natural cause of death. The fact that he plowed into the palm trees and his car exploded? That was after the attack."

"And you can tell that from your autopsy?"

"What autopsy? We didn't run one. He was burned beyond recognition. What the hell would an autopsy show me?"

"I don't know, that's why they run them."

"Do you know who you're dealing with?"

"Yeah, I do."

He waited for me to explain, but I was hoping irony might win the day.

It didn't.

Wade figured that out before I did. "We're trying to understand, Gerry," he said, "why there's a set of bones you're trying to cremate, a set of bones with a cratered cranium..."

Gerry blanched when he heard this.

"... that you listed as 'death by natural causes' when it would appear that the cause of death certainly might be homicide. And now Reed Lockhart's car goes straight into the only set of palm trees on *Vista del paseo*, and that's also 'death by natural causes.'"

Gerry tried to stare down Wade, but that's like going eyeball to eyeball with a Rottweiler. And Wade wasn't even pissed. Yet.

"Look," Gerry said, "the Chief ordered it, so that's what I did."

"What about the law?" I said.

"Around here he *is* the law, you dumb shit. You lived here all this time, and you still haven't figured that out yet?"

"No. And I hope I never do."

Gerry shook his head at my impenetrability of the order of things in Paraíso del mar.

"You know why he did it? Because Reed was his best friend. He wanted to save Leah a lot of pain and people talking. Cancer was going through Reed's body like wildfire. I doubt he would have lasted two months." Gerry straightened a folder on his desk. "The Chief thinks Reed drove into the palms on purpose. So he wouldn't have to face what was coming."

"So natural causes wipes the slate clean? That how it works?"

"This way Leah collects on the insurance without all those assholes asking her painful questions." He pumped his fist with each word for emphasis. "Now that's a fucking friendship."

59

"Hey, bud," Zak said. "I'm buried on this project for...uh, anyway, I'm buried."

"So you won't be able to get any info on the building?"

"I'll get it. I just need some more time."

"Crap, we really need it, Zak."

There was a silence of several moments, which is like an eternity in any communication with Zak. He's always talking. Wade calls him the Steven A. Smith of computers.

"Matt, I know you look out for my moms at the beach there, and I appreciate the solid. And that you helped me get this gig, but, dude, these guys, my bosses, they—"

I cut him off.

"I check on your mother because she's a nice lady. I don't do that expecting to always ask you for info. And how many times have I said, I'll pay you."

"Aw, shit, man, I'm not asking for money. I just need more time."

"You got it. Get back to the keyboard."

Wade looked at me for an explanation.

"Looks like both Duncan and Zak have now put us on a pay-as-you-go plan." I headed for the Building Department. "We're going to have to gumshoe this one ourselves."

"Interesting that they knew about the ID bracelet so soon," Wade said.

"They don't know shit. That was Hal talking. He's fixated on those bones."

"Imagine that."

The Building Department takes up most of the second floor in the new City Services Complex. You go up a set of winding stairs, flooded with natural light from the numerous skylights set in the roof, and enter a wide-open space jammed with people on opposite sides of a long, circular granite counter.

Actually, only one side of the counter is jammed, the other has around twenty staff members whose criteria for employment is a pernicious, anal-retentive mindset, and an ability to alienate Mother Theresa. The jammed side is filled with architects trying to get their blueprints approved, contractors pissed off that their house didn't pass their last inspection, carpenters, plumbers, electricians, and every other kind of tradesman trying to understand the latest changes in city codes. Scattered among these professionals are the odd homeowner who wants to add on a bedroom and bath over the garage and is about to fall down the rabbit hole of rules, codes, regulations, and coastal construction criteria.

After waiting twenty minutes, getting sent to another region of the granite counter, being told that we needed to see the supervisor, then another ten minutes before learning the supervisor wasn't in today would you like to make an appointment, a tall, angular woman with a permanent squint, either from smoking or poor glasses, came to our rescue.

"Hi, I'm Eileen."

Wade and I introduced ourselves and shook hands with Eileen whose grip was also angular and sharp, then explained our problem. Eileen typed on her keyboard, frowned at the screen, squinted even harder, and then said, "Shoot, you're out of luck here. Paradise Enterprises, LLC is our last entry too."

But before I could ask where our fortunes might change, Eileen said, "But there is hope. Way down to the right is one of the gates to this counter. Why don't you follow me down there and I will give you magical entrance into the wonderful kingdom of the Building Department."

We did, and when Eileen admitted us passage, there was an alarming look from several of her coworkers, who didn't seem to have anything in common with Eileen, other than they worked for the city.

Eileen took us to a door at the back, and we followed her down to a small room.

"Paradise's non-computerized records."

The walls were filled with shelves filled with thick, dusty notebooks. Eileen searched for a few moments and then pulled down a notebook. She flipped through several pages and then replaced it.

"This was before my time. But I do remember there was a building boom back in the early sixties. Lots of GIs back from 'Nam, getting government loans. Big influx of people from the Midwest and back east." For a moment, she drifted away. "*That's* when this really was paradise. Before all that..." She pointed upstairs.

She shifted over a few feet to another bookshelf, looked at the top row, then bent down to the bottom row and extracted a thick notebook There was a stack of cartons in a corner, she put the notebook on them, opened it, and flipped through several pages.

"Tah-dah." She moved aside so Wade and I could see, and pointed to a page.

"L and B Partners, Incorporated," I said. "Who're they?"

"Only the two biggest power players in town. Or at least used to be, now they're just half of that."

"Mayor Lockhart and Chief Black?"

"Bingo. Only back then they were just Sergeant Black and Councilman Lockhart."

I read through the document. "There's a third partner indicated, but not listed?"

Eileen checked the document. "If it's not here, I can't help you. But Ollie over in Business Affairs might. Ollie's the oldest employee Paradise has ever had. If you want to know the real truth about our town, just ask Ollie."

60

"Just like I told you," Ollie Robberts said, "Bill MacEllroy the Third. I knew that without even having to look it up." Ollie waved a thick, yellowed finger at the legal document with all of the information about Reed's and Ben's corporation, then turned his head and hacked and coughed for about ten seconds.

I saw a pack of Camels on the counter, so that explained the yellow fingers and probably black lungs.

"See right here," Ollie said and flipped through several pages of legal documents. "Those three owned the primo parts of Paradise. And kept going after it."

"Ben's the muscle, Reed's the front man, where's MacEllroy fit in?"

"Used to be a detergent called Rinso. Rinso Blue actually. That's what they called Bill. The Rinso Man."

Wade looked at Ollie.

"I think he taught Louis B. Mayer how to do the books."

"I'm not following."

"You know how a movie like *Alien* will do a couple hundred million in the box office, and it never makes a profit? Because those Hollywood types form an LLC for just that movie, then charge that movie all kinds of distribution fees, fees that they're collecting from the movie, but also doubling back on them? That was Bill MacEllroy did the accounting for Ben and Reed. Rumor was he taught Louis B. Mayer how to cook MGM's books.

Ollie looked longingly at his pack of Camels.

"You want to go outside, have a smoke?" I said.

Ollie looked at me like I had mysterious, magical powers.

"Yeah," he said, grabbed his smokes, and headed for the exit.

Once we were outside, he fired up and took a huge deep hit, then exhaled in a long, harsh puff. "If they'd have started the 'No Smoking' inside years ago, I'd have probably quit. All this bullshit just to have a smoke."

"You were talking about William MacEllroy," I said.

"I didn't forget," Ollie said, a little indignant. "I just wanted to inhale some more carcinogenic fumes first." He took another long hit, exhaled in a long double hit where the smoke curled up from his mouth back into his nostrils.

"Old Bill didn't just work magic with the books. You needed a weekend trip to Vegas for granting a change of title?" Ollie snapped his fingers, and the hard, calloused tips popped loud and hard, like striking flint. "Want a couple of Howard Hughes' finest little starlets to put lead in your pencil? Blondes or brunettes? Just state your preference. Or maybe one of each? Not a problem. Some folks call that graft or payola. Bill put that under 'research and development.'"

Ollie took another deep hit, examined the tip of his cigarette.

"Yeah, I've seen a lot of shit go down and through this place."

"Is that true you're the oldest employee around?"

Ollie looked at me and laughed. "Shit, I passed oldest years ago. I'll be seventy-eight next week."

"Isn't there a mandatory retirement policy?" Wade asked.

"Goddamn right. But if you know a thing or two, there's ways around anything. I learned that from Bill MacEllroy."

Ollie took another hit, crushed the cigarette on the heel of his shoe, and tossed the butt into a nearby trash can.

"But enough's enough. Next Tuesday I collect my last paycheck, and I am officially cashiered out. Grace, that's my wife of sixty-two years, something, huh?"

"Absolutely."

"Anyway, Grace and I bought us an Airstream Trailer. 1976 Ambassador model. Thing looks like it just came out of the factory. So we're hitching that up to my Chevy Suburban, and we're hitting the road."

Ollie moved to head back to work.

"I ain't going out like Bill MacEllroy."

"What happened to him?"

"Heart attack. Right in the middle of a federal tax investigation. One minute he's talking circles around those government twits and the next his face is in the middle of all the accounting records. Damn IRS fellas couldn't believe it."

"Those accounting records still around?"

"Maybe. Bill's wife, Sophia, is still alive. She might know."

"Blue skies and green lights," I said. "Have a great trip."

"I intend to. Grace and I deeded our house over to my son. So once we hit the road, we ain't looking back and we ain't coming back. One or both of us will probably have our odometers stop out there someplace on the highway." He shrugged. "We're all bound for the final trip."

He looked at me and Wade. "*All* of us. You young studs got a lot of time ahead of you. But it's still a finite amount of time." He shook hands with us. Then sang a song as he went back into the building, "*Enjoy yourself, it's later than you think. Enjoy yourself…*"

"Shit," Wade said, "that was depressing."

"Yeah. And not just because he knows most of his life is behind him."

"And the other reason?"

"When he passes, so does the secret history of Paraíso del mar. And I'm not sure if that's a good or a bad thing."

61

"A pretty young thing," my dad said, "that sure as hell was Sophia Kent MacEllroy. You may remember, Matt, her father owned Kent's Jewelers. Hell, it was three doors up right here on Marine."

"Not really."

Wade and I had gone over to the Marine Diner, met my dad there, and filled him in on the events.

"No matter. Sidney Kent had a great eye for diamonds and rings. Best place around to get fine jewelry, and not just in Paradise. Then he had a stroke, her mom couldn't run the business, and they lost everything."

My dad took a bite of his sandwich and stared off into space.

"Hell, right after, that's when Bill scooped up Sophia." He chewed slowly. "Maybe she figured she wanted to keep having the finer things of life."

"Worse decisions have been made, "Wade said.

"For sure," my dad said. "But Sophia was gorgeous. She was signed to Warner Brothers and some hotshot producer was going to make her the next Elizabeth Taylor. But then she married Bill and that dream went by the boards."

"So, you have any thoughts on all of this, Dad?"

"Yeah, I think you two have stumbled on a Japanese Puzzle Box. You may have to squeeze things in the middle, you may have to turn it upside down, and getting to the secret center's going to be complicated."

I must have looked confused because my dad said, "You do know what a Japanese Puzzle Box is, right?"

Wade did.

"They were first imported back at the start of the nineteenth century from the Hakane region of Japan. They're called Himitsu-Bako." Wade looked at me and shrugged. "Benefits of a classical education."

"The best ones are very complex, and you go nuts trying to open them if you're out of sequence. That's what you guys have here."

My cell rang. It was Zak.

"Hey, the original partners were..."

"Reed Lockhart and Ben Black."

"Whoa, how'd you get that?"

"Sometimes gumshoes work out."

"Gumshoes? Those some new kind of soles from Cole-Hahn?"

"Goggle it, dude," I said and clicked off.

Wade looked at me. "He didn't know what gumshoes were?"

"Sometimes you've got to stop looking at the computer and experience life."

We finished lunch. I Googled Sophia's address, called her, and then went over.

My dad was right. Sophia must have been a vision because even now when she had to be in her early seventies, she was still striking. She had ice-blue eyes and a thick head of stylishly cut shiny, silver hair. Her skin was smooth with only some deep wrinkles around her eyes and some parenthesis around her full lips when she smiled. Most likely a nip and tuck here and there, but hard to tell.

She was happy to see me, but I got the feeling that was because she didn't see much of anyone these days. The house was in the "Hill" section of Paraíso del mar, so when we walked through her spacious living room, the view over the rooftops to the water was impressive as hell.

We passed a huge Steinway, its closed ebony top clustered with silver-framed photographs, mostly of a younger Sophia, probably when she was under contract at Warner Brothers.

She stopped for a moment and pointed to a dramatic black and white close-up of her looking seductively over a bare shoulder at the camera.

"George Hurrell," Sophia said. "He was *the* only photographer you wanted to have snap your picture. That is, if you were serious about your career."

"Very beautiful," I said.

"George said I had more presence in my photos than Liz or either of the Jeans. You know, Tierney or Harlow." She traced a finger over the edge of the frame. "But I'm sure George told all the girls that."

She smiled at me. "Onward to the dungeon. At least that's what I call the room where William's records are."

The room was a small, dreary place tacked on to the back of the garage. It was stuffed floor to ceiling with stacks and stacks of meticulously labeled boxes, the writing slight and faded with time.

"Lord knows every year I tell myself to throw them out, but I just never get around to it." Both of her hands went out in a helpless gesture of resignation. "When William passed, well, this was his life's work. And they just moved all this stuff from his office and jammed it in here."

This looked daunting. But I said, "Thanks, Mrs. MacEllroy."

"Oh, please, call me Sophia. I'll be in the den if you need anything."

Two hours later I felt like I needed a flamethrower. I couldn't find a goddamn thing. I'd gone back through the boxes by years and found nothing. Then I'd tried by project. I was tired and hot, and my nose kept twitching from all the damn dust.

The door opened and Sophia appeared with a silver tray that held a pitcher of lemonade, its glass frosty with tiny rivulets of condensation running down its curved sides, and a small tray of almond cookies.

"I thought you could use a break."

"Thanks," I said and gulped down the glass of lemonade she poured. "I'm sorry, I didn't mean to take up so much of your time. I'll be going."

"Oh, no bother at all. Would you mind if I asked what you're looking for exactly?"

"A project that L and B, LLC did over 3309 Laurel."

"Oh, Lord, that hellhole."

Ten minutes later I had all of the information I needed. The hellhole project wasn't in among all of the boxes but inside William's study. This set of boxes hadn't fit into the dungeon room and had been jammed into the closet.

"Can I make a copy of these?"

"Just take them. Lord knows it's time to get rid of it." Sophia walked me to the door and picked up a large manila envelope from a small table. "Here," she said, almost shyly. "I had an extra, and you seemed to like it."

"Thank you," I said without looking at what I knew had to be one of the photos.

Sophia opened the door. "I autographed it."

82

62

"Why do I have to sign this?" Mayleen Santiago said, her voice plaintive and worried through the cell.

"It's just a formality, *Señora*. It's to try and help you and Ritchie."

"How can a man swabbing the inside of my cheek be helpful?"

"We think..." I stopped because I didn't want to offer even the remotest chance of hope and then have it all come crashing down. So I did what most people do. I lied. "It's about the insurance."

"There is a problem?"

"No, I'm sure it will all be fine."

"But this is something I see on TV, no? They rub a swab inside your cheek and then run your DNA. Why would they need to do this for me and Ritchie too?"

Shit. Moral crossroads here, Singer.

"It's for the insurance, but it's..."

"Miguel!" her voice went up an octave. "*¡Oh, mi Dios, que no puede ser cierto!*" I could hear her gasping, catching her breath. "Is this true, *Senor* Matt?"

How the hell did she jump to that idea?

"I...it's possible, but I don't want you to get your hopes up, *Senora*."

"*¡Oh, madre!* Oh-oh...you...you don't..." She took a deep, calming breath. "All these years, I held out this secret hope that Miguel's *activities* with all those women of the town had forced him to run away. Maybe to Mexico or someplace far away. And that one day he would find a way to contact me. Because that is what families do, they take care of each other. And then, after the time kept passing and the years went by, I knew he was *muertos*."

Then her courage broke, and she started sobbing.

Way to go, Singer.

"Hey," Ritchie yelled, his voice loud through the phone that he'd taken from Mayleen. "What the fuck, dude? What'd you say to my mom?"

"It's a long story."

"Man, you're fucked."

"*Ricardo!*" I heard Mayleen warn him.

There were some shuffling sounds and then she came back on the line.

"You have found his body? No, after all this time, *Sus huesos?* His bones?"

"I think so. We're running tests, and we need your DNA for a match."

"Yes, just like on television, I understand. But, *perdón, por favor*, why Ritchie?"

"That's for the insurance."

Mayleen was quiet for a few moments.

"They need to prove that Ritchie is Reed's son?"

"I'm sorry, you know how insurance companies are."

"*Si*. Greedy." She held the phone away from her mouth and said, "Ritchie, let this man do his job." Then she came back to me. "They are greedy, but they will lose. Because he is definitely a Lockhart."

"I didn't doubt it. So, hopefully, this will just take a few days."

"Okay, *Senor* Matt," she said, "now I am going to hang up since this man is so anxious to stick his thing in my mouth." There was a small intake of breath, and the *Señora* giggled. "*Perdón*, sometimes my English is not so good."

And I was pretty sure I heard her giggle again before the connection was broken.

It was the giggle of a twenty-year-old *senorita*.

A Hispanic beauty sweeter than the *dulces* she brought to her brother's worksites who had unerringly pierced the hard armor of Reed Lockhart's heart with Cupid's ancient arrow of love.

63

"You gotta love it," Wade said, "the sheer brazenness of what they did."

We had been going through the thick box of documents Sophia had given me on the Laurel project for a couple of hours. There was definite proof that Miguel had worked this job—lumber invoices, receipts for galvanized pipe delivered to the job, several official Paraíso del mar building code cards, all with Miguel listed as the contractor of record.

More than half of the box was filled with receipts and cancelled checks, all neatly ordered and filed, all signed in MacEllroy's tight hand, a flurry of paper and disappearing funds.

"He writes a check to Miguel from L&B LLC for $2,345.16. Then this Seafarer Development gives Miguel an invoice for $1,125.16, which he pays. And Seafarer – Surprise, surprise -- is a wholly-owned subsidiary of L&B."

"So that was the kickback from Miguel to get the work."

"No free lunches," Wade said.

"Seems to me," I said, "it would have been easier to just pay Miguel the lesser amount."

"Easier, yes. Less expensive? No." Wade opened an account ledger book. "And here we see a charge-off for L&B for 'services rendered' for the $1,125.16 from Seafarer."

"So the money cancels itself out?"

"Yeah, on paper they have losses equal to the money they're making. So it looks like they've got zero balance. No profits, no losses, and no taxes. But, unless somebody really looks closer, like the IRS did, they've really hidden that $1,125.16."

"Seems like a lot of work."

"It is. But you have a hundred of these transactions on every project, all tax-free, it's a small fortune. Remember this is forty years ago when everything was a helluva lot cheaper. And not as difficult to slip things pass the tax men."

"No kidding," I said. "Did you see this?" I held up a copy of the original Deed of Trust for Laurel. "They bought the property for $29,000. You know what it's worth today? Over $6.5 million. The purchase price wouldn't even cover the taxes now."

"Okay, we can prove Miguel worked there, but the rest of it?"

"How much motivation you need? Miguel kicks a cop's ass. That's a reason for a beatdown from the boys in blue. Maybe it started out as punishment and got out of hand."

"Maybe. Miguel was a pretty tough guy. I'm thinking more than one cop."

"Black and Lockhart, partners in business, partners in crime."

"That's some secret to keep all these years."

"Which makes you wonder what happened. Why now after all this time?"

"You're thinking about when you saw them arguing?" Wade said.

"They were ready for blows."

"If you're right, it went way beyond that."

"But even with the resurrection of Miguel's bones, they pretty much had that covered too. I mean, if we don't stick our noses in it, Miguel disappears for good in the crematorium. And there's no proof."

"Well, the Chief be knowin' we be stirrin' the pot." Wade smiled at me. "And de pot be boilin' ovah. And dat means they gonna be a mess and somebody's gonna get burned."

I wet my finger and touched Wade on the shoulder.

"Tsshhh," I said. "We're red-hot."

64

"I'm feeling chilly," Leah said. "I'm going to my car and get a sweater. Please start without me."

She was having dinner with Wade, my dad, and me at *La Grenouille* restaurant, the town's most pretentious eating establishment, but still damn good food.

"All that money and all that pain," my dad said.

"She doesn't know the half of it," I said.

"You think you'll ever tell her?" my dad asked.

"Depends on how things go."

"Assume they go in the toilet," Wade said. "Just in case. Besides, I thought we already agreed that Duncan should drop that bomb."

"That won't be a 2,000 pound blockbuster, that will be Hiroshima."

Two waiters appeared with our food, another refilled our glasses, and they left in a haughty swoop. My dad looked at his food. "Nice-looking dish." He took a forkful of his *sole menuire*. "And speaking of dishes, what'd you think of Sophia?"

Wade just rolled his eyes.

"Dad, she's in her late seventies."

"So am I, almost. And she's still a handsome woman. If you had seen her in her prime…"

"I did. Her entire piano is covered with pictures of her when she was a star."

"She was never a star, just a starlet. I got the feeling her acting chops weren't all that great." He shrugged. "Just saying what I heard back then."

I took a savory bite of my *coq au vin*. Wade was already deep into his *poulet rôti provençal*. Leah was also having the sole, and I thought about having the waiter put it under a cover when she appeared.

"Sorry," she said and slipped into the booth next to me. "This looks delicious."

"It is," I said through a mouthful.

"I stopped in the bathroom and had the weirdest conversation with a woman in there."

"Not bathroom humor while I'm eating, please," my dad said, laughing and taking a big swig of his wine.

Leah took a bite of the fish and nodded that it was good.

"Apparently she met some guy in the bar last week at the Marriott. I guess he was real charming and they hit it off. And she was drunk. So they go up to his room, kiss a little, and he says I have a business partner to meet, but I'll be back in an hour."

"What the hell kind of guy does that?" my dad said.

"Oh, it gets stranger," Leah said. "So she orders extra towels, goes in and takes a long shower. By the time she's ready and slips into the sheets, almost two hours have passed. She calls down to the bar, he's not there. She tries the guy's cell, he never answers."

"Maybe he was married and got cold feet," I said.

Leah took another bite of the sole, had some wine, and continued. "That's what she thought. Because the guy never showed."

"Never?" Wade said.

"Nope. She woke up the next morning, and the other side of the bed was untouched. He never came back. So she ordered a huge breakfast, a gift robe for herself, took another shower, and left the room around 8:30."

"Enterprising gal," my dad said. "She didn't get the rod, but she got the robe."

"Dad!"

Leah smirked, Wade did his *heh-heh*, and I watched my dad beam and grin like the mischievous kid in fourth grade.

"Ah, hell," my dad said. "What kind of guy does that to a woman?"

"A guy with something…to hide," I said.

I jumped up out of the table. "What's the woman look like?" I said.

"What?" Leah said. "Why?"

Wade got it at that moment too. "Let me out, Mario," he said.

"The woman," I said, "where'd she go? What's she look like?"

"She's got this amazing red hair, and she's wearing a blue dress, why?"

My dad had stepped out of the booth, as confused as Leah.

Wade was past my dad and heading for the bar.

I held out my hand to Leah. "C'mon, I need you."

My dad looked around. "Matt, what the hell's going on?"

"Tell the waiter to keep our food warm, we'll be right back."

Joanie Dumas was in the center of the bar and definitely the center of attraction. She was surrounded by three salesmen types, had to be from out of town, just the way they were dressed and how stupid and nervous they acted around her.

Of course, we didn't know her name was Joanie at that point, only that she was as attractive as Leah had said. Wade slowed down and waited for us.

"You need to talk to her right away," I said to Leah.

"I do? About what?"

"I'll explain as we go along."

Leah cut straight for the group. And just as I had thought, these bozos had probably never picked up a woman outside of their local bowling alley back in Nebraska or Mississippi or whatever bum-ass town they called home, because Leah was standing next to Joanie before they could react.

A sharp guy looking for beautiful women would have *sensed* Leah before he saw her, and he would have seen her at least twenty feet away. Not these guys. One minute part of their brain is thinking about how incredible it would be to go to bed with this redhead, and the other part is thinking of what they're going to tell their buddies back home, the ones who aren't part of their lucky trio. Then the next minute, their luck has doubled! Because there's Leah!

Wade and I had moved back and waited just outside the entrance to the bar so the outsiders wouldn't suspect we were part of the rendition. Although, I doubted they suspected anything other than they wished they lived at the beach.

Leah said something to Joanie, who excused herself from the boys and walked back toward us. The shitkickers from Middle America still couldn't figure out what the hell had just happened.

After the introductions and Wade and I maneuvered as delicately as we could through Joanie's weird night, I asked if she had her cell phone.

"Yours isn't working? Sure, you can use mine."

"No. I just need you to use yours. Scroll through your calls."

She pulled it from her purse. "And what am I looking for?"

"The guy's number who stood you up."

"I'm not calling that asshole."

"No, I am. I just need you to show me the number."

She scrolled through several pages of calls, obviously a popular or very talkative woman, and came to the number. "There," she said. "John Q. Asshole."

Only that isn't who answered.

"Hey," the voice message said, "it's Stephen McDougal."

65

"It's always the husband," I said. "Always."

"Right," Wade said, but somehow his voice lacked conviction.

"Crime Stoppers, rule eighty-two."

"You think anyone else your age remembers Dick Tracy?"

"What?"

We were hauling ass to the airport since McDougal's neighbor had told us Stephen was taking a long trip to Rio de Janeiro. I took a fast turn on Century Boulevard.

"You think Dick Tracy's *passé?*"

"You only know it because your dad used to read it. And I only know it because you're always telling me this shit."

I slowed down as the guards at the LAX entrance roads did their security check. One of the guards motioned for us to stop and to roll down my window. His name ID read "Alexander." He scanned us quickly and assumed we weren't a threat to national security and waved us through.

"Excuse me," I said.

I felt Wade tense and mutter "Shit" under his breath.

The guard was slightly more alert.

"You ever hear of Dick Tracy and his famous Crime Stoppers?"

"You're kidding, right?"

He was either insulted or incredulous. Could go either way.

"Prune face? Flattop? B.B. Eyes?"

"All right," I said.

"My dog's named Chester Gould Alexander. What do you think?"

"I think you just proved an excellent point I was trying to make to my unenlightened friend."

Alexander leaned in, checked out Wade, then said, "There's always hope. Long as he's not B.O. Plenty."

I smiled all the way to the "Exec-Ride" parking lot. Wade and I had left our weapons at home, so we were out and running for the terminal as soon as I cut the engine.

"Okay, now," I said.

And as we pounded for the Aeromexico boarding area, cutting around people who were pushing suitcases and tugging children, Wade called Glenn Remington, the lieutenant everyone figured would replace the Chief, if the son of a bitch ever retired. We called Remington because we knew he'd do this right and fast.

Okay, we should have called Remington the minute we found out the slick maneuver McDougal had pulled, but we had a score to settle with Stephen.

And if this worked out, then Glenn would get the credit for the righteous bus, and it wouldn't get sucked into the Chief's vortex of power.

"Okay," Wade said as we made the main doors and slowed down. People get nervous when they see men running in an airport. Especially two dudes like us. Okay, a dude like Wade, who was a black flowing mountain. "Remington's on board."

"He didn't bitch about calling him so late?"

"He doesn't know it's late. Yet." We slipped around a group of Asian tourists. "But he will eventually and we'll deal with that then."

We came up to the security section for Aeromexico. I looked past the guards and saw Stephen already through the x-ray machine stations.

"Shit," I said to Wade, who was just behind me.

"Yeah," Wade said. "Think the guards will let us through?"

"Worth a shot."

But when we showed the guard our licenses and explained that we needed to talk to our client, he didn't say a word, just smiled like we were inmates let out of the sanatorium, and shook his head. "Next please," he said, looking past us.

We stepped to the left, away from the crowd filing through the gates, and I waved to get McDougal's attention. I tried it a couple of times and got weird stares from passengers and a very annoyed glare from a very heavyset female guard. When I waved again, she chugged over for me.

Wade stepped in front of me and gave her his biggest smile. A smile that ignored the fact she could be in one of those LAP-BAND weight-loss infomercials—definitely as the "before" subject. He flashed his smile then he flashed his license.

"Our client there, that tall man in the all-black outfit?"

"Shawna Howard," that's what it said on her ID, didn't even bother to check out what McDougal was wearing. "I'm sorry, sir, but you cannot make those kinds of movements in the airport."

"Yeah," Wade said, "we didn't mean it. It's just that Mr. McDougal has had a terrible tragedy in his family that just happened and he can't get on this flight."

Wade can be very persuasive just by his size, but when he's wearing his sincerity face, he's devastating.

But not with Shawna.

"If Mr. McDougal doesn't want to board this flight, that's his decision. It will be a very expensive one since Aeromexico doesn't allow this kind of last-minute cancellation."

"I don't think money's the issue here," Wade said. "But he can't make that decision if he doesn't know it needs to be made."

Shawna was about to protest again, but Wade went into drill sergeant mode. "Get him and get him now. Or I'll talk to Adrienne Gilroy, and she'll ask you,"—and Wade purposely stared at her name tag—"Ms. Shawna Howard, why you didn't save one of Aeromexico customers a load of grief."

Wade was eyeball to eyeball with Shawna. And she blinked first.

She didn't say a word, just turned slowly, like an aircraft carrier in high seas, and went back for McDougal.

"Who's Adrienne Gilroy?" I said.

"Used to be head of security, dark ops, for the airport. I wasn't sure if she still worked here."

"Obviously she still does, or Shawna thinks she does."

Before she got to McDougal, Wade and I split up and moved in opposite directions out of his line of sight. If he saw us on that side of the security divider, he might not come across.

We watched while Shawna talked to McDougal. He looked at her like she had the wrong man, then looked out to where we would have been, talked some more with Shawna and finally, and obviously reluctantly, headed back our way.

To come back, you had to go way to the left side where several guards were positioned so no one could get past security the wrong way. Shawna and McDougal came through the border, and she pointed in Wade's direction. Wade gave McDougal a big wave and smile and motioned for him to come over. I was already moving, closing the gap, from McDougal's blind side.

McDougal hesitated a second, then spun around to head back, right into me.

We collided for a momen, and I slipped Stephen a little gift in his side coat pocket.

"Hey, Stephen, there've been some new developments and…"

"Fuck you," he said and shoved me away a little, then walked as fast as he could back into the line to go back through the checkpoint. He had two people ahead of him. Then one.

Wade came up. "You make the exchange?"

"With bells on."

And I meant that in every sense of the word.

Now it was Stephen's turn. Just before he went into the zone, he looked back at Wade and me and flipped us the finger.

And then all hell broke loose.

Lights started flashing, one of the head guards must have hit a button because at least four burly guards came racing over. Two of them pulled their batons, and they grabbed Stephen and escorted his ass away, his black Falke luxury cashmere socks barely touching the floor.

The rumor and news went through the place like wildfire. Guy had a machete, guy had a straight razor, guy had a bazooka.

None of them true. All our guy had was a Smith & Wesson "Baby" S.W.A.T. automatic knife in the side pocket of his Hugo Boss sport coat. It was my knife, but somehow it had just fallen out of my hand into Stephen's jacket. Imagine that.

"That should keep him grounded until Remington, and his troops get here."

"You gave him the S&W, right?" Wade said. "The cheap one?"

"I am prudent, if somewhat devious."

As we headed for my car, three Paradise squad cars and two motorcycles screeched to a sto, and eight cops rushed for the Aeromexico gates. Two of the cops, I noticed, were my former Academy classmates, Alan Bartle, and Jim Tucker. Two badasses that were just the ticket.

66

"Parking stub please," the attendant said.

I handed it over.

She was very attractive, probably Creole, judging from her *café au lait* skin and turquoise eyes. "Twenty-eight dollars and seventy-five cents please," she said, looking past me to Wade.

"What?"

"Twenty-eight seventy-five."

I looked at her name tag. "Moesha, how can that be?"

She focused those startling eyes on me. "First twenty minutes is $18.50, then $10.25 every ten minutes thereafter." She pointed to the sign. "Says right there."

I forked over the money. "Are all the lots around here this expensive?"

"Nope. We the champs."

"And what makes you champions?"

"We chauffeur you right to your terminal and hand-deliver your bags."

"But we didn't have any bags."

"That ain't my problem."

As we drove out, there was a bright flash of light. And I saw a sign that read, "Auto Photos for Security." I stopped, opened the door, and called back, "Hey, Moesha, you take a photo of every car?"

"Yep. Coming and going. That way we know exactly who came in, what time, and when they left."

We pulled into traffic. I asked Wade, "You notice a flash from the cameras when we came in?"

"No, but then we were concentrating on getting Stephen."

I shifted into second and passed several cars. "And get him we did."

"Who you think's going to win? Airport or Paradise?"

"Tough call. My guess is Stephen spends a few hours denying and accusing me and eventually they let Remington's boys arrest him."

Wade smiled.

"What?"

"Moesha likes me."

"Christ, you think every woman of color likes you."

"Not just of color."

My cell rang. I answered, and the call went to Bluetooth, putting the caller on speaker.

"Hello," I said.

"Matt."

"Glenn. You didn't have to call and say thanks personally."

He ignored my jibe. "McDougal says you planted a S.W.A.T. knife on him."

"Really?"

"Says you and Wade..."

"Hey, Glenn," Wade said.

"Hello," Glenn said in return, not quite sure how to parse his words. "Anyway, McDougal says you two lured him outside with some bullshit story that there were changes in his case, a story corroborated by a..." I think he was checking his notes.

"Shawna Howard," I said. "He's right, his case did change. He went from a slick, conniving bastard who was about to flee the country where extradition is impossible, to a prime murder suspect. We didn't bullshit him. We just didn't tell him what lay ahead for him."

"It's always best to stay out of the fortune-telling business," Glenn said. "So, you know nothing about this S.W.A.T. knife?"

"Nope."

"Curious. Because he'd cleared security without a hitch before. Then he comes outside, spends ten seconds with you two, and next thing you know he's setting off alarms, and the airport guards pounce on him."

Neither of us said anything. After a long pause, Glenn said, "We'll sort that out later. Right now, we're trying to convince the airport folks that instead of having to go through all the hoops to charge him, get him downtown, attorneys, and so on, it's faster and more secure to just let us arrest him."

"Sounds like a plan."

"And you have the cell phone of this Joanie Dumas?"

"No, she wasn't about to give it up to us, but she promised us she'll store it in a safe place. You got her home address, right?"

"We did. Okay, got to go. Looks like they're moving McDougal." He hung up.

"Always good to score brownie points with the next chief," I said.

"Assuming we can bank them that long."

"Chief Black's run is over."

"Just remember, somehow that man do endure."

67

"It would have been a long time before they got McDougal," Wade said.

"Probably never," I said. "If he boarded that flight, he was a free man."

Wade and I were having coffee at Marie Calendar's. I was also having pie. Lemon meringue.

"Free from jail, but not from the guilt," Wade said.

"I don't think he'd feel that way for a second. Son of a bitch was coldhearted."

"Charming, but chilly," Wade said. "The city's going to have to go through all the bullshit from McDougal's attorneys. And I'm assuming Bags won't be the only mouthpiece working for him, but in the end, he goes down."

I took a sweet mouthful of pie. "Not even Duncan could save him."

"Might get him life, avoid the death penalty, but still, McDougal's gone."

"And it looks like Paradise's finest detective team retains its crown."

"By sheer luck."

"Luck is the residue of great planning," I said.

"Only residue you got is some meringue next to your lip," Wade said.

I cleaned up. "You're right, we caught a break on this one." I took a sip of coffee. "Of course, it took a brilliant mind to make the connection from jilted Joanie to McDougal."

"Two brilliant minds," Wade said. "When we clickin', we think as one."

He gave me a big cheesy smile. "You thinking of calling Denis Titlebaum?"

I'd forgotten all about him.

"I'm sure he'll get the news eventually."

"Think he'll call you?"

"Not a chance. That would admit to the possibility that he might have been, ah, insensitive."

"In a church no less. Fuck him." Wade took a big swallow of his coffee. He looked toward the entrance. "Aw, goddamn it."

I looked to the door. "Fucking Purdy."

"You think he's just here for coffee?"

"Do you?"

"Hell no." Wade signaled to the waitress for the check.

But Purdy, in spite of his limp, made it to our table damn fast.

"You two assholes got a lot of fucking nerve, pulling that shit," Purdy said.

Wade signaled for the waitress again. I just looked at Purdy.

"You get a lead like that, you fucking call it in, let the officers handle it."

"You saying Glenn Remington's not capable?"

"That's not the point."

"Actually," Wade said, and stood up fast, moving Purdy back a half-step. "It *is* the point. We called the best cop on the force." He stared right at Purdy. "Oh, shit," Wade said, "you meant we should have called *you*?"

The waitress came, giving Purdy a moment to think about a comeback.

But he didn't know what to say. Proving Wade's point.

I handed the waitress a twenty. "We're good," I said and stood up.

"The Chief is going to be on your asses," Purdy said.

"For giving a tip that captured a murder suspect before he left the country and wouldn't have ever come back? Really?"

Wade and I started for the door.

Purdy followed, like some snarling dog, ready to bite, jittery with fear.

"He thinks you guys knew about McDougal all along. Then you figured you'd eventually get caught, so you dropped the dime on him."

Wade spun back around, again moving Purdy back. He stumbled a little on his bum leg but recovered. I turned around too, so we were both looking at him.

"The Chief thinks that? Or is this something you've told him?" Wade said.

"The Chief listens to me."

"And who're you listening to, Purdy? You hearing things since you got your bell rung?" I said.

Purdy's face changed color, so the acne scars took on a dark purplish hue. "You fuckers."

"Purdy, you have any idea how fucking stupid you are? Do you ever think about the shit that comes out of your mouth before it comes out? Because according to your brilliant legal mind, we staked out his wife, looked the other way when he killed her, then at the very last possible second, when he's already through customs, when in another three minutes he's on the goddamn plane and isn't ever coming back, we suddenly changed our minds?"

"It's possible," Purdy said. "Guy's got a boatload of money. Maybe he paid you off."

Wade did something I've never seen him do. He grabbed a police officer by the shirtfront. And twisted it hard enough to pop two buttons—snap, snap—they arced out and bounced off the tile floor.

"You can question our brains and talent," Wade said. "But don't ever question our integrity."

"Get your fucking hand off of me. You're under arrest for assaulting an officer."

Wade rubbed his hand on his pants like he was wiping off a stain.

"Impossible. First, a real police officer would have to show up." Wade leaned in close to Purdy. "And if that's you, Purdy, go ahead and do it. Take us in."

Purdy blinked first.

And Wade and I walked out of Marie Calendar's.

Totally satisfied.

68

"It's confirmed," Duncan said the next morning. "The bones are a match to Mrs. Santiago."

"Wow, that was fast," I said. "And gratifying."

"Would you like me to notify the family?"

"Thanks, Duncan, but I think Wade and I should do that. In person."

"I concur. I assume she will want the remains transferred to some cemetery of her choosing for a proper burial so we can arrange that."

"Great. And great work too, Duncan."

He didn't respond, I guess he was still pissed off that I'd brought up an attorney's main drive in life—money. Although to be fair, while Duncan has wealth beyond the dreams of avarice, he does a lot of pro bono work, takes on and wins charity cases that seem hopeless, and gives many rah-rah speeches at law schools around the country.

"And as to the 'natural causes' issue?" he said.

"Many theories, a few facts. We're trying to connect the dots."

"I should think the chief dot is colored Black."

And with that little metaphor he hung up.

An hour later, Wade and I were driving back to Pacoima. But it was close to noon and the traffic was terrible. So by the time we got to the Santiago's house, Wade and I were both irritable.

And life is timing.

Just as he and I got out of the car, Ramón and his *compadres* turned down the street, making enough noise for a Mexican fiesta. Ramón's stereo was booming out some *cholo* gangsta rap, announcing his arrival. When he saw us, he hit the shocks modifier button, and his Chevy bounced, and the front wheels levitated two feet off the road. The car rocked several times settling down and stopped twenty yards away.

The doors opened, and two seriously steroid-enhanced bangers got out. They were each wearing an XXXL T-shirt with the sleeves ripped off. Their lats were like batwings in full flight, pushing their enormous tattooed arms away from their body. Each man carried what looked like a Mossberg pump shotgun. Serious shit.

They stepped away from each other and flanked Wade and I, mirroring the move we'd made just a few days before.

Ramón pulled in behind my car and got out, all smiles and sly looks. "So, *amigo*, you have my five thousand?"

"No."

"What the fuck?" he said.

"But I've got your four thousand. Like we agreed."

I sensed Wade's slight head turn at me, probably repeating Ramón's *what the fuck?*

"So, if we're going to do some business," I said, "call your boys down."

Ramón checked me and Wade out for a moment, then signaled the two beef trusts to relax. He sauntered up to about three feet from us. "So, I don't see no bag."

"You thought we were bringing cash? Here?"

"You don't like my neighborhood? You don't think it's safe?"

"I'm sure it is. Just like mine. But even on my own block, I don't walk around with four thousand dollars in cash."

"Shit," Ramón said and pulled out an enormous roll of money with a thick rubber band around it. "You know how much I got here?" He held it up between his thumb and forefinger and twisted his wrist several times. "Six grand."

"Maybe," Wade said and took a small, quiet step toward Ramón.

"What?"

"Might be a Texas Roll," Wade said and closed the gap again.

"What the hell's that?"

"Where you have a hundred wrapped around a roll of one-dollar bills."

"Fuck you, *esse*," Ramón said. He undid the rubber band and fanned out the bills, which, indeed, were all one hundreds.

But occupying both hands and his attention was Ramón's mistake. Because by the time he had the money out, Wade had his automatic out and up against Ramón's temple.

Ramón couldn't believe it. "You fucked now, *pendjo*, you…"

And then he couldn't say much because Wade's huge arm was around his throat.

The two bodyguards moved, but I was already in firing position on one knee, and Wade had turned Ramón around and was using him as a shield.

"Call them off," Wade said and relieved the pressure on Ramón's neck.

"*Joder estos chicos!*" Ramón said.

"No," said Wade, "you don't want to fuck these guys." He imitated Ramón's accent perfectly. "*¿Crees que eres el único que habla español?*"

"Yeah, he speaks Spanish," I said to Ramón, never taking my eyes from the two guys in the street.

"And French, and passable German," said Wade.

"I do the Italian," I said.

"We be the Berlitz of detectives," Wade said, putting on his sharecropper's accent. "So, tell your boys to lay down their weapons and step away from them and go sit on the curb." Wade dug the barrel deeper into Ramón's temple. "Now."

Ramón did as ordered, but wasn't happy about it.

His unhappiness increased when Wade took the roll of money from him and handed it to me.

I removed twenty of the one hundred dollar bills and put them in my pocket. I handed the remainder of his roll back to Ramón. "Okay, *esse*, here's the four grand Ritchie owes you."

Ramón struggled against Wade, but it was futile.

And then the damn screen door opened and Ritchie came bounding out.

"What the hell's going on?" he said.

Wade didn't move the gun or his eyes from Ramón but yelled at Ritchie. "Get back in the house, Ritchie."

But Ritchie didn't listen and ran across the lawn. When he was even with me, I swept his legs out from under him. And for the second time seeing us, he landed on his lard ass.

"You sit and don't move."

He was about to say something when we heard, "*Oh, Dios, no, no. ¿Qué está pasando?*"

"It's okay, *Señora* Santiago, nobody's going to get hurt."

She stopped and stared at the scene, afraid to say or do anything.

I told Ritchie, "Go stand by your mother."

"*Venga, venga,*" she said.

After Ritchie was with the *Señora,* I said, "Excuse me for a minute," and picked up the weapons. The two bodyguards just glared at me. I reached into my car and pulled out an even more dangerous weapon— my checkbook.

"These are nasty," I said when I reached Wade and Ramón. "Which Mossberg is this?"

I signaled to Wade, who released his armlock and backed away, his automatic still on Ramón.

"They're the Rolling Thunder models," Ramón said. You could hear the pride in his voice. "Twelve-gauge, got the barrel stabilizer and that little thing on the end? That's the Heat Shield."

"Okay, Ramón, here's how this goes down." I walked over and held out the other two thousand. "That's your original six."

He just stared at me but took the money.

I flipped open the cover of my checkbook and quickly scrawled out a check.

"And here's what I said I would pay you, four thousand."

Ramón took the check like he suspected some kind of trick.

"Don't worry, I'm getting it back from Ritchie."

Ritchie laughed at this, but his mother backhanded him in the chest.

Ramón looked at the check and then me, "This ain't going to bounce, is it?"

"Only thing bouncing is your crate."

"Hey, you like that, huh?"

"It's cool."

Ramón waited, not sure what to do. "What about the Mossbergs?" he said.

"Father Damien will have them for you at the church."

Ramón nodded in agreement.

"And you should seriously consider making a donation to the good father's church. I think ten percent is the usual tithing."

Ramón did some fast calculations. "My six, your four makes ten grand. He gets a thousand?"

"The numbers add up."

Ramón considered this a moment more. "Okay. My little sister Rosita takes Communion there, so it's cool."

And then he did something that surprised both Wade and me. He held out his hand to shake. First Wade, then me.

"You're good," he said in his Spanish-flavored Bogart. "You're very good."

69

"*Esta es una mala noticia*," Mrs. Santiago said. "Very bad news."

That threw me. I thought that once we'd told her we'd found her brother Miguel she'd be happy.

And then she started crying, the tears coursing down her face. "I am happy they have found him, but to think of all those years, lying in the dirt, buried like some animal." She motioned to Ritchie, "*Un pañuelo, por favor.*"

Before Ritchie could move, Wade handed over a handkerchief.

"*Gracias.*" She dried her tears and put the hanky in her lap. "I will wash this and return it," she said.

"It is yours," Wade said.

She nodded her thanks, and then said, "How did he die, Miguel?"

"They are working on it," I said. I looked at Wade, and he gave me a slight head nod to tell her. "And...the medical examiner has it listed as natural causes."

"That would mean he died from a heart attack or a stroke?"

"Yes."

"And this is how they do things in Paraíso del mar? A man dies, as they say, naturally, and they bury him in a construction site? With no priest? Without saying anything to the family?"

"That's why we're investigating," I said.

"Natural causes, my *culo*. He was killed," Ritchie said.

That put Mrs. Santiago over the edge, and she sobbed into the handkerchief, her body heaving.

"I'm sorry, Ma," Ritchie said. "I didn't mean..."

"We'll find out the truth, *Señora*, I promise," I said.

She quieted down, dried her face, and looked at us.

"I told Miguel that he should be careful. They liked his work, but to them, he was just a... *Mexican*. So he needed to know his place in their society. The single women were dangerous enough. But when he started seeing that woman, that *puta!* A married woman. And she was so free and easy with her favors to Miguel."

The *Señora* leaned back in her chair, overwhelmed.

"The wife?" I said.

"*Si*, the Chief's wife, Lorraine."

70

"Migraine," my dad said. "Instead of Lorraine."

"Why?" I said.

"Migraine, because she was either having one or giving you one."

My dad was making lunch for Wade and me at his house, which for my dad meant ordering a couple of pizzas and beer. We'd figured he was the best source of information for us.

"Yeah," my dad said. "Lorraine Black. She was pretty and smart. How the hell she wound up with Ben was a surprise, especially considering…" He didn't finish but took a bite of pizza.

"Considering what?" I asked.

"His legendary schlong for starters. I imagine once the excitement of marriage faded, enduring that telephone pole would have been a real pain."

"C'mon, Dad."

"I'm just spitballin' here. But forget that. Think about Ben and his attitude, his personality." He took another bite of pizza and smiled, so I knew he was going to be clever. "Hell, if she didn't have to worry about his big prick, she had to deal with him being one." He drank some beer. "Probably why she claimed she had so many migraines. Although when he wasn't around, Lorraine could be a lot of laughs."

"She sleep around?"

"Not around here that I can remember. Although as bad as he treated her, I wouldn't have blamed her." He finished his pizza. "Goddamn Ben considered her just another of his possessions, like one of his goddamn cars. He wouldn't let you drive one of his cars, and he sure as hell wouldn't like you even looking at his wife. He was very jealous. Back then, sometimes people went out to the valley, to the Palomino Club. Western bands, shitkicker stuff. And some drugstore cowboy asks Lorraine to dance. I think it was a square dance, so you never touch your partner. Ben catches the guy in the restroom and beats the shit out of him. Claimed the guy made an advance at him when he saw his equipment."

"So what happened to Lorraine?" Wade said.

"I think that Palomino Club started things and she saw the writing on the wall. That maybe the next face he beat in would be hers. So one night when Ben was out doing whatever he did, she took one of his Cadillacs and drove straight through to Vegas."

"Ben go after her?"

"Nope. She didn't ask for anything, and you know in California, especially back then, wives got anything and everything they wanted. Migraine only wanted the Caddy. And that was it. I don't even know if she's still alive."

We all ate in silence.

"Okay, we have Miguel's head caved in, body buried so no one would ever find it. We have Miguel sleeping with the Chief's wife. And we have…the Chief. What are we missing?"

"Proof," Wade said.

"Yeah," my dad said. "Unless you can get Ben to confess, you're pulling a *Don Quixote*. And even if you could somehow get enough to even start an investigation, Ben would lawyer up and the case would never make it to court. Not in his lifetime."

"That's the problem," Wade said. "His lifetime. It's been too long already."

My dad and I looked at Wade. It was so unlike him to say something like that.

"It's true," Wade said, noticing our stares. "Man's the Chief of Police, supposed to be the personification of the law. True, pure. And the mutahfucka is dirty to the core of his black soul."

"Jamal," my dad said, "I've never heard you say something that strong."

"I guess I was thinking about the *Señora*. Having to suffer all those years, not knowing, wondering."

"And closure doesn't make it any easier," I said. "Because then you have the reality. They aren't coming back."

"Yeah," Wade said. "I don't know, she reminds me of my grandmother."

My dad looked at me and nodded his head slightly.

For Wade, like most of us, nothing is more important than family and blood.

So we knew.

I mean, family and *Sicilians*?

71

"Italians make the best cars in the world." I heard the Chief say to somebody in the hallway. "And the best clothes."

I stopped and did a U-turn and went back for the door.

"And their food," he said.

I had gone down to see Hal Bartkowski after we'd talked with my dad, but sure as hell didn't want to see the Chief.

I went through the door and looked to my right. There was the Chief's Ferrari, looking like it had just come off the line at Maranello, Italy. I wondered how many miles it had on it.

I jogged over, checked the building and hoped the Chief didn't come out at just that moment and tried the GTB's door handle. It was unlocked, because who the hell would dare steal the Chief's car? I opened the door and ducked my head inside. It smelled just like a brand-new wallet, all soft leather and reeking money.

I checked the speedometer: 14,516. Whether that was kilometers or miles, it hadn't been driven much. I quietly shut the door and got the hell out of there.

I found Hal a few minutes later, his eyes glued to a microscope. He jumped when I came into the room.

"Shit, you scared the hell out of me."

"Sorry. But I thought you should know since you asked me to give you any advance storm warnings."

"Storm warnings?"

"Yeah, as when the shit is about to hit the fan."

Hal turned off the power to the scope and waited.

"They got a positive ID on the bones. Miguel Santiago." I waited to see if that name meant anything to Hal. It didn't. "He was a hotshot construction worker, forty or so years ago. Built a lot of the biggest and most expensive houses in Paradise."

"And he didn't die of natural causes," Hal said.

"They're still examining that."

"What's to examine? His skull was crushed, his arm was fractured in two. Whoever did it was big and strong and probably berserk." Hal gathered his papers together and put them back into a folder. "Talk about a cold case. How the hell you going to prove something from that long ago?"

"I don't know."

"You got any suspects?"

"Just some theories, none of them clear enough to talk about."

"Kelly's going to have a coronary. And the Chief? This isn't just a storm warning, this is a gale force shit-storm in the making."

"Right, so we keep this between us."

"Automatic," he said.

"Thanks. I'll keep you in the loop, Hal. I appreciate your cooperation."

"Let me know if there's anything I can do. And I mean anything."

I left Hal and was heading to my car when I saw Jim Tucker walking for his motorcycle.

"Hey, Jim," I called.

He looked over and tried to pretend he hadn't heard me, but I ran over before he could mount up and ride away. He just looked at me.

"Hey, the other day at the Mayor's funeral, one of the guys said you had a five-in-one ticket. That true?"

"Who told you that?"

"I don't remember, but shit, five-in-one, that's awesome." I almost held out my hand for a high-five, but couldn't make myself do it.

Everybody's a sucker for praise, especially overcompensating, steroid-popping motorcycle cops.

"Yeah," Tucker said, a smile splitting his broad face. "Fucking fiver. But I had to give it up."

"What? No way, why?"

"Driver was delivering a Ferrari for the Chief. Fucking Big Ben finds out I gave the guy who brings him his car just one ticket, much less five violations at once? Shit, I ain't riding this baby anymore."

And with that, he fired up the Harley. He revved it a couple of show-off times and then said, "Yeah, I'd be on parking patrol."

He dropped the visor on his helmet and accelerated away.

I went home.

I remembered that Clarice had said he'd bought the Ferrari from La Modena Motors in San Francisco. I Googled it and got the number.

I was expecting a sexy, throaty Italian *bella donna* to answer the phone. Instead, I got a nasal man who sounded like he was from Brooklyn. "Chuck Elster here."

"I was calling La Modena Motors."

"You got it. What can I do for you?"

"Yeah, my Chief, uh, Ben Black, bought a Ferrari last week, a…"

"A 275 GTB/4," Chuck said.

"You remember it just like that?"

"Because I don't sell many like *that!* And I don't mean because it was so expensive. Thing was absolutely perfect. And I don't know, but that red, I think they did something different to the paint because the damn thing shines, unlike any other Ferrari I've ever sold or seen for that matter. And I also remember like that because he fucking busted my chops on it."

"He's a tough negotiator."

"Wasn't the money, in fact, he paid me sticker. No, what he busted my chops on was the arrangements to pick it up. He had some private jet fly him up at three in the morning. Three o-fucking a.m. I asked him why couldn't we do it doing normal business hours, and he exploded. Yelling and screaming, cursing."

"That's our Chief."

"So I met him at four when he landed, drove him over to the garage, signed the paperwork, and he drove off. Said this way he'd beat most of the traffic."

"You remember the name of the jet company?"

"DonnJet or something like that."

"You remember what the mileage was?"

"Yeah, why? I'm sorry, who is this?"

"Jim. Jim Tucker. I work *for* the Chief. I'm a motorcycle cop."

"Hey, you into motorcycles? I mean, you riding a Hog and all? Because I've got an Indian for sale that's unbelievable. It's a 1917 Twin. One of the rarest Indians around. The only Hedstrom engine model made after Indian switched over to the Powerplus engine in 1916.

Matching engine and frame numbers. Totally rebuilt. Thing runs like a Swiss watch. I could let you have it for right around sixty."

"Sounds tempting, but it's way over my budget."

"You're kidding. I mean your Chief books private jets, spends over seven million dollars for a car, hell, sixty thousand is chump change."

"Maybe for the Chief, but not for this chump. Sorry. But about the mileage?"

"Why's he need that?"

"Insurance company. They insist on the actual miles when he bought it."

"Yeah, insurance companies will screw with you every chance they get. Hold on a minute, let me check it on the computer. But I'm pretty sure it was right under fifteen thousand. That's incredibly low mileage."

I could hear keys clicking on his keyboard.

"Why didn't he just give them the sales invoice?"

"He couldn't find it. Probably put it in a file and forgot."

"You want me to email you a copy?"

"That'd be great, but could text it to me, too?"

"You got it."

"Driving that car would be a dream," Chuck said, "around town, short trip. But these machines are investments. That's why I couldn't understand him driving it all the way down to L.A. Why not just ship it? We're only seven miles from the airport."

"Yeah," I said. "You wonder why."

"I was right," Chuck said. "Under fifteen thousand: 14,483."

72

The numbers didn't add up.

There were only thirty-three additional miles on the Ferrari's odometer. So the Chief didn't drive the Ferrari down. He'd shipped it. Just like Chuck had suggested.

Then once it landed at LAX, they'd loaded it onto the car carrier. And the truck driver had run into Jim Tucker.

That meant the Ferrari had flown, and so had the Chief.

Fifteen minutes later I was pulling into the Execu-Ride parking lot, and there was my newfound friend, Moesha, the attendant. She looked at me suspiciously, like maybe I had a complaint.

"Hi, Moesha, remember I was in here the other day."

"Oh, I remember you. But mostly I remember the brother that was with you."

"Wade. My partner. Handsome dude."

Shit, he'd been right.

"Loved his dreds."

"You said the lot takes photos of every car that comes and goes?"

"Every one. Coming and going. Why? Somebody hit your car?"

"No. Uh…Wade and I are partners…"

"So you said. Partners in what?"

I handed her a PI business card. She read it. "So, Mr. Singer…"

"Call me Matt."

"Okay, Matt, what are you investigating? And why here?"

"Last time we were here we had to stop a guy who'd killed his wife."

"Really?" I didn't think Moesha was quite convinced.

"Yes. You probably heard it on the news. The husband figured his wife was cheating on him, snuck back and killed her."

Moesha reflected back a moment. "*That* was your guy?"

"Yes. We managed to delay him from getting on his flight to Rio and then the cops came and now he's in jail."

"Good work. But what's going on this time?"

"We think another murderer trying to slip away."

"Where do you live?"

"Just back at Paraíso del mar. Paradise."

"Sounds like Hell to me."

A customer drove up in a silver Jag, paid his ticket, and as the gates went up, the bright photo flash recorded his departure.

"How long you keep the photos?"

"About a month. They're digitally recorded. Recycles automatically."

"Any chance I could go back a few days? I'm looking for a particular car."

"No, no way. That's confidential material, property of the company."

"Moesha, I could really use some help. Is there anything you could do? Or that I could do for you?"

Her bright eyes flashed a little, and she smiled. She looked at my business card. "This number? That how to reach your partner?"

"Absolutely."

I didn't tell her every call went to me and then I called Wade.

"You have another card?" she asked.

"Sure." I handed one over, not sure why she needed two.

She pulled a pen from a pocket and wrote on the back of the card. "You give this to him. Soon as he calls me, you can look at the photos."

I walked away from the booth so Moesha couldn't hear and dialed Wade.

"Pick up, pick up," I said as the phone rang, then rang again.

"Yo," Wade said.

"Listen to me, don't ask any questions and just do what I say."

"You been kidnapped?"

"No. Remember that parking lot attendant at the airport?"

"Moesha? Yeah, why?"

"I didn't think you noticed her, much less her name."

"A good detective has ways of sleuthing not easily discernible by civilians."

"I'm going to give you a number. It's Moesha's..."

Heh-heh. "I told you she was checking me out."

"Right. You need to call her right now so that I can look at the pictures."

"Dirty pictures?"

"Just call her, damn it, I'll explain later."

I barely made it back to the booth when Moesha's cell rang.

She answered and was all smiles and joy. "Oh, hey Wade, how you doin', baby?" Wade said something and Moesha said, "Oh, Jamal. I like that name."

I motioned to Moesha about the pictures, and she pointed to a monitor at the side of the booth, handed me a remote.

So while Wade and Moesha talked, I looked at the photos.

And they might as well have been dirty pictures, the way Moesha was giggling, saying things like, "Oh...really? Now, you being naughty, Jamal..."

And so on.

I reversed back at high speed until I got to the right day and then went through the snapshots until I came to the one I knew, deep down, *had* to be there.

A tuxedo-black Mercedes S600 with a personalized California Environmental design license plate: PARDSE 1.

73

"It's my license, so what?"

The Chief was glaring at me as we stood in Reed Lockhart's lanai room. I'd figured that Leah had not taken the key from its hiding place, had let myself in, and then left the door open for Big Ben.

"I hope you didn't bring me down here to talk about personalized plates."

"No, I brought you down here to talk about murder."

"You know I can't talk about the McDougal case."

"This isn't about McDougal."

He was getting irritated. "Okay, what fucking murder are you talking about? Because the last time I looked, that was the first murder we've had in a couple of decades."

"Not true. We had another one just last week."

He shifted his weight. For a big man, the Chief is amazingly fast and graceful. I'd seen him screwing around with a couple of cops, doing martial art moves, and he was snake-quick.

"Look, Matt, I'm not sure whether you're still suffering from your concussion or you're just trying to piss me off, but this is over. Nobody got murdered last week."

"Reed Lockhart did."

"Jesus Christ."

He turned to go.

"And you killed him."

That stopped him, and he looked back at me, and then snickered. "You're fucking hopeless."

"Maybe, but you're going down for it."

He put out both hands in a gesture of acceptance. "Okay," he said, and then he laughed, shaking his head, humoring the village idiot. "Okay, tell me how."

"You shot Reed and I happened to walk in on it, and you blindsided me and then set me up to look like I was drunk and had a concussion."

"Stop," he said.

"That way, whatever I said about the fake car crash, you could blow off that I was hallucinating."

"You're beyond help."

"Then you had your in-house toad, Kelly, list Reed's death was from natural causes."

"You think we should have put down suicide?"

"You should have put down the truth! That you shot him, you bastard."

He went for his gun, but I was faster.

I had my .45 trained on him before he'd even reached the grip on his Berretta.

"You are under arrest, Matthew Singer," he said.

"Fuck you, Benjamin Black, you cocksucker."

He stared at me for a long, long moment.

"Okay, Matt, let's just calm down here. Maybe I've been a little too harsh with you, maybe I've been a little too resentful of the past. But there are things going on in Paradise, big things you don't know about, that are beyond your control. And you just need to let them happen."

"Like what?"

"Reed was riddled with cancer. Started in his pancreas, spread like wildfire. It had metastasized in his brain. He may have had five weeks left. And not a good five weeks."

He shifted his body a little, but I tracked him with the gun.

"I'm sure that's why he took the car into the palms. To save him and Leah all that torture. Putting cause of death down as from natural causes lets everybody breathe easier, feel better."

"Reed would never have done that."

"I knew Reed all of his life. Longer than you've been alive. And you're telling me you know what he'd do better than me?"

"Reed wouldn't have committed suicide, and you know it too. You're only saying that to cover the murder."

"And why the fuck would I murder my best friend?"

"Because of those bones."

A flash of recognition passed his face, but he covered it well.

"The bones?"

"The ones that were found on Laurel. The bones you had Kelly list as the same way: from natural causes."

"The bones you had your goddamn attorney remove from my city for some supposed DNA match? *Those* bones?"

"Unless you've killed somebody else we haven't found yet."

"Yeah, I'm just a one-man crime wave. Those bones had been there for a long time. Nobody knew who they were, or how the man died. Natural causes was the best way to handle it."

"Right. That way, the lovely town of Paraíso del mar doesn't get any bad publicity, and property values stay high and whatever scams you're pulling keep moving forward."

"Progress always has its bumps."

"And calling it death by natural causes would have been okay if having your skull caved in by a Colt .45 automatic is natural."

"What do you want, Matt?"

"Justice."

"For who?"

"For Reed. For the Santiagos."

Hearing the Santiagos got a bigger "tell" from the Chief.

"You know the Santiagos," I said. "The family that's been wondering all these years where their brother Miguel was."

"And who is Miguel Santiago?" he said.

And he said it so calm, you would never know the volatile links he had to it.

"The man that your wife Lorraine was fucking."

"You…"

He lunged for me, but I moved back and to his left and kept the .45 on him.

"Don't make me kill you, Ben."

"How dare you talk about my wife like that?"

"Truth hurts, I know."

"It's not true!"

"Sure it is. Miguel played with fire. All the ladies loved Miguel. And as long as it was just single women, you and Reed looked the other way since he was such a terrific contractor for all your projects. But when Miguel beat the shit out of Reed over his sister Mayleen, it was just a matter of time before you served your own brand of justice. Then when he hooked up with Lorraine, or more likely, Lorraine went after him because you were such a prick, that was the tipping point. That's when you took him out."

"You are certifiable."

"Not are. *Am*. I *am* fucking crazy. No telling what I might do."

The Chief looked to his left as if he heard or was expecting something.

I glanced there quickly but didn't see or hear anything.

"Reed was terminal," I said. "And was feeling guilty about all the shit you two pulled. He knew his time was running out. Maybe he thought he could be forgiven for his sins at the last minute. Repent and be saved. And then when Miguel's bones turned up, that put him over the edge. I saw and heard you two arguing in front of his house a few days before you killed him."

"I didn't kill him. On the day Reed committed suicide I was up in San Francisco buying the Ferrari. Call the dealer."

"I already did."

Another surprise for him, but he covered it well.

"And what did he tell you? That I left at 4:30 in the morning and spent the day driving down here."

"You left at 4:30, but you didn't drive almost three hundred and fifty miles from San Fran to here. You drove six miles to the transportation company and gave them the Ferrari. Their manager drove you to the airport, you got back on the DonnJet plane, arrived here at 5:25. Then you picked up your Mercedes at Execu-Ride and left their lot at 5:48. You drove back to town and figured you were safe."

"Safe from what?"

"From anyone being able to prove you killed Reed."

"You're out of your fucking mind."

"You've already said that. But hear me out. I walked in just after you'd shot Reed, that was probably 8:15. You wacked me on the head, called Purdy, and he wrangled me out to the north end of the Strand, poured booze all over me, and left me there."

The Chief blinked hard at that. Good. That'd been a wild guess, but it had hit home.

"Meanwhile, you and one of your other corrupt fuckers, probably Gerry Kelly, sneak Reed out and store his ass while you're scrambling to come up with a cover story, which is when you came up with the fake car crash, making sure that his gas tank, which was nearly empty, explodes and supposedly he burns to death. That about right?"

"Jesus Christ. You should give up this bullshit private investigation shit you're doing and go write screenplays. That's the wildest fucking story I have ever heard. Totally unbelievable, but hey, Hollywood will buy anything. In fact, I still know a couple of guys from my days with Howard Hughes. Maybe they could help you."

"You killed Reed in cold blood. And I can prove it."

"How?"

"With this."

I tossed a copy of Tucker's voided parking citation toward him. He didn't even flinch when it was in the air. It floated down and landed on the ultra-clean new rug.

"What is it?" he said, not taking his eyes from me.

"The five-in-one ticket Tucker wrote and then buried because he didn't want you up his ass for busting the transportation company that delivered the Ferrari."

"All that's going to prove is that you're so fucked up, they've got a room waiting for you up at Atascadero."

"Maybe. But that ticket, and the invoice from La Modena showing the mileage on the car, plus Moesha Matheson's testimony should be enough."

He only blinked several times, which was pretty fucking amazing, considering I'd just hammered him with three knock-out blows of information.

Then cool as a riverboat gambler he said, "And who the fuck is Moesha?"

"Parking attendant at Execu-Ride. Where you parked on the day, you killed Reed. And where they photographed your Mercedes, license plate PARDSE 1."

I threw the photos Moesha had printed for me of the Chief's Mercedes—both coming and leaving the lot. They were terrific photos because they showed the car, the plates, and sitting smugly behind the wheel, the Chief.

"Do you know what the fuck you're dealing with here, Matt? Goddamn it, think. Reed and I built this town, we busted our asses, yeah, and sometimes we busted heads, but we made Paradise what it is today."

"A living hell."

"We couldn't lose everything."

"So you killed him."

"Reed was the living dead. I saved him all that pain."

And then the noise the Chief had heard to his left appeared.

"Leah! Jesus," the Chief said, "how long you been there, darling?"

"It's true?" she said.

She walked toward him like she was in a trance.

"You killed him?"

"No, no, that was just…Matt's just…" He coughed violently, huge wracking bursts that doubled him over. He dropped to a knee and faster than I would have imagined, the Chief pulled his .38 from an ankle holster and had the barrel up against Leah's temple.

"Don't even think of it," he said.

Leah struggled to break free, and *whack*, he clubbed her in the head. She sagged against him.

"Now your turn," he said. "Put it on the floor and step away from it."

For a nano-second, I thought I could shoot him before he had a chance to react, but then slowly put the .45 on the carpet.

"Purdy," the Chief yelled.

Ken Purdy limped in, his Beretta out, all smiles and revenge.

"What the fuck were you waiting for?" the Chief said.

"I almost ran into Leah, so I had to double back."

"Get his gun," the Chief said.

I looked at Leah. She was slightly dizzy, but she was tensed with anger. She looked at me and nodded and rolled her eyes down toward the Chief, signaling me.

Then her right hand moved for the impressive bulge that makes the Chief "Big Ben" and she yanked with everything she had.

He roared in pain, shoving Leah away.

Giving me that split second to jump him. We struggled for the pistol. Goddamn, he was strong. And somehow the barrel turned down and…

Bang!

The Chief staggered back, blood flowing from his crotch.

I spun for Purdy…but…

Bang!

Purdy dropped, his knee shattered.

And Wade stepped into the room, calm, ready to shoot again.

We looked at the Chief. He was on the rug, his legs splayed out. A fountain of blood was soaking through his pants, and more blood running down and out his cuffs onto the brand new carpet. Looks like it would have to be replaced again. He fumbled with his zipper, but it was a losing battle.

He looked at me, his eyes getting glassy.

"Great police work, Big Ben," I said, "you just shot yourself in the pendulum."

74

Tick-tock, tick-tock.

Time moved slowly for the next few days.

Wade and I had to explain everything that had happened. And having Duncan on our side sure as hell helped, no matter how expensive his bill was going to be.

Glenn Remington was the interim Chief until the city council had a hearing, but it was a slam dunk that he was the new man in charge. And since we'd helped Glenn, like Wade had said, having a few brownie points banked didn't hurt.

Purdy was in the hospital for a few days while we proved that he had been part of the cover-up for Reed's murder. He'd do some serious time, but would probably get the charges reduced if he cooperated, which, being Purdy, he would do in a heartbeat. It was less than he deserved.

Gerry Kelly blew out of town before the wheels of justice rolled up on him. Maybe he was smarter than he looked. Now *that* was a natural cause—a rat leaving a sinking ship. Hal Bartkowski got promoted, which was justified since he was better on his first day than Gerry was his entire career.

Leah and I spent many days together and talked of so many things. Telling her about her half-brother wasn't one of them.

Duncan said he would do that, in time. Maybe. If the need, meaning Ritchie, arose.

A week after all of this, Wade, Leah, my father, and I drove out to Pacoima for Miguel's funeral in my dad's Fusion. Leah was going to hire a limo for us, but when I explained how small the church and the ceremony were going to be, and that we would be the only guests who weren't from Pacoima, she understood.

"I'm still learning," she said. "All that money, you feel compelled to spend it."

"A lot of slick people will try and help you do just that, so you'd better find two good financial advisors."

"Why not just one brilliant one?"

"I like two, so they can check up on each other."

Señora Santiago looked lovely in what I assumed was a genuine antique Mexican black skirt encircled by a beautiful handmade leather belt with turquoise stones, and a long-sleeved white blouse, with a black shawl covering her hair.

Ritchie had cleaned up too. He was wearing a dark suit, highly polished boots, and a white shirt buttoned tight to his neck, no tie.

There were eight other guests in attendance. Seven of them looked to be close to the *Señora's* age, and the other was a *chicka* in a tight-fitting screaming-yellow dress that rode way up on her chunky thighs. Ritchie's squeeze.

Father Damien started his service referencing the stained glass window of Jesus with the lost lamb, and I thought, *Oh, brother, here we go.*

But the good Father was more than good. His words were clear, precise, not maudlin, and very comforting. It was a speech to be proud of, whether you were Catholic, Protestant, or whatever higher source you called upon.

Miguel had died twice. Once when he was murdered by Ben Black, and the second time when every trace of him was removed except memory.

Father Damien didn't mention Reed Lockhart since this was Miguel's funeral, but Reed had also died twice at Ben's hands—shot and then burned to death.

At the gravesite, *Señora* Santiago said that she was happy her brother had finally come home and was now at peace.

Father Damien said that while Miguel's bones and physical presence were finally back with us, his spirit had long been with God in heaven. His closing words came from John 11:23-26, when Jesus comforts the grieving Martha, *"Your brother will rise again."*

Then he gently dropped some dirt on Miguel's shiny mahogany coffin. We each followed Father Damien and tossed our handful of dirt and filed out across the white carpet runner laid down on the green grass.

Señora Santiago was waiting for us at the end of the carpet.

She shook hands with my father, then Leah, then Wade.

She said something to Wade and he bent down and kissed her cheek.

Finally, it was my turn. She grasped my hand in both of hers, stood up on her tiptoes, and kissed my cheek.

"Gracias, a mi hijo."

Thank you, my son.

That's a pretty good way to be paid in my book.

The End

WANT TO KNOW WHAT'S NEXT FOR MATT AND JAMAL?
HERE'S AN ADVANCE PREVIEW OF THEIR NEXT CASE.

Paraíso Lost

1

"Yo," Jamal said on the phone. "We still in business?"

"Which business? Selling or sleuthing?"

"Either or both."

Singer & Wade Real Estate had been slow for a few months now.

The market had slowed down, mostly because in the last year, homes had soldat a record pace in Paraíso Del Mar, our chic, *uber*-rich beach town. People were flipping homes and driving the prices so high there eventually had to be an adjustment.

We were in the adjustment period.

It will come back. It always does, that being the cycle. But when you're trudging down in the valley, you can't see that far ahead and everything looks bleak.

Our other business, Singer & Wade Investigations, was also slow. Actually, it was worse than that. No one had hired us to investigate anything for several months.

"Mebbe we too good at stopping crime," Wade said. Wade's a *summa cum laude* grad from Emory, so he can speak excellent English. And Spanish, French, and a passable German. I do the Italian. As he tells people, "We be the Berlitz of detectives."

"Well," I said, "we almost had a job."

"Almost?"

"A guy came in, said he'd heard about us, and wanted to hire us."

"Only wanted?" Wade said. "Meaning he didn't?"

"Hey, this is *my* story."

"Okay."

"So then he asked what our rates were."

"For real estate or investigations?"

"Investigations."

"And?"

"And I told him."

"And?"

"He said, 'Your rates seem high.'"

"Only at the start," I said.

"Meaning what?" he said.

"We deliver."

"Is it negotiable?" he asked.

"Yes, I can raise it."

"That's absurd," he said.

"Getting pissed," Wade interrupted.

"Seemed like it. But I didn't comment since it's hard to discuss absurdity without being stupid.

"What if I don't like the results?" he said.

"You can hire us again."

"If you fail, why should I hire you again?"

"Depends on how badly you want results."

"I *expect* results, that's why I would hire you. So if you don't find her, then I shouldn't have to pay."

"I assume by *her*, you mean a wife or girlfriend?"

"Neither."

"A daughter, then?"

"Isn't that all that's left?"

"Unless you've lost a female pet."

"If you are trying to be funny, you aren't succeeding."

"I'm here all week, and let's have a hand for the band." I waited a moment, then said, "I would like to help you out, if possible. So why don't we start with the basics." I stuck my hand out for a shake, "Mister…?"

He didn't want to shake. Instead he said, "I think if you don't find her, I shouldn't have to pay."

"Then we can't work together."

"Why?"

"Because if someone doesn't want to be found, they won't be."

"Not even by you guys?"

I gave him my most dramatic sigh. "Not even by us."

"Dat be true," Wade said, interrupting my story again.

"I think he actually sneered at me and left," I continued. "And he slammed the door behind him."

"Man, you always know how to handle people," Wade said.

"I am a silver-tongued devil," I said. "But he'll be back."

"Doubt it."

I saw a shadowy form appear at the glass of the office door, and the man opened it and walked back into my office.

"No, I have a feeling he'll be back," I said. "Bet you a lunch on it."

"You're on," Wade said and hung up.

The man sat back down in the same deck chair that he'd sat in before and looked at me.

"If I could tell you where she is, would you reduce your fees by half?"

"If you could tell me where she is, then our fees would double, maybe even triple."

"What?"

"If that were the case, you wouldn't need an investigation team. You'd need a family counselor."

"That's pretty harsh."

"Sleuthin' ain't pretty."

I drew our standard contract from my desk drawer and signed it. "Shall I fill in your name, Mister…?"

"I want to think about it."

"Think about your name?"

"No, and I don't understand why you're so flippant about a serious issue."

"You're right, Mister…"

"Finneran," he said. "Peter Finneran."

"Well, we're making progress then, Mr. Finneran," I said, and filled in his name and pushed the contract to him. I didn't want to try another handshake. I don't handle rejection well.

"This isn't correct," he said.

"What isn't?"

"The name."

"I'm sorry, you did say your name was Peter Finneran."

"Yes, but that's not who you would be working for."

"So, this is a mystery about a mystery." I waited for him to say something, but he was suddenly very interested in the contract. "Are you going to tell me who we *might* be working for?"

"If and when it's appropriate."

"Okay."

Mr. Finneran stood up. "And even if it's a pass, I've enjoyed discussing Keynesian economics with you."

"Is that what we were doing?"

"Yes, one component of it anyway. That of inflexible pricing."

"Oh. I thought we were doing James Taylor's version."

"Excuse me."

"From his song, 'You Make It Easy.'"

I sang it for him. "I'll provide the satisfy, you provide the need."

He didn't wait for another chorus, shook his head, and clomped—and that is the appropriate word because he walked with a damn heavy step, out of my office. And he slammed the door. Again.

He'd probably gotten mad because I'd switched the words around. Sure as hell couldn't have been my singing.

NOTE FROM THE AUTHOR

Word-of-mouth is crucial for any author to succeed. If you enjoyed the book, please leave a review online—anywhere you are able. Even if it's just a sentence or two. It would make all the difference and would be very much appreciated.

Thanks!
Jack

About the Author

Private detectives Matt Singer and Jamal Wade's plan to sell real estate as a side business explodes into murder when their client is brutally slain in a house they've listed for sale.

In their search to find the real killer, Matt and Jamal are trapped in a Chinese puzzle box of cover-ups and corruption that goes to the very top of the southern California beach town known as paradise.

Before this case comes to its shattering conclusion they will uncover a man's crushed skull and shattered bones buried forty years ago .. the Mayor's illegitimate son who threatens to destroy his father's reputation .. a political assassination disguised as an accident .. and the most devastating discovery of all – that the truth is far closer to them than they'd thought possible.

Thank you so much for reading one of our **Mystery** novels.

If you enjoyed our book, please check out our recommended title for your next great read!

K-Town Confidential by Brad Chisholm and Claire Kim

"An enjoyable zigzagging plot." *–KIRKUS REVIEWS*

"If you are a fan of crime stories and legal dramas that have a noir flavor, you won't be disappointed with *K-Town Confidential*." – *Authors Reading*

View other Black Rose Writing titles at www.blackrosewriting.com/books and use promo code **PRINT** to receive a **20% discount** when purchasing.